IDENTITY

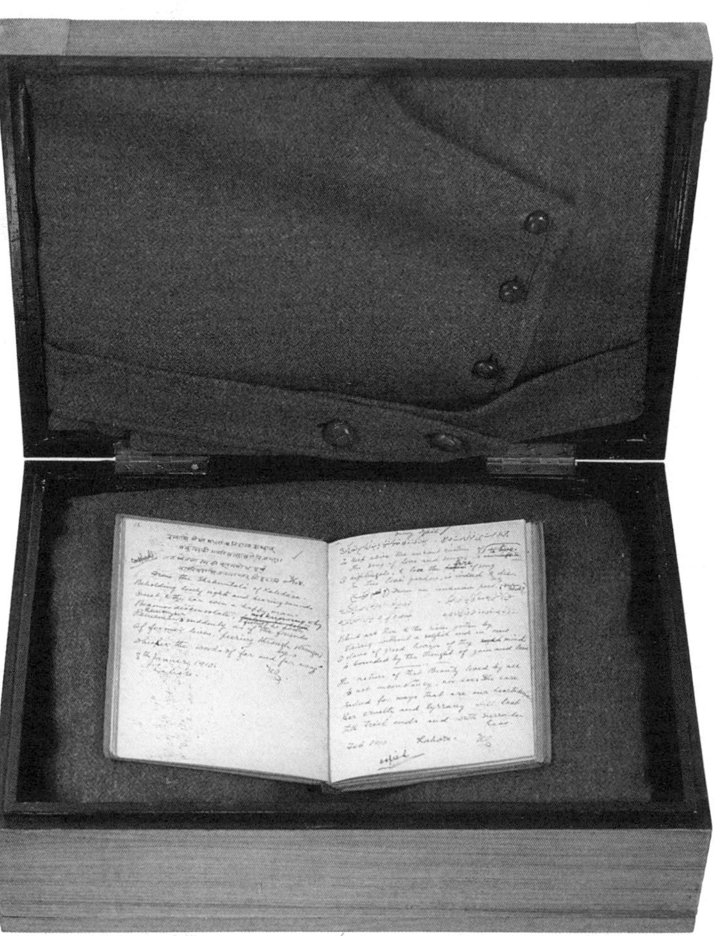

---

*This issue of **GRAND STREET** is dedicated to the memory of* **William S. Burroughs**, 1914–1997.

"So how does one face death head-on? . . . without flinching and without posturing—which is always to be seen as a form of evasion, worse than flinching because covert. For the man who flinches and runs away, like Lord Jim and Frances Macomber, there is hope. But not for him who sticks out his chest and wraps himself in a flag."
—**William S. Burroughs**, in *My Education: A Book of Dreams*, published in ***GRAND STREET** 51* in 1995.

FRONT COVER Shirin Neshat, *Offered Eye*, 1997. Silver-gelatin print and ink, 10 x 8 in.

BACK COVER Pepón Osorio, *En la barbería no se llora (No Crying Allowed in the Barbershop)* (detail), 1994. Mixed-media installation.

TITLE PAGE Vivan Sundaram, *Box One: Father*, 1995. Teak-board box fitted with woolen lining and notebook of Umrao Singh Sher-Gil, 19 11/16 x 13 3/8 x 17 11/16 in.

TABLE OF CONTENTS Juan Rulfo, *Untitled*, circa 1950. Silver-gelatin print.

"Like an Old Elephant" by Marcello Mastroianni. Copyright © 1997, Baldini & Castoldi International, Milan. Translated by Vicki Satlow.

"From *The Apple Tree in the Corridor*" by Can Xue. Copyright © 1997 by Deng Xiao-Hua. English language copyright © 1997 by Ronald R. Janssen and Jian Zhang. Reprinted by arrangement with Henry Holt & Company.

Grand Street (ISSN 0734-5496; ISBN 1-885490-13-5) is published quarterly by Grand Street Press (a project of the New York Foundation for the Arts, Inc., a not-for-profit corporation), 131 Varick Street, Room 906, New York, NY 10013. Tel: (212) 807-6548, Fax: (212) 807-6544. Contributions and gifts to Grand Street Press are tax-deductible to the extent allowed by law. This publication is made possible, in part, by a grant from the New York State Council on the Arts.

Volume Sixteen, Number Two (*Grand Street* 62—Fall 1997).
Copyright © 1997 by the New York Foundation for the Arts, Inc., Grand Street Press. All rights reserved. Reproduction, whether in whole or in part, without permission is strictly prohibited.
Second-class postage paid at New York, NY, and additional mailing offices. Postmaster: Please send address changes to Grand Street Subscription Service, Dept. GRS, P.O. Box 3000, Denville, NJ 07834. Subscriptions are $40 a year (four issues). Foreign subscriptions (including Canada) are $55 a year, payable in U.S. funds. Single-copy price is $12.95 ($18 in Canada). For subscription inquiries, please call (800) 807-6548.

Grand Street is printed by Hull Printing in Meriden, CT. It is distributed to the trade by D.A.P./Distributed Art Publishers, 155 Avenue of the Americas, New York, NY 10013, Tel: (212) 627-1999, Fax: (212) 627-9484, and to newsstands only by Bernhard DeBoer, Inc., 113 E. Centre Street, Nutley, NJ 07110, Total Circulation, 80 Frederick Street, Hackensack, NJ, 07601, and Ubiquity Distributors, 607 Degraw Street, Brooklyn, NY 11217. *Grand Street* is distributed in Australia and New Zealand by Peribo Pty, Ltd., 58 Beaumont Road, Mount Kuring-Gai, NSW 2080, Australia, Tel: (2) 457-0011, and in the United Kingdom by Central Books, 99 Wallis Road, London E9 5LN, Tel: (181) 986-4854.

GRAND STREET

EDITOR
Jean Stein

MANAGING EDITOR
Deborah Treisman

ART EDITOR
Walter Hopps

POETRY EDITOR
William Corbett

DESIGN
J. Abbott Miller, Paul Carlos
DESIGN/WRITING/RESEARCH, NEW YORK

ASSISTANT EDITOR
Julie A. Tate

ASSISTANT ART EDITOR
Anne Doran

ADMINISTRATIVE ASSISTANT
Lisa Brodus

INTERNS
Laurel Gitlen, Michael Lumelsky, Hilde Werschkul

ADVISORY EDITORS
Hilton Als, Edward W. Said

CONTRIBUTING EDITORS
Dominique Bourgois, Colin de Land, Mike Davis
Raymond Foye, Jonathan Galassi, Stephen Graham
Dennis Hopper, Hudson, Jane Kramer, Erik Rieselbach
Robin Robertson, Robert Storr, Katrina vanden Heuvel
Wendy vanden Heuvel, John Waters, Drenka Willen

FOUNDING CONTRIBUTING EDITOR
Andrew Kopkind (1935–1994)

PUBLISHERS
Jean Stein & Torsten Wiesel

THE MILKY WAY

CRISTINA PERI ROSSI

The night Mauricio looked at the sky and discovered the notion of infinity, he got dizzy and then fainted. Later, life would afford him other thrills, preserved by tradition from time immemorial, such as: first communion, grade school, masturbation, military service, dominoes, exams, soccer games, generational conflicts, certain diseases, dream analysis, the need to get a job, inflation, mandatory voting, marriage, chronic sinusitis. But all those pleasures were awaiting him in a time zone called the future; for now, the most urgent thing was the fainting brought on by the notion of infinity.

The day had been like any other. Mauricio's mother had had the tact not to send him to school under one pretext or another. When Mauricio turned three, she said he was awfully small and though some of the neighbors disagreed, she managed to impose her will. She made every possible effort to stop Mauricio from growing up. He was her only son and she had no interest in his ceasing to be little. She had observed what happened in the vast majority of cases: the moment the mothers looked away, the children stopped being children, they grew up, became men, and sought to lead an independent life. So in her daily prayers, she included a plea that Mauricio remain forever three, the age she considered ideal to be conserved for life. Not entirely convinced of the effectiveness of prayers, she consulted a medical specialist who assured her that despite the great developments in science over the last years, particularly after the experiments carried out during the two world wars and myriad local wars, there was still no adequate procedure to make a child remain indefinitely three years old.

"Then what good were all the experiments carried out on the blacks, Indians, anarchists, and other political prisoners?" asked the woman, who, while lacking precise data, was under the impression that thousands of buffaloes,

Chileans, chimpanzees, Uruguayans, and other animals had been consumed in scientific tests in gigantic laboratories in the North American deserts of Nevada and Oklahoma.

"Science is lamentably slow, my good woman; it does not advance as swiftly as we would like," the doctor said.

As for Mauricio's father—who had become a skeptic after his quest to become the president of a state failed because the presidencies were occupied for life by career militarists and other upstarts—he believed that medicine was not a science but rather just an empirical discipline and unable, therefore, to conserve Mauricio's three golden years for the rest of his life.

"You will have to make do with a third year that lasts just three hundred and sixty-five days," he told his wife. "And bear in mind, dear, that every day that passes will be one day less of three years and one day more of three years," he added, because he enjoyed showing his wife the strict limits of reality.

To him, reality was a square. To her, reality was a circle. They had debated those conceptions of reality substantially before getting married. It seemed to him that the marriage of a person for whom reality was incontrovertibly represented by a quadrangle to another person for whom reality was indubitably a circumference could not end well—unless the circle or the sphere could be subsumed within the square, with which it would have certain overlapping zones, retaining, however, extensive surfaces with no contact or, on the other hand, unless the circle could absorb the square, thus leaving empty spaces without communication, inside the sphere.

The discussion ended when she, who was at times capable of extraordinary lucidity, despite her conception of reality as a circumference, told him that the only outcome that could be hoped for in any marriage—whether between a rhombus and a triangle or an octahedron and a pyramid—was a distant and peaceful cohabitation—without the dubious extolling of passion—and procreation, for which they had been physiologically prepared long before knowing each other, and which enjoyed the approval of generals, the blessing of the Church, the credit of the State, private financing, official bibliography, the support of tradition, and the consensus of public bystanders.

He believed that the work of fertilization could be carried out without great effort, by which his square would be definitively inscribed within the infinite context of reality's parallel squares, and she believed that, in that way, her circle would join the series of spheres that had rotated indefinitely in space since the origins of the universe, in perpetual motion without beginning or end.

Mauricio believed that reality did not exist outside our perception of it, so he refused to represent it under any determined form. Until now, nobody had asked him about his particular vision of the world anyway, as he was still not of an age to marry.

When his mother could do nothing to prevent it, Mauricio had four more birthdays and grew to age seven, but she still refused to send him to school under one pretext or another. One winter it was his tonsils, another it was an epidemic, one month it was anarchy, another the class struggle, but she always figured out a way to keep him at home. The other kids envied him and, when they saw him on the street, they threw rocks at him to forget the fact that he didn't go to school.

As for the notion of infinity, he acquired it almost spontaneously while looking at the sky. One dusk, he saw a cluster of shining stars. He was sitting behind the white painted grating while his mother, illuminated by the light of the garden lantern, knitted a blue sweater for him. He was bored; he had already incited a war between the snails he gathered from plants and studied the route of the ants, watching their comings and goings for half an hour. He had thrown rocks into the well of stagnant water and eaten two or three kinds of herbs growing around him, both acidic and milky tasting. Then he saw a cluster of stars and counted them. There were fifteen from north to south and eight from east to west. But the second time he counted, there were seventeen from north to south and twelve from east to west. He thought he must have made an error in addition by counting some of the same stars twice. He couldn't touch and separate them, leaving the ones he'd already counted aside. That must have been the mistake. The third time he counted, he obtained the following figures: twenty stars from north to south (and one small blue point of uncertain identity, star or fleck of dust on his retina) and fifteen from east to west (though he thought he discerned another tiny, innocent, imprecise one, number sixteen, twinkling between number eight and number nine). It seemed like an inconsistency of the heavens.

"Don't worry, son," his father explained. "No matter how many you can distinguish, thousands of miles away from them, light years, my boy, there are many more, invisible to us, but detectable with the right apparatuses.

Telescopes and things like that."

"And behind them?"

"Still more, my boy. Behind the stars are many more stars, in huge quantities."

"And behind them?"

"Still many more."

"And behind the last ones?"

"Too wide a space," the man answered.

Mauricio closed his eyes. He opened them unexpectedly, contemplated the first layer of stars, then the second, then the third. Exerting an enormous effort, he could find hundreds, thousands of little luminous points that exuded their twinkling light in the middle of space, and space, the blue, profound, too wide space, with no beginning or end, that never ended and that all together could not enter the retina of his eyes. Then he got dizzy and fainted.

When he woke up, it struck him that space was an invisible, warm, and friendly entity that surrounded objects, plants, and things. Houses, furniture, animals, banks, plazas, and sweaters knitted by mothers.

"I am surrounded by space," he told his father with satisfaction. He was a tiny star that quivered upon moving and filtered a celestial or golden light, but around him the air comprised a limitless space without borders and revolved according to certain constant, solid, secure, and unknown laws. He liked sitting quietly on the warm, serene summer night, knowing that despite his apparent immobility, he was shifting imperceptibly in accordance with a planned orbit and that the plants, the moist, green leaves of the ivy, the garden's shiny rocks, the wood-framed, white windows, the velvety couches, and the birds sleeping in the branches spun with him.

The dictionary said: "Infinite: that which does not and cannot have an end or conclusion." That which does not. And cannot. Have. An end. Or conclusion. He repeated it several times. He decided to test it. He sat behind the gate at dusk. The sky was starry. His mother was knitting a sweater. He didn't know when she had started or if she would ever finish. He couldn't ask her questions. He could only watch and observe the slow passing of the yarn from one needle to another, so slow, so imperceptible that its movement could well be stationary in the end. The yarn came and went and, when it was going, nobody could really say whether it was going or coming and, when it was coming, nobody knew whether it was actually going. He opened his eyes wide and decided to compute just one section of space. He chose an apparently less populated section, for fear of making mistakes and later having doubts. His father was reading the paper not far away in a white rocking chair. The paper had a beginning and an end; it was not infinite, and yet, many variations could be made with it, so that the text read was not just one, but rather, via multiple and varying combinations, diverse texts appeared, different, new, not yet conceived by the editor and not set by the linotypists. The yarn ran and, if it didn't run, the yarn stopped in one place, sublime and warm. The strip of space to be observed had to be carefully delineated. Once he had selected it, he looked for points of reference to establish it. One star in the north, solitary and distant, that shone almost steadily, could serve as a real limit. The empty space to the right established a neutral field, a resting zone, a stellar landing where the ship of the eyes could dock when it tired of sailing through the universe of twinkling stars. He looked for a southern limit, a base, a place to anchor. He finally discovered a dog's ear comprised of a small stellar formation—a sculptural grouping, you might say—that would serve as a reference. Page four of the paper rustled when it was folded and several letters spilled onto the surface of page ten. As for the left side, it was easy to be guided by three stars mounted almost on top of each other. They were small and seemed human.

Once the perimeter to be analyzed was delineated, the limits fixed precisely, and the coordinates of observation established, he had to study carefully but without fixing his eyes too much. If he fixed them, the effort made by the eyes could accept the apparition of blurred points, possible errors of an imprecise identity. Over the text read, an infinity of other texts could be read at random, mixing the symbols, sentences, as the yarn that came and went constructed, in its movement, different dance steps, structures of changing air, energy that moved sinuously in multiple forms. He would start counting from west to east, as if he were following the course of a ship. Then he would do it from north to south, not shifting or moving his head, not closing his eyes. What kind of information could a text provide if it was enough to move or change just one of the parts of the sentence, or even less, if modifying the position of just one of the written symbols was enough to turn the message into something else? His mother could just as well be knitting a sweater, a net, a bag, or a scarf, the wool came and went with a pendular and perpetual motion, once she had started, yes, she had started but nobody now remembered when or how; nor did anyone know how it would end, or what form it would end up assuming, after having been successively an anchor, a knot, a rudder, a saber, and a spur. *The Naming of a New Minister of Finance.* Twelve from west to east. *Political Prisoners Deported. Air Catastrophe.* Fifteen from north to south. Fifteen. Fifteen self-assured stars, shining in the firmament, defiant. The Naming of Political Prisoners. Air Finance. Catastrophe of a Minister. What had she wanted to knit in the beginning? In what beginning? In the beginning of infinity? The first layer seemed defined. Twelve from west to east and fifteen from north to south. *President of World Chess Federation Resigns. Public Transit Scandal.* But surely, there were other layers behind it. Other, apparently invisible layers, difficult to detect in a simple and innocent vision of reality.

"If it were a square," she had said before getting married and many times after being married, "there would always be the risk of bumping into the sides, colliding with them. A line launched from any point inside the square would unfailingly end up crashing into some angle, a straight line, and no matter how much you insist, the way a fish insists inside a fishbowl, knocking, licking the cold edge of the glass, there would be no way to transgress those specific limits placed by who knows whom."

"If it were a circle," he argued, "it would spin indefinitely your whole life, without receding or advancing, with no notion of progress or regression, the different molecules would mix in a terrible confusion or the points inside the circumference, launched in diaspora, would simply dance an inconclusive and meaningless dance, lost in space, floating and minuscule, whether dispersed or coordinated in repulsive concubinage."

Air transit, world scandal, public federation, chess resigns. As far as the second layer, the whole thing was blurrier. Everything was more vague—as when in the distance you can make out a white ship that could also be, why not, a snow-covered island, a low cloud, a huge animal lying down (when did she start knitting? when did she determine the movement of the yarn, from left to right or right to left?)—and the light was increasingly diffuse. It was extremely hard to count the stars in this second layer; he suffered frequent vacillations, was unsure whether to move on to the next or go back to revise the previous computation. *Eight Miners Dead and Twenty-three Missing. Several tremors of medium intensity shook southeastern Iran today. It is assumed that the majority of the seven thousand missing so far this year—a partial figure, since denouncing the missing has been prohibited—have been executed and their bodies have not been found. The price of petroleum by-products has gone up. With the goal of maintaining a professional relationship with the Armed Forces, the State Department will continue for the moment to offer its assistance in matters of security and torture.* Is she knitting or unknitting? Is she leading the yarn to the sea of celestial points or unraveling the hot threads, sinking them in the tide of the seas? It is assumed that the majority of the missing have gone up the by-products of the State Department. And suddenly, the limits chosen precisely, expertly studied, suddenly the established limits and guides were becoming blurred; they oscillated, mixed with others; the solitary and distant star in the north appeared surrounded by other solitary and distant stars or had he just not seen them before? And the empty space, the neutral zone to the right, seemed scattered with eyes, the pupils flickered, the dog's ear had melted into a wheel of spinning points, the dog no longer barked and page ten of the paper was furrowed with stars for letters. It will continue for the moment to offer its assistance in matters of security and torture.

He had lost the visualization of the limits completely. The first stars mingled with the second and the last ones, if he looked—and if there was anything he was sure of it was that he could not stop looking. The silvery points of the stars were reproducing, multiplying, as if they had always been there, as if they had never moved; some stars joined others, and there was less and less neutral space between them; the stars had been defeated by lust, they mounted and straddled each other, and there were so many stars, he felt that they were not only entering through his eyes, not just flooding his pupils, his retina, his iris, his eyelashes, and the lake of his eyebrows, the stars were suddenly invading him through his ears, assaulting his inner ears; they were filling his head, his hair, the air in his mouth, he had stars on his fingers and under his nails and his pockets were full of stars and, if he stepped with his feet, he squashed twinkling stars.

"Circular like a sphere," his mother had said with total confidence.

"Square like a box," his father had answered firmly.

And after twenty, came twenty-one and then twenty-two and twenty-three, he had to hurry to be able to count, he had to run to catch up to the stars, infinite running, infinite counting. I will die before I count them all, he thought, because stars kept appearing, they took up the whole space, they filled the air of the sky and the air of the earth and started to rest on the boughs of the trees and in the thickets, in the watchtower and the streetlamps, the stars that no longer found a place in the firmament were falling a little; they slipped down to the point of penetrating the atmosphere closest to the houses, and they were going to occupy his room, the bed, the closet, all the furniture, and three hundred forty-eight, *has devalued its currency by 389% in one year*, the chickens would start squawking when they invaded the henhouse, the paper full of points of stars, *military specialists starve a rat over several days until the animal turns carnivorous*, the yarn coming and going, going and coming, in a continual rocking; *later they insert him in the intestine of his victim*. And if one fell from the highest tree branch, what would happen? Would it stop shining? Would it lose its light? Could he approach it slowly to touch it? As he had never touched his mother's blue knitting—she didn't like him to—as the letters of the paper that seemed fixed blended together? *By that method, Father Pablo Gazzardi, for example, recently died.* And when it fell, would the house collapse? His father's rocking chair? Would the garden flowers be squashed? *Photo: Daniel Gluckman. Copyright: Le Nouvel Observateur*. One thousand two hundred three, one thousand two hundred four, life is short, a whole night isn't enough, one thousand two hundred seven, tomorrow they will leave, that is certain. It is a relief to know, to know that tomorrow they will leave and won't be there anymore, *missing*, seven thousand, denouncing the missing has been prohibited, even though he didn't have time to count them all and life wasn't long enough, he wanted to, he was going to keep counting all night, but still he could stand it because tomorrow no more, with the light of dawn they would leave and maybe they wouldn't come back, not every night, not every day, and he could tell his mother: "Mama, they're not there anymore, they've gone, they won't come back, sleep well, knit your yarn, read your paper. They won't be back." No more rats eating intestines over several days. Four thousand eight hundred fifteen, four thousand eight hundred sixteen, specialists in, method of dying, numbers weren't enough, there weren't going to be enough, but no matter what, even if he now had to start with 1-A, 2-A, tomorrow they'd be gone and he could sleep peacefully.

Translated from the Spanish by Laura Dail

Requirements for an Addiction to Movies

though layering macaroni and cheese
the woman is thinking of Hitchcock's layered motifs

friendship and betrayal
the grotesque and the ordinary

horror blended
with humor

for laughs
she dyes her water Purple Nightshade

and drinks it like a movie star
in black silk pajamas

she attracts birds to her garden
with a giant projection of a black-and-white bread crumb

at night if the moon isn't there
she makes one from a round Albanian prop that reads

Gone to America
on vacation she visits theaters

The Silver Eye
The Dollar Shadow

at dawn she soaks in the image of a bubble bath
like an exhausted but beautiful murderess

she uses just one emblematic capful
of sharp-focus concentration

ROBERT RAUSCHENBERG

SEEN OF THE CRIME

GENCY

[PAGE 17]
Catastrophe (Arcadian Retreats), 1996.

[LEFT] Early Edition (Arcadian Retreats), 1996.

[ABOVE] Florida Psalm (Anagrams [A Pun]), 1997.

Wrong Distance (Anagrams [A Pun]), 1997.

R.R.

SEEN OF THE CRIME

WORKING WITH MY CHRONOLOGY FOR THE GUGGENHEIM WAS AN AWKWARD EXPERIENCE, HAVING DIFFICULTY READING AND NO HISTORICAL SENSE. THE EVIDENCE OF MY EXISTANCE SEEMS TO ME LIKE AN INTERESTING ADVENTURE HAD BY A STRANGER THAT I WOULD LIKE TO MEET. CRITICISM HAS NOT WORKED IN MY DEVELOPMENT, BECAUSE IF IT WAS GOOD I CONSIDERED IT FLATTERY AND IF IT WERE BAD I THOUGHT OF IT AS MISUNDERSTANDING. I NEVER WORK WITH ANY IDEA OF RISK, GROWING UP "HAVING NOTHING, WHAT DO YOU HAVE TO LOSE". HAPPILY, COURIOSITY HAS TEMPTED ME TO DO ANYTHING THAT HAS TO BE TRIED TO BE REALIZED. PEOPLE ASK ME "TO WHAT DO YOU CONTRIBUTE YOUR SUCCESS?" I USED TO SAY "LUCK", BUT I THINK IT IS "I DONT GIVE A FUCK BUT CARE A LOT" I LOVE WORKING, THERE IS AN EROTIC SATISFACTION WITHOUT SEXUAL LIMITATIONS OR REFERENCES THAT CLIMAXES IN AN UNEXPLAINABLE JOY. RECENTLY I WAS ASKED BY AN OBVIOUSLY UNINTERESTED VEIWER "HOW LONG DID IT TAKE TO DO THAT" MY ANSWER WAS "IF YOU DONT COUNT THE FIRST 20 YEARS, WHICH WEREN'T WASTED, ABOUT 50 YEARS". THERE IS NO ART ACT TOO SIMPLE OR COMPLEX NOT TO BE VALID IF HONEST. ONE OBSTACLE IN LABOURING THIS EXHIBIT IS THAT MY TIME HAS BEEN SPENT ON MY PAST INTERFERRING WITH MY NOW. I AM HAPPY BECAUSE HOPEFULLY YOU CAN LOOK FORWARD TO MY BACK. LOVE

LAIRD HUNT

Dear Sweetheart,

Three people by a house under a frowning moon have joined all the other colored chalk drawings on the sidewalks of the city. Someone passes. Stops. Starts again.

All evening in the center of streetlights amber stutters between stop and go. At the dinner table another kid cuts her finger and doesn't cry. *This is the church . . . This is the steeple . . .* becomes confusing. Requires a new configuration. Digits recompose. *This is the earth. This is the crack . . .*

Dear Sweetheart,

I go to see a famous ventriloquist who is making cardboard children, sitting cross-legged in a circle, tell ghost stories. Every few minutes all but one of the cardboard kids cough. Then I cough. Then I am sitting down next to the ventriloquist on the ventriloquist's bed. Watch, I say. Only I know I haven't actually said anything because I don't know what it is we're going to watch. Then the lights dim. And there are only candles and a few coals in the fireplace. Watch, I say again. I watch. Glowing in the shadows, sitting opposite each other, are a chimera and a sphinx. Cute, I say to the ventriloquist. Then I realize that I am the ventriloquist. Cut that out, I make myself say. I am myself again. Then I am the ventriloquist. This repeats until I'm confused about who is saying what. I said that, says a voice. No, I did. Then the sphinx says, stop. And now I am sitting opposite the sphinx. Hello, says the sphinx. What do you want, sphinx? I say. I want an answer, the sphinx says. To what? To the riddle. That's an old one. It's a new one. So what is it? I realize my lips aren't moving. I am watching the sphinx and the chimera. We are talking. We are sitting at the center of a huge stage. A wind rattles across us. We are made of cardboard. We glow. My lips don't move. Neither do theirs. I tell the riddle. I listen to the riddle. I answer it. There are only three of us.

Stories
of the Early Earth,
Guatemala

NATHANIEL TARN | MARTIN PRECHTEL

In 1952, anthropologist, poet, and translator Nathaniel Tarn traveled to Atitlán, in the highlands of southwestern Guatemala. There he became interested in the ways in which the encounters—peaceful or conflictual—between elements of the Mayan worldview and elements of the Spanish Colonial worldview four centuries ago may have left traces in the contemporary Atiteco Mayan-Christian religious synthesis.

In the early 1950s, Catholic priests seriously interfered with local worship of the Maximon deity (a version of the traditional Mayan god, Mam), and the ensuing 'scandals' have echoed down to the present day. Protestantism, capitalism, socioeconomic change, and the recent violent civil war have all done much to destroy the fabric of age-old Mayan religious life and to threaten traditional Mayan identity in the Guatemalan highlands. The Mam, however, continues to be of major importance in his almost incredible multivalence.

Tarn's work chronicling local history and beliefs began in 1952 and 1953; it continued in 1969 and 1979, when he joined forces with Martin Prechtel. The following are several excerpts from their oral history, Scandals in the House of Birds, *which details various versions of the origin of the Mam. At first sight, the story, which has complex relations to the great Highlands classic text* Popol Vuh, *does not seem to be so much a tale of the world's beginning but rather a tale about social order breaking down when men are too long away from home, and it may reflect the problems of a society of traders. The main parts of the story of the Mam, however, involve the origin of order in the world as a whole—a major, if not the major, story told by virtually all tribal origin myths.*

Tarn records the following story, told by his teacher Nicolas Chiviliu:

In the very old days, when men were small, dirty, and poor, we the Atitecos were capable of prophecy and knowing about the rain before it came. Among these ancients there were—now . . . was it twelve or six? It was six, yes, six—who used to go on regular trips east to Antigua which, in those days, was the capital of Guatemala. You know the town: it is still there, tourists love it. The ancients were traders and fishermen and, after fishing the fish from the lake, they went on three-day journeys to Antigua and then came back to Atitlán. They did the journey very quickly until they arrived at the two volcanoes.

These men had six sisters—some say wives—who were very clever, but also poor and dirty. In Antigua, the men were always treated as "Indios" and "Ixtis" and "dirty people" . . .

LEFT The Maximon as Judas, hung by the Telinel on the Atitlán church porch, 1953.

The Lake Atitlán Area, Department of Solola, Highland Guatemala.

Pascual Mendoza, a shaman and "miracle worker," is given to frequent outbursts of crying and is nicknamed Weep Wizard. He explains:

We have a group of women, the *nawal taq exji* or *taq iyoma'*, the Power Women. They are pure, steadfast, ideal women. They have their husbands—the Power Men, the *nawal taq achi*—although they are as solid as old maids. We call old maids *rilaj q'apoja'*: venerable maids. These women used to go southwest to the coast every day, taking the road past the crossroads, the *kolo' be*, as you leave the village, passing Xokexom and Chicacao and then on down to San Miguel Panaj and San Antonio Suchitepéquez. That road is a killer. Most men who go down in Holy Week, for instance, take three days. A woman doing it today is unthinkable.

Our Power Women go down carrying huge baskets. They are winds and clouds going down to the coast and coming back by return flight that very day. They take salt down from Sacapulas in the north and trade it for cacao. Also tropical fruit.

At the same time as the Power Women traveled southwest, their men would catch fish in the lake and take them all the way east to Patzun, on the way to Antigua. It's said they went so fast, the fish were still alive and jumping when they got into the highlands. Some of them would go as far as Panq'an, which is our old name for Antigua.

Prechtel adds:

He is not saying it in the story, but the men put one foot on one volcano, then the other foot on the next, then another, then another. The story only says that they went very quickly so that the fish would remain fresh. The men and women moved in a continuous cycle. When the men came back in the early morning, the women would have already gone. And when the women came back in the afternoon, the men were already gone. Some say the men and women were siblings and they each had husbands and wives. Most say that the men and women were married but did not see each other too often. Cabezera* says they made love only once every twenty days—the Mayan calendrical cycle has twenty days.

Weep Wizard:

In the story of the Power Women, we have the Power Men passing between the volcanoes: Volcano-Volcano (Volcano Atitlán) and Volcano-Her-Children (Volcano Tolimán). There was a place, below Sajkab, where they would test their weapons. The weapons were called *hwit*. They were magic sticks or staffs. They would throw a *hwit* at a wall and it would boomerang back: the wall would be all sliced up. They had no other weapons since all other arms were prohibited by the government.

The Power Men went up every day and could read their own palms. They could also make their *hwit* stand up and it would divine for them what was happening at home. One day, they were at Tz'anch'oj, which is just behind Volcano-Her-Children.

The Power Men are going along. Some say there are twelve men and some say three. The older people seem to prefer three. The first man was Poklaj, Dust; the second Batzin, Thread; and the third was Ch'eep, the Ultimo. Well, they are

* The head of Atitlán's Indian officials.

climbing away and the older brother, Dust, says to the younger: "Hey, don't you feel a bit ridiculous, a bit ashamed?"

The Ultimo asks why.

"Well, because there is another man messing around with your wife," says Dust.

"I didn't know that," says the Ultimo.

"I think we should 'play a game' on the next trip, don't you?" said Dust. So they agreed on it.

The next trip, the Ultimo left in his house the box that we usually place inside our carrying frame. When they got to Tz'anch'oj, he turned back, leaving the other two to go on to Godinez and sleep there. At midday, the Ultimo gets home and knocks on the door. No answer. He knocks again. Eventually his wife's voice, asking "Oooooooooouuuu! What are *you* doing here?"

"I just forgot my box," says the Ultimo.

The wife goes on delaying by asking questions and he says she should just let him in to get his box. She lets him in; he has liquor and some food. He tells her to tell the friend to come out.

"*Friend*," she says, "*what* friend? What do you mean? Whom do you mean?"

"Oh, the guy lying under the bed wrapped in a mat, of course," says the Ultimo. "Is that what you do to your friends? Is that how you treat your turkeys, shoving them under the bed?" he asks his wife. The wife begins to apologize; her husband tells her not to worry. They should all have lunch together and then he will be off again. The lover comes out all colors, feeling terrible: the husband tells him to sit down and not feel bad and not run away. The husband offers the lover a drink; the lover thinks he is going to kill him with that drink.

"Why should I kill you?" says the Ultimo. "You are a man just like I am. You saw a fruit, you smelled it, you found it good and wanted to eat it. Any man would have done the same: there is no fault in you." The wife is crying. He tells her to pass the food and liquor around; they all get soaked. The Ultimo then picks up his box and departs.

He gets back to his brothers; they talk about it. The brothers argue that they cannot let this go on: pretty soon the whole village will be at it. Obviously the wife is informing on them and has joined "the other side." She has turned *q'isoum*, transforming witch. They will have to be cunning, to "play a game," *tz'aniem*, and risk themselves against these devils. But they cannot do it alone. They will have to make a form, toy, doll, instrument, weapon: an *itzbal*.

Now Dust, Thread, and the Ultimo decide they will have to call a convention of the Power Men and, after selling their wares in Antigua, they make for Atitlán and on to the center of the world. We call that center Cerro de Burro*. It's a small hill among those that separate us from the coast, just southwest of our village. There they call all the Power Men and Power Women together. Then, they all give *razón*, which is like they're saying what should be done about a case and why, and Dust is first: some even call him Santiago because Santiago is our "first" saint. Dust-man they call him. "Well," someone begins, "it seems as if the earth has gotten a little different: the sons and daughters** have gotten a little bit out of hand and the order of things is beginning to break up. Virgin boys are starting to marry widows and widowers take virgin girls to

---

* Burro's hill.

** The ordinary people, especially the uninitiated.

wife; married men are sleeping with other men's wives; people are taking things that don't belong to them; Indians are trying to be *ladinos** . . . All this has got to stop and we are the ones who must stop it."

Each one gives his or her views. One of the Power Women told a story about her human husband: how he got worms in his testicles so that they rattled and how she cured him. This was a case of female witchcraft. The whole village was suffering from female witchcraft as a matter of fact. . . . Well, in one way or another, enough evidence was collected at this Power Conference for something to get done.

*The Central American term for *mestizo*, non-Indian locals or foreigners.

Nathaniel Tarn in Atitlán, 1952–53.

The Telinel, an official who looks after the Mam and whose nickname is Loincloth, tells the story differently:

A long time ago, there were many Power Men. And there was one woman: Maria Magdalena. She was very powerful: number-one crazy woman and also an incredible witch. She would spend eight nights with a man and then switch to another and so on down the line. She would get hold of someone's husband and run him so ragged he would turn into a *nikanik*, a crazy guy, a kind of village idiot, and very soon die. But the guy who was looking after her more than most was Diego Tzaa'j*—for he was very rich and lived inside a hill. No one could help being attracted to her. And the world had only just begun.

There were three shamans, diviners-of-days, who wanted to cure this woman and set the world straight: while this woman was in the world with all these guys buzzing around her nothing could happen right. The best thing they could do, they thought, was to put her in a sweat bath. To sweat her up. That is the way you get rid of *ch'ojlal*, the lust sickness. They tried it one time. When they woke up, all the men were tucked inside the sweat bath and she was gone! Another time, one of the three diviners became her lover, he was that attracted. He was also very strong and told her that, no matter what happened, she would not be able to do him in. But she got him all right: she slowly turned him into a *nikanik*. Once he tried to get her with the *isote* plant—which was used against transforming witches—but she turned it around against him and drove him crazy.

* *Tzaa'j* is a taxicoba tree.

It was at that point that they decided on making the Mam.

Weep Wizard:
In the great council room, the Power Men and Power Women were debating. Francisca Batz'bal, that is, Francisca Thread, gets up and says, "I believe that we should make a form."

Juan Ajcot, nicknamed Red Banana, says:
"I believe we should make a *cha'jalniel ruchiliev*, a guardian of the earth," said First Merchant. "Let's make a helper, a machine; let's ask a tree —we'll make an image from the tree and give him wisdom and set him up as caretaker of the earth."

Weep Wizard:
Another answers, "Yes, but with what?"

Francisca says, "Let's try rock."

And they tried rock and the rock wouldn't stand up. They tried mud, rubber, and other substances. Then, they saw that the obvious thing was to make it of wood like a *santo*. "Okay, let's do that," said one. "Let's use cedar." The women said that cedar was too purely good: it lacked spunk, fire, death—and how would they get rid of female magic if they used cedar? But nevertheless they went to the place Xejuyu to ask the cedar. They talked to him, gave him food and candles, but he said no. He did not want to have anything to do with woman-magic.

The session went on as they discussed each wood in turn. "Let's try the cypress," they said. The cypress said that he had killed the jaguar in the old days, but he was no good at killing woman-magic. So they said, "Well, let's go talk to the *tzaa'j*." But the tree said he was good for beds and house-corners because he didn't rot, but he also didn't move very fast, and no, thank you.

Red Banana:
The merchants come upon six coastal trees: the white guayava, the guanacaste, the ceiba, the chicharro, the cedar, and one other I forget. They talk to each tree in turn, making their offerings and ceremonial speeches and requests. Each tree says he cannot give up his own spot: his boss will be mad at him is the excuse. The trees are thrones of the rain angels. The last tree says, "Why don't you try Pkok?"—that is, the Corral—which is the name we give here to the home area around the lake.

So the merchants go to Pkok at Xesiwan; they talk to *chaj*, the pine tree, to the cypress, the *okuy*, the *kuxin*, and the *tzaa'j*. But each of these trees is a throne. Better: the thrones are connections between sky and earth, like ladders going up to heaven. The upper part of the tree, where the angel sits invisible, belongs to sky; the lower part to earth. It is like an office: the angel sits in the tree and picks up his mail.

Weep Wizard:
So each tree claimed to have its own work to do and to be already busy helping the world to thrive. They went to the bat tree who said, "I glow at night in the people's fires: what would they say if I became a killer?" They went to the pine tree who said that he lit fires and kept them going in the hearths and adorned all the fiestas and celebrations: how could he mess with woman-magic? There would be no good odors in the forest anymore! And the *okuy* tree also refused. And all these Power Men were trees,

you understand, so what they were actually doing was asking each other.

As they got to the south side of Volcano-Volcano, they found the *hornillo* tree, from which they make the marimba and some of the drums. They said, "This tree's wood is hard; he has a note and can sing: his secret is that he is the spirit of the song-men." And they asked him. But the *hornillo* tree said no. He would willingly help to make the form stand up if they ever found it, but, as for him, he was hot shit and used only by angels.

Red Banana:
The *tzaa'j* says the same. "We can't believe it! We have been through eleven trees!" say the merchants. They are giving the whole thing up for lost, walking around in circles, their arms behind their backs, shaking their heads. Suddenly the merchant Tzaa'j has an idea. "I have a friend who lives on Volcano-Her-Children," he says. "He's over there and maybe *he'll* do it." They wander around, up through Bekan and Chupral. They go all over that place but they can't see anything special. Then they come on an alder tree, a smooth tree with few leaves.

Right next to it stands a *tz'ajtel*, a coral tree, but it has bad wood, is dumb-looking and soft. "This is just the *worst* scene possible," they think, so they go through the whole business with the alder. They begin to hear the coral tree panting uneasily. Its heart is almost jumping out of its body, it is so anxious to talk to them. As for the alder, it claims to belong to the sons and daughters to keep them warm: it will definitely not give up its body to the merchants. But the coral tree seems to be more than willing.

Well, the merchants make to go home and the coral tree is weeping and weeping.

"Why don't they talk to me?" he says, and, as they go off, he whistles.

So the First Merchant calls to his Ultimo and says, "Hey, did you whistle, Ultimo?" Well, they find out it isn't Ultimo, it's the tree. They tell this tree he's no good, he rots, he's soft, he's valueless, he won't burn.

"Yeah, I know," says the tree, "but I'll do the job you need."

So First Merchant has a list of questions. "Well, are you ready to take pain? Fire? Glass? Bullets? The heat of day? The cold of night? Wet? Damp? Mud? Slings? Arrows? Outrageous fortune? Everything?"

"Yeah, yeah, yeah, I am, I am, I am," says the coral tree.

"Are you ready to turn into a man? Into a woman? To do everything we say?"

"I am, I am, I am," says the tree very quickly.

"Without slipping in anything that *you* want to do yourself?"

"Yeah, yeah, yeah," says the tree, quicker and quicker.

"Without getting paid? Without any reward? Without anything to show for anything?"

"Yes, yes, yes! Absolutely! I'm just sick and tired of being here and nobody wanting me!" said the tree.

"Okay," said the merchants. And they quit questioning the tree.

So the merchants go home and they get something to eat. "He doesn't look so good, he doesn't cut much of a figure," they decide, "but he's our boy." They all get their files the next day, to sharpen their machetes. But the Ultimo has had a dream.

The Maximon as Judas, hung on the Atitlán church porch, 1953.

"This tree doesn't want sharp machetes: rub them on rocks to make them dull," he tells them. It's true: if you put a sharp machete into coral wood, it will stick just like cork. So First Merchant comes up to the tree and asks if he is ready for this pain. The tree says he is.

"Remember everything we told you yesterday because we are your makers and we will take you apart if you disobey us," First Merchant says.

So they give him a first stroke on his feet, *plaaam*. With each chop, they give him an order. They get to his head and the head is going up and down, nodding, like this. *Plaaam*.

"You feel that?" they ask.

At every stroke they hear the tree going, "Ah! Eh! Oh! Oh! Ay! Ou! Ah! Eh!" while they are making and shaping him. When they have finally carved him out, he is about this big.* "Well, can you stand up now?" they ask. "He looks pretty good this man made of pain," they say to themselves in congratulation.

Weep Wizard:

Then Dust called all the Powers and they came in a big wind. Dust announced that they had found "it."

"*This?*" the Powers asked sardonically.

But Thread came forward and said, "Yes, yes, this is him. I recognize him perfectly! Okay, everyone in order give him seven strokes of the hatchet." So Thread directed the making of the figure; it was not Dust who did it.

Loincloth:

At this point, the old ladies, the Power Women, will come and say, "This tree will be the one to cure our world because all it does is tell lies and that is exactly what we need! We need something that can put witchcraft into something else and kill it." They will divine the right day on which to make the figure. The women will say that it cannot be carved—it has to be sung into being. They will charm it with the first song. With each cut, they will make a prayer and will work inside clouds to be invisible. The diviners will teach the women to get food each day from the village: they will not be hunting anymore. And also to bring them their pipes and chocolate and liquor. With each word there will be 260 questions*, with each cut they will ask him:

"Are you willing to go inside a man and kill him?"

"Yes."

"Are you willing to become a wall?"

"Yes."

"Are you willing to become a spine?"

"Yes."

"A woman."

"Yes."

"A man?"

"Yes."

"A wasp?"

"Yes."

"Smoke?"

"Yes."

"Are you willing to become all things that have smell and taste on the face of the earth?"

"Yes."

"Are you willing to go up? Are you willing to go down?"

"Yes."

"Are you willing to go underwater? Under the

* About four feet tall.

* A calendrical number.

trees?"

"Yes."

"And under the earth?"

"Yes."

And so on and on, until the end of the questions. So, finally they will come to an end but the figure will not be able to stand up. The two women will take off their headbands, wrap them around the legs and up the body and around the arms and head, and the figure will move. They will sing; it will stand up and begin to dance. The headbands will give it the power. Then they will begin to test him.

Weep Wizard:
Batzin gives him the power to tie knots; Ikaj, the axe, the power to chop, cut, and make lightning; and so on down the Powers. One gives *naoj*, intelligence, savvy, the power to connive and be wily: some say this is Dust and some say it's Tzaa'j. Many of these things we do not remember exactly anymore. They give him the power to name the days and divine: his is the tree of the divining seeds, which, from now on, will be taken from the coral. They give him the power to make rain, wind, lightning, storm, and to ruffle the waters.

When the Power Men have given him their powers, the Power Women line up and give him theirs. They give him the power to turn into a woman, to make himself beautiful, and to change forms. They give him food, drink, and clothing. "You have a thousand faces, forms, words, prayers—of each a thousand," they say. "A thousand prayers, a thousand songs, a thousand compassions," as the *ajkuna** later say.

* The shamans or native priests.

"You can be the head of butterfly, bat, hawk, double-headed eagle, jaguar, snake, bee, wasp, and all those woman powers."

Nicolas Chiviliu:
After he is made, he is very, very hot: his chest grows into a hot sun disk. His face and chest are glowing; he is bright like the sun. He thinks he is the sun. Later they will have to blow mist into his eyes. When they begin to punish him, they will have to blow clouds over the sun.

Weep Wizard:
"You are our dog, our servant," they make sure to tell him. He is feeling a bit inflated because he has not yet gotten up. They begin to play the second song.

Francisca Thread gives the last cuts on his feet, forms them, and sings, "Stand up, boy, stand up, man!" so he stands up. They ask him if he can talk.

"Ha, ha! I'm the best of speakers! I speak better than any of those sons of bitches!" he cries out. So they said that they would have to test him.

They went to the village and found a *nikanik ala*, a real dumb little guy who had never opened his mouth and they brought him to the Mushroom Place. Well, the new figure gave this guy a piece of mushroom with mineral water—kneeling down and praying over him before he did that—and suddenly, no question about it, the guy could *speak*! The figure had turned instantly into a sort of demigod. Then they had to make him dumb again and so they blew mist into his eyes. The guy could still talk and so on, but he no longer had that divine knowledge.

Francisca Thread said that they had to dance the figure a second time and they created the second song. They danced him in the four directions in order to orient him: "This is where your father comes from and this is where your mother rests," they said to him. The third song was for the woman: she picked him up on her shoulders and danced with him, just like a Telinel does today.

They created a table for burning candles and incense there and wanted to test him some more. His root stock stayed there—and is still there at the Mushroom Place up high, back of the village —but they sent him to the south side of Volcano-Her-Children and told him to make rain. He made rain after flying there like the wind, but he stood under the rain and got all wet. They all roared and roared with laughter and asked him what sort of a god he was, the knucklehead, the *rubenom acha*, the manufactured man, the one who had not been born, who couldn't get out from under his own rain!

"You don't have any flesh—where the hell are you?" they laughed and laughed. "You will kill yourself if you make lightning and it shoots *you yourself!*" They roared. "When you make rain, stand *on top* of the clouds," they said to him.

"Oh, I didn't know that," said the being. So they made him try it again while he was still all wet and shivering.

Then they told him to come down out of there and instructed him to change into a dog, a man, a leaf, a woman, and all sorts of things. Then the Ultimo asked him if he remembered his wife—the Ultimo's, of course—and the figure said yes, he did.

"How the hell can you *remember?*" said the Ultimo, but the other just went "*ooouuuuuuu . . .*" Then the Ultimo told him to get on his wife's case because she had messed him up.

"But I thought you were going to . . ." said the older brother, Dust.

But the Ultimo said, "Well, no, we have a form now," so the figure went down the hill. They had this great procession to carry him into town. So he went down the hill to do his first job.

EUGENIO DITTBORN
MILAGROS DE LA TORRE
ROSÂNGELA RENNÓ

Eugenio Dittborn, *Airmail Painting No. 78, The 7th History of the Human Face (The Scenery of the Sky)*, 1990.

[ABOVE]
Eugenio Dittborn, *Airmail Painting No. 05, To Hang*, 1984.

[RIGHT]
Eugenio Dittborn, *Airmail Painting No. 15, Shadows, Nothing*, 1984.

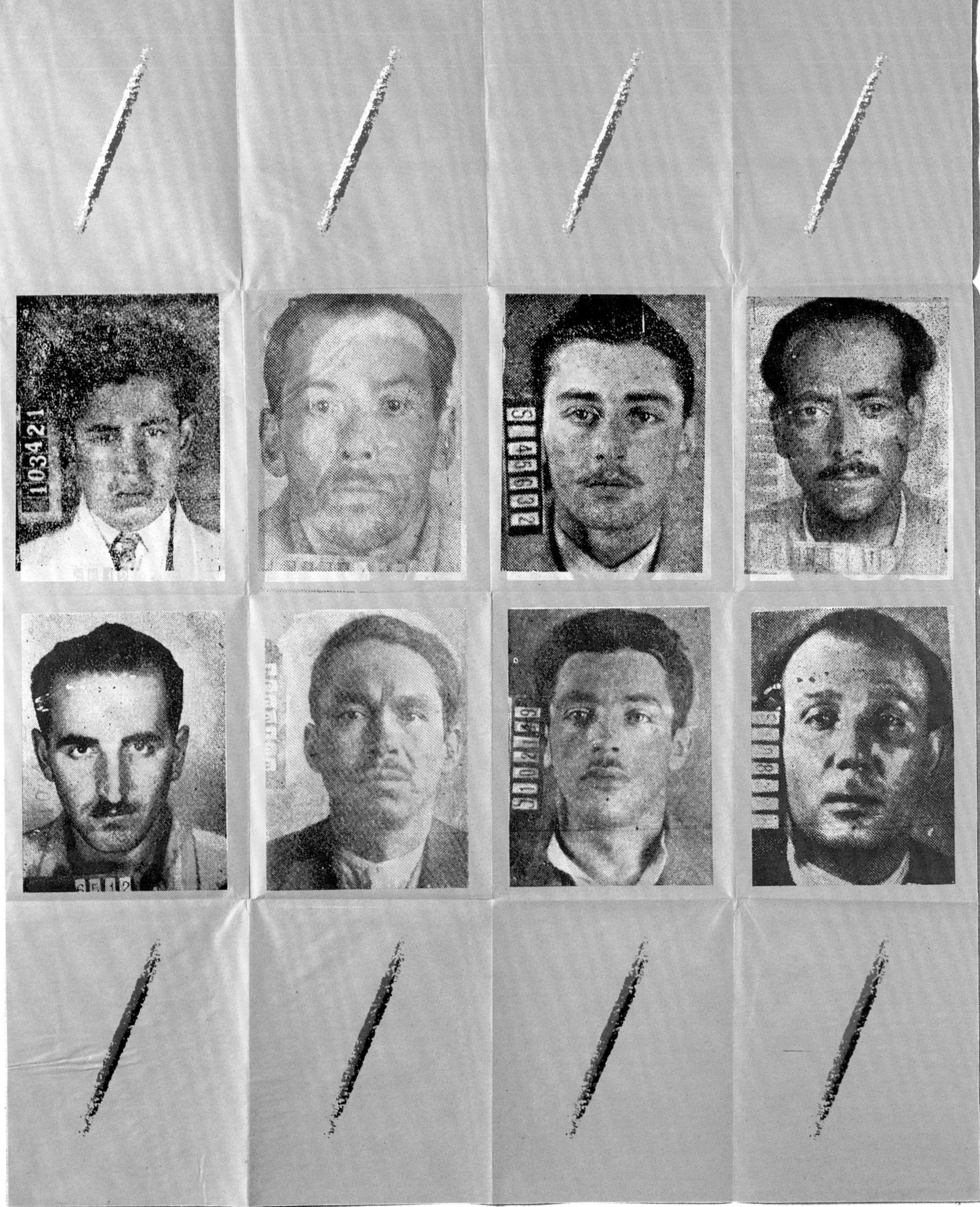
103421

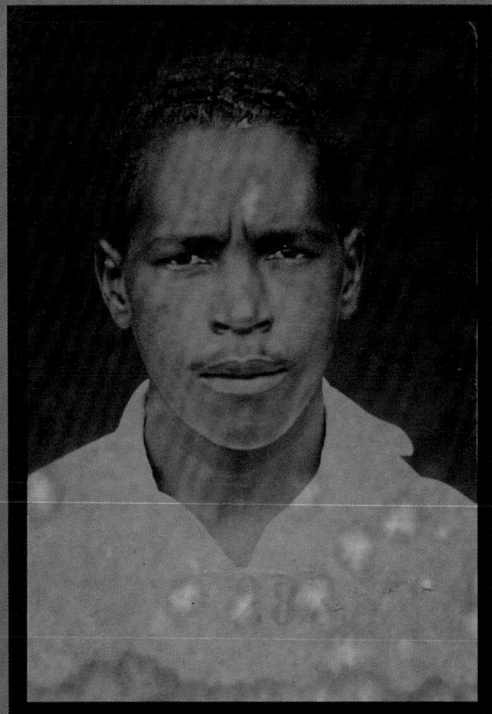

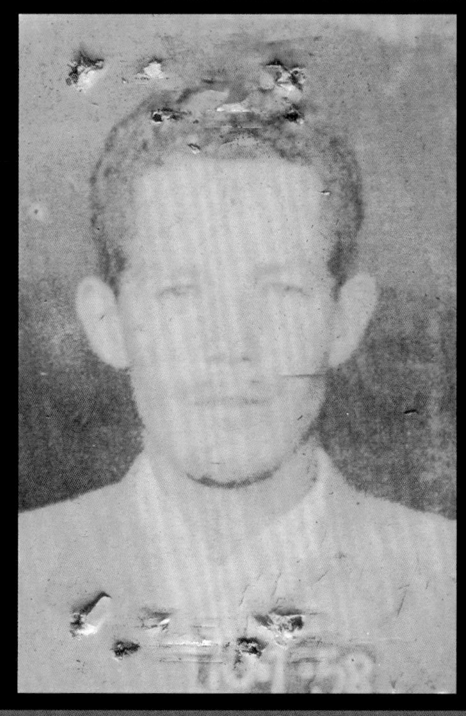

Rosângela Rennó, from *Imemorial*, 1994.

MILAGROS **DE LA TORRE**

Knife fabricated from prison bed frame.

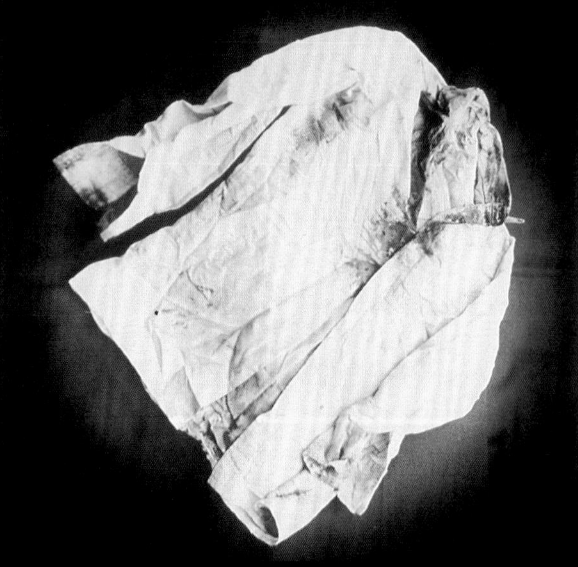

Shirt of journalist murdered in the massacre of Ucchuraccay, Ayacucho.

All images from Milagros de la Torre, *Los pasos perdidos (The Lost Steps)*, Lima, Peru, 1996.

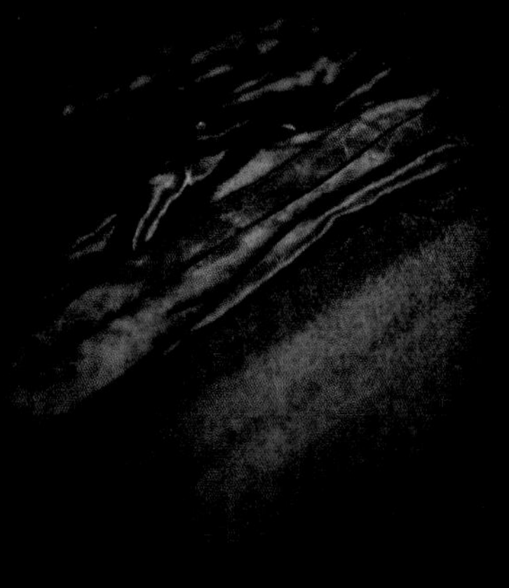

Skirt worn by Marita Alpaca when she was pushed by her lover from the eighth floor of the Sheraton Hotel in Lima. In the autopsy, she was found to be pregnant.

Belts used by psychologist Mario Poggi to strangle a rapist during police interrogation.

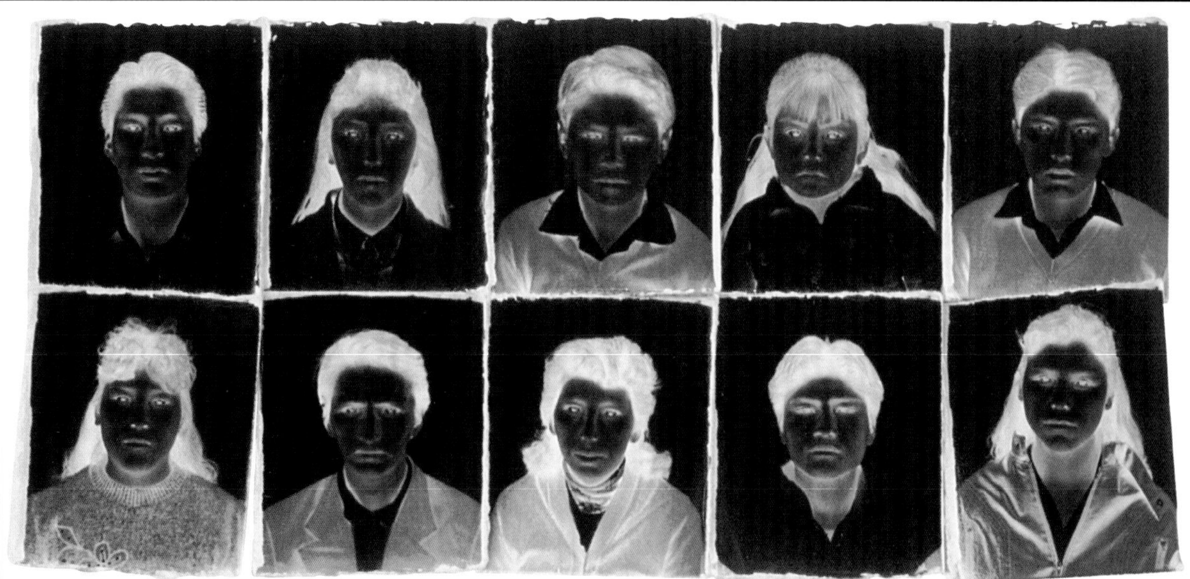

from *Bajo el sol negro (Under the Black Sun),*
Cuzco, Peru, 1991–93.

This project was inspired by the low-cost, rudimentary techniques of Peruvian street photographers, who often apply Mercurochrome to paper negatives in order to lighten (and thus

The historian Pierre Nora has written that "modern memory is, above all, archival. It relies entirely on the materiality of the trace, the immediacy of the recording, the visibility of the image." Photography is critical to the practice and authority of the archive, insofar as it folds together history as representation and representation as history. Transferring the world to image, photography as a representational structure produces a certain archival *effect*. And, like photography, the archive gains its authority to represent the past through an apparent neutrality, whereby difference is either erased or regulated. Both the archive and photography reproduce the world as witness to itself, a testimony to the real, historical evidence.

Eugenio Dittborn of Chile, Rosângela Rennó of Brazil, and Milagros de la Torre of Peru have all worked with the concept of the archive. Through their work, they seek to rezone the cartography of memory and to restore a past that has been erased from the historical record. While Dittborn's work dates from the 1970s through the period of Pinochet's dictatorship, the work of both Rennó and de la Torre began in the murky wake of a period of state and civil violence. They use photography precisely to destabilize its authority as a technology of remembrance, a technology that participates in constructing seamless narratives of identity. Each of these artists works with the notion of the unsanctioned or unlawful body of the nation as a way to address the violence that characterizes the inscription of history. They use photographs that represent the moments before which the body becomes absent. In so doing, they question how and what it is that photography remembers and forgets and for whom and what purpose.

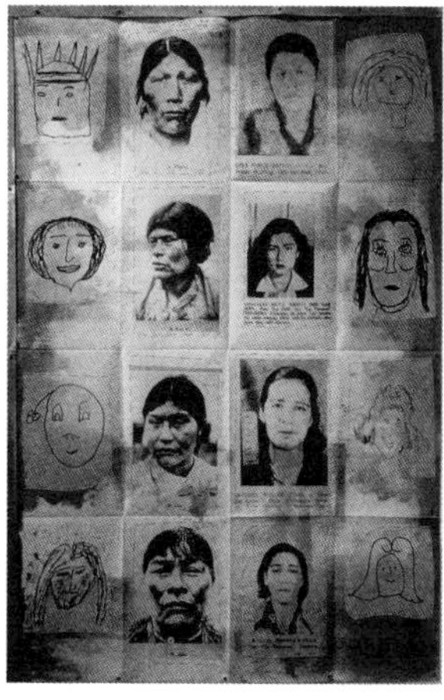

Eugenio Dittborn, *Airmail Painting No. 95, The 13th History of the Human Face (the Portals of H.)* (detail), 1991.

Since the late 1970s, Dittborn's project has been to return to circulation the marginalized and erased figures of Chilean history. His work points to the the archive as a container that preserves but, at the same time, buries the subject. In his extensive series of *Airmail Paintings*, Dittborn has brought together anthropologist Martín Gusinde's 1920 photographs of indigenous peoples of the Tierra del Fuego, who, after a long history of extermination, were on the point of disappearance; ID photographs of petty thieves and prostitutes taken from police files and published in cheap detective magazines of the 1940s and 1950s; identikit pictures; images of archaeological remains; and drawings of faces made by Dittborn's younger daughter. This work of exhumation recovers the body of Chilean memory and history and places it back into circulation. Folded and transported to new points of destination, the unfolding of these figures makes them visible and combats the oblivion to which they had been consigned.

As it exposes us to those whom the government had defined as transgressive, criminal, or primitive, this work fractures the seamless and monumental history of the nation. It becomes an allegory of life under the dictatorship of Pinochet, a regime that committed violence against its people in the name of the nation and national identity.

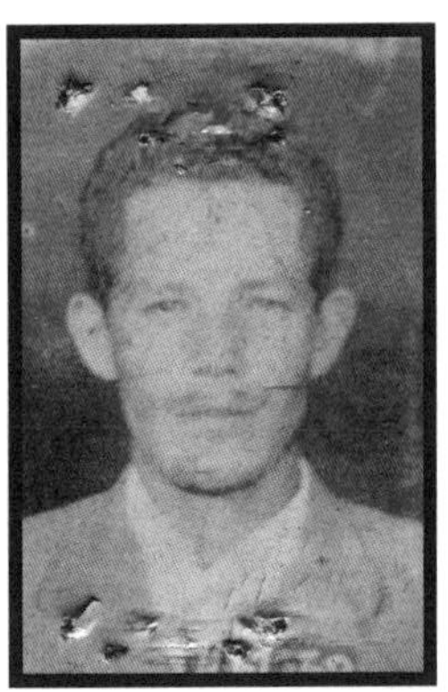

Rosângela Rennó, from *Imemorial*, 1994.

In her series *Imemorial* (1994), Rosângela Rennó showed an installation of fifty photographs that yield dark portraits of the workers and children who built Brasilia, the capital whose architectural design was championed for its utopian vision. In a warehouse of the Public Archive of the Federal District, Rennó found suitcases of more than 15,000 files concerning the employees of the government construction company Novacap. In *Imemorial*, she used stories that told of a massacre in the workers' barracks and of dozens of workers who had died in the building of Brasilia and been buried in the foundations. In the archives, these workers were classified under the heading "dismissed due to death."

An example of Walter Benjamin's warning that not even the dead are safe when only the victors tell the story, Rennó's work engages in a struggle over the ownership of memory. The experience of seeing is itself subject to the forces of forgetting, and the labor of reading traces is equivalent to coming to terms with the past. Traces of identity are captured in the moment prior to the subjects' disappearance, a recognition of difference brought out of the shadows of a suppressed history. The installation represents a redemptive gesture, a resurrection of fallen bodies, those sacrificed in the building of the future.

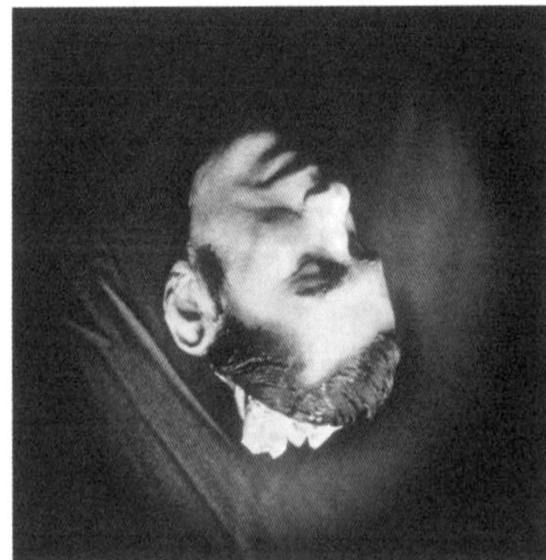

Milagros de la Torre, *Police identification mask of criminal known as "Loco Perochena"*, from *Los pasos perdidos (The Lost Steps)*, Lima, Peru, 1996.

In 1996, Milagros de la Torre produced a series of fifteen photographs of objects taken in the archive of *cuerpos del delitos* at the Palace of Justice in Lima. The title of the series, *The Lost Steps*, refers to the name given to a hallway in the Palacio de Justicia through which detainees pass on their way to receiving their condemnation. Under the guidance of long-term archivist Manuel Guzman, de la Torre was led through the mountains of files, boxes, and evidence hidden away in the recesses of the Palace. The objects she photographed are the evidence of crimes committed, the remaining traces of tragic stories of passions, beliefs, and illusions gone awry.

There is no bright light of revelation given to these objects. Rather, they are seen in an obscure or uncertain light. Death haunts the photographs. They are witness to what is absent from the scene. The strange illumination de la Torre gives to her photographs—as if they are lit by the darkness that has befallen them—represents the objects' entombment in the archives and a memory that, swiftly buried, lies deep within the shadows of history. One may propose that the effect of de la Torre's work in the archive today functions in part allegorically. It suggests something that has passed, but which, by being brought back into the present as the image of a ruinous history, becomes emblematic of the fate of things to come.

In the wake of a long period of violence and unrest, the concepts of identity, freedom, and justice, as defined by government, have become a guide to measuring the possibility of democracy. Their artistic expression represents an intervention in the archives of a nation. As these images bring identities into the light and expose us to the stories they embody, they are mute witness to the fate of the individuals who, by entering the public record, have been written out of history. At a time when histories of identity and nation are being rewritten, these images are a timely reminder of the instrumental power of state institutions to control, if not determine, the lives of its populace. The photographs become a memorial, a site where memory and forgetfulness can face each other.

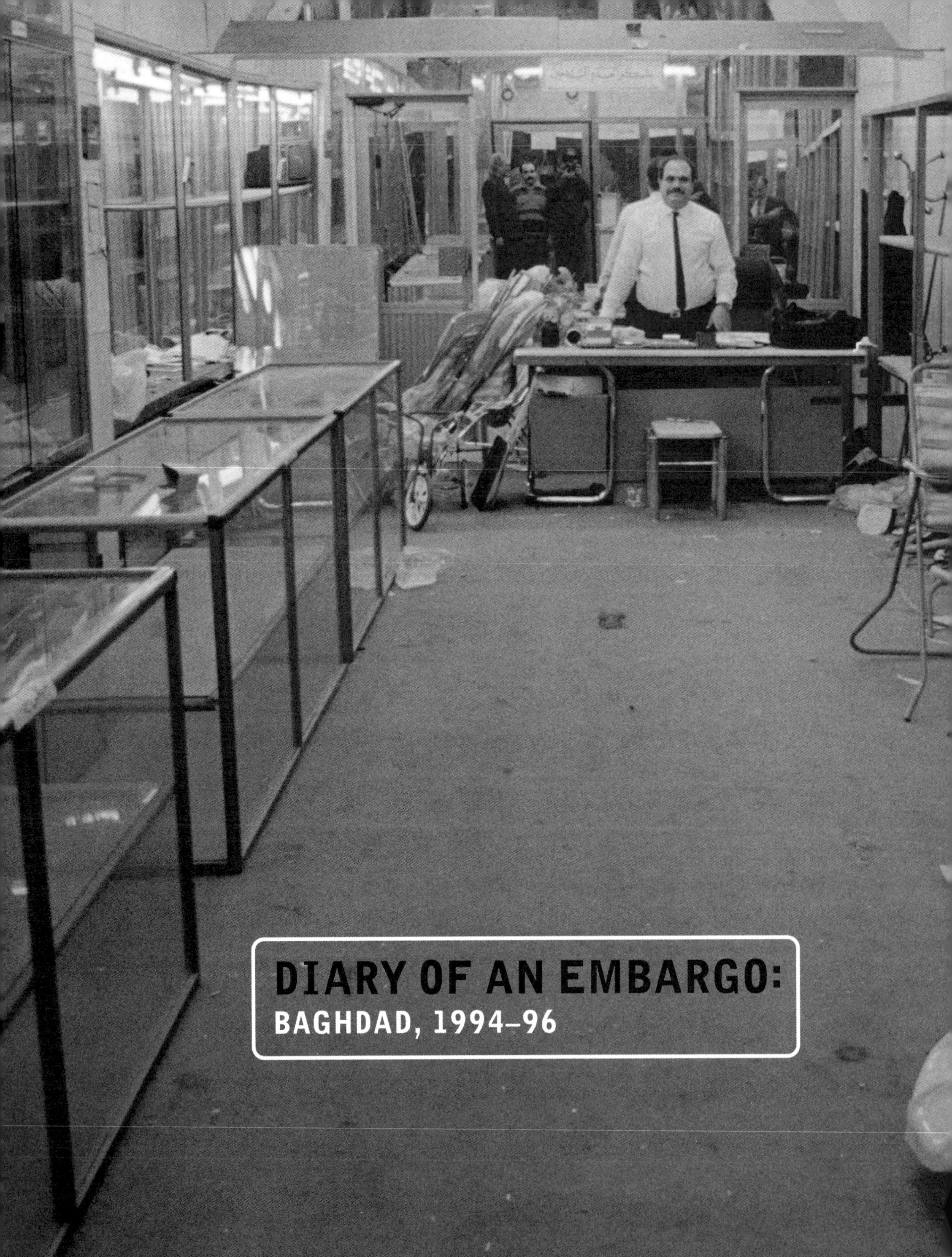

DIARY OF AN EMBARGO:
BAGHDAD, 1994–96

NUHA AL-RADI

The following passages are taken from a diary kept by Iraqi artist Nuha Al-Radi, during two years of the UN embargo on trade with Iraq, which began in early 1992.

BAGHDAD

1994

November 3 The first thing I noticed coming into Bags at four in the morning after being away for ten months was how wide, clean, and well looked-after the main streets were. I'd forgotten that. Naturally, there was not a soul on them. At the border they took a blood sample for an AIDS test, luckily with a disposable needle. The guards there looked well fed, but they still wanted something to eat. Heard a few good stories—the best about a woman who took a whole cooking pot full of drugged or poisoned dolma (stuffed vegetables) as a present to the guards of the Abu Hanifa Mosque. The guards slept and the whole place was robbed—carpets, chandeliers, everything. It took one of the guards two days to wake up. Imagine the quantity that was administered.

LEFT **Baghdad, December 1992. Mehdi al-Jilawi, owner of Baghdad's biggest toy store, faces empty shelves after a rush by shoppers to buy imported goods before a government ban on sale of luxury items went into effect.**

My neighbor Hashim says he will give my car to a friend who will renew the license. That's what he did for his own car: he gave him 1,000 dinars* and a bucket of yogurt, a strange combination.

November 4 A lot of talk about food and prices. An egg costs sixty dinars**—even during the war a dozen eggs only cost four dinars! My new car battery is going to cost 16,000 dinars. Cars crawl around the streets of Bags, their tires as smooth as babies' bottoms—not a ridge left on them. People are living by stealing and cheating. Leila and Hatem, who live down the road, had all four tires stolen. Their car was propped up on bricks and parked at their front door—the thieves also took their washing off the line in the garden. Jassim's ex-nanny, who now works at the "palace," says they keep the staff on starvation rations and watch them like hawks in case they steal (or use poison, I added). She said that, when someone was caught stealing, they gathered the staff together and brought in a doctor who chopped off the guy's hand and immediately dunked his arm into boiling oil to cauterize it.

November 6 I have been homebound because the car is battery-less, though a battery has been bought. A new law came into existence in my absence which stated that Japanese cars had to have a number etched on them, like cattle. I'm surprised that they haven't started doing that to Iraqis: a stamp on our foreheads would be most fetching. Better not to even think of such an idea or someone with a sixth sense will pick it up and, before we know it, it will be law, then God help us.

* Then equivalent to U.S. $1,818.

** Equivalent to U.S. $109.

November 7 Tarik Aziz* is called Tarik'aza by the Christians in Bags. *Aziz* means dear but *'aza* means mourning. . . . Today there was another bomb scare in a Christian children's school in Karradi. I wonder if it's the fundamentalists getting at the remaining Christians—it always seems to be in that same area.

November 9 Went and ate fish in Abu Nawas street with the Italians at night, streets full of little kids aged from five to twelve selling Chiclets and shining shoes—sad, haggard, forlorn, and listless faces.

If one deposits money in the banks these days, they weigh it in bundles. People go in and out all day with gunny sacks in their hands. If the bank tellers had to physically count these millions they would only be able to manage four customers a day. It is really funny-looking photocopy money.

November 11 People are being warned by their doctor friends against having an operation in Bags. The anesthetic is bad, it makes the patient hysterical upon waking up. The embargo has been on against Cuba for thirty-two years, God forbid that we have to wait that long. I would love to go there and compare notes.

November 12 While I was waiting for Paolo to finish his papers at the museum, an employee there started telling me about a retarded nephew of his who disappeared for a week. Yesterday the army called them up and told them that they had him and that he was listed as a deserter. They threatened to chop off his ear if the family didn't

* Deputy Prime Minister of Iraq.

come and show proof that he was exempted. Anyone who catches a deserter gets 10,000 dinars, so all types are getting caught up in the mess.

November 15 Everyone seems to be dying of cancer. Every day one hears about another acquaintance or friend of a friend dying. How many more die in hospitals that one does not know? Apparently over thirty percent of Iraqis have cancer, and there are lots of kids with leukemia. They will never lift the embargo off us.

Suds* appeared on TV this evening stating that Albright's speech was a pack of lies.** "Nothing is in my name," he said, "it's all for the state." True enough, he doesn't need to put anything in his name—the whole country is his.

My great-aunt Thamina, as usual, was wonderfully funny with her throw-away remarks, talking about immigration. "Everyone is leaving," she said, "and we were never a country of immigrants. Now you can't even find a first-rate prostitute in town, they too have gone." I asked her how she knew that. She said, "Look at the terrible singers we get on TV now!" Twenty-one members of her family have left, only eight remain in Bags. Her daughter said that a lot of kids have stopped going to school because the parents can't afford to buy exercise books and pencils. A friend of hers who lives in Mansur told her that her thirteen-year-old daughter had locked herself in her room crying because she wanted to walk down the main shopping street and her mother said no. "I can't afford to let her," she said. "Everything costs in the thousands. I can barely afford to give her a sandwich to take to school." This is a middle-class family living in a good neighborhood, and reasonably well-off.

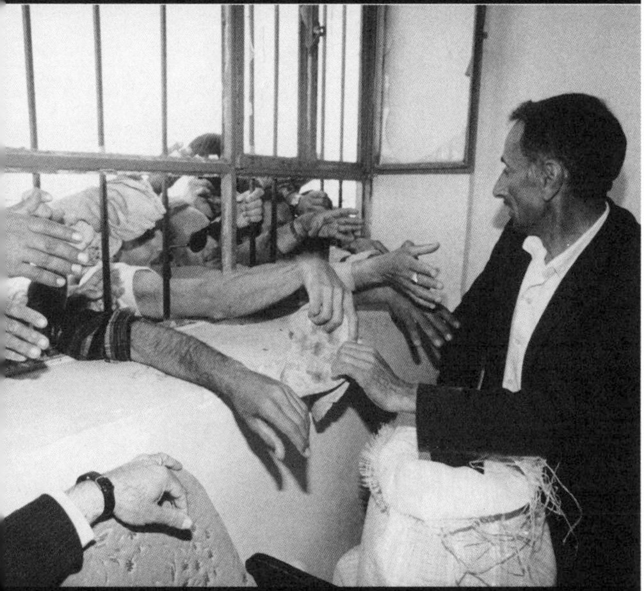

Zakhu, Iraq, April 28, 1991. Iraqis scramble to receive flat breads that are handed out from the police building.

* Nickname for Saddam Hussein.

** On November 14, 1994, the UN Security Council decided unanimously to continue sanctions against Iraq. This decision was partly based on the assertion by Madeleine K. Albright, then U.S. Ambassador to the UN, that Saddam Hussein had spent half a billion dollars on the construction of private palaces for his family, rather than using available funds to feed the general population.

There is a popular music video on TV that shows a boy lying on his bed, dying. He has just cut out his kidneys and is handing them out for love. It sounds grotesque. We are weird even when showing our ardor.

November 17 My handyman Abu Ali passed by today. He has two sons in the army now. One is in a military prison because he was so hungry he went home to eat, but was caught as a deserter and locked up for three months. The army doesn't feed or clothe its soldiers anymore. The other son, Ahmed, is out in the middle of nowhere guarding an arms depot. Poor Abu Ali, he looks worn out. He has tried to get his sons out of the army but has been unable to do so; it's a presidential decree that all young men should be in the army.

Went and visited Fulayih, the man who handles the orchard next door. He has just spent four months in jail. He said it was frightful and wished he had been in for murder rather than stealing. "How could you say that?" I said. "Well," he said, "if one has to be put away for something, with us Arabs it's more honorable to kill than to steal."

Something strange is happening—little business enterprises are being started up by seemingly ordinary individuals who take your money, invest it, and promise a thirty- to seventy-percent profit in a month. It starts off well enough, and the first investors duly get their profits. Slowly word gets around and more and more people put in their money; some even sell their houses and valuables. All this without a paper changing hands: your name is simply written in a ledger. After a few months the government clamps down, the person running the enterprise is put into jail, the money is confiscated and the investors lose everything. My theory is that it's a government mafia scam organized to steal from the people. After all they have the printing machines to print out the money—they can afford to hand out a few thousands and then collect them and the people's money too. They may even pay the salaries of their civil servants with this money.

Sarsank, Iraq, April 29, 1991. Saddam Hussein's summer retreat palace sits on top of a hill, complete with landscaped gardens, a three-yard-high security wall, and two ornamental lakes.

One of these enterprises belongs to the wife of one of Suds's bodyguards—they even advertise it on the TV. Perhaps this is their way to curb rampant inflation! The latest joke circulating around Bags goes as follows: a guy is stopped on the street by a beggar asking for money; the guy answers, "Go to Sam Co." (the latest enterprise to have crashed). "They have my money." The beggar answers, "They have mine too."

A strange abnormality: many new babies are being born dumb. It's probably better for them that way—they won't have a chance to talk against anything.

December 11 Although all sorts of statistics are being gathered on Iraq, scientists need seven years of observation before they can be positive about the accuracy of their data. Baghdad and Basra got the worst of the bombing in an operation called Watertap when the U.S. experimented with barium bombs. Apparently, these do not make a big bang but just let out a lot of smoke. Some die immediately from the effects, others linger on for years. They were experimenting. In years to come, history will show how destructive toward us the West's policy was.

December 15 The UN has found that we were hiding something else—a Chinese radar installation and chemical germ warfare stuff, seven tons of which seem to be missing. Sanctions will be kept on.

December 16 I am off to see my friend Naila who had a horrible adventure the other day. She was driving her car and had stopped at a traffic light when a man opened the side door, got in, said hello, and proceeded to try to shove her out of the car. Since she is large and he was small, they had a good tussle. He punched her in the eye, she grabbed him by the throat, they struggled, and he ended up running away—all this on a main street at seven in the evening. She now has half a black eye. Her cousin asked her whether the guy was trying to steal the car or making a pass at her.

1995

January 3 Loma was telling me about her university classes; she teaches computer studies. She has sixty students. They have no paper and no pencils. They write on the backs of receipts, pharmacy bills, account books, anything that has a blank side to it. The university does not supply her with paper to photocopy the exams so she has to write the exam on the blackboard; those in the back cannot see it so, when the ones in front have copied the questions, those in the back move to the front. There are only ten working computers, so they take turns on the machines; some students even do alternate years at the university as their parents cannot afford to pay for their studies. They work for a year and then come back to study for a year. A lot of them fail on purpose so that they don't have to go into the army.

January 25 John Lancaster, a correspondent with the *Washington Post*, came to dinner. I'd never met him before. I said, "Would you like to meet a bunch of women?" "Absolutely," he said. So we had my mother, Needles, Amal, Suha, Ass, and myself—six women in all. He got an earful. The major topic of conversation was whether Iraq could be divided. We all agreed on the following: that Iraq is situated on crossroads; that all Iraqis are of mixed blood, Kurdish, Turkish, Persian, and different religions, Sunni and Shia, Christians of all sects, and Yazidis; and that this diverse group has been living fairly amicably together for centuries. How can they now divide us? The West tried to encourage the Kurds to rebel against this regime because it was so cruel to them. Mind you, only Iraq has given the Kurds autonomy—the Turks have been killing them off for years. Now, after having been dumped on by everyone and turned against each other by various political factions, the Kurds have no recourse but to come back into Iraq. So what was the whole thing about anyway? Maybe oil.

January 26 Ninety percent of the human population of Iraq is ill with some kind of flu, fever, or allergy. Our paranoia is so strong that we all believe that a bug has been introduced into our environment by the U.S. of A. I think that all Iraqis suffer from Gulf War Syndrome.

Terrible rumors circulating around Bags about the ultimate fate of the people involved in the recent attempted coup . . . Their leader was apparently tied to a horse and dragged around the parade grounds; the others were thrown to starving dogs, trained to maul.

One sees the strangest people begging these days—embarrassed hands stretched out by very respectable-looking people. They can't make ends meet no matter how hard they work because salaries are so low.

January 31 John Lancaster came to say good-bye. He had gone to the brewery and seen that all the vats had been marked for specific use by the UN inspection team. "Yeast" on the yeast vat, etc. Utterly ridiculous—what a waste of time and money this whole exercise is. I heard that the UN team frequently turns a blind eye because they don't want us to be completely defenseless, just under control—their control.

February 11 Medhat, a friend of the family, had to go and have a hernia operation at the government nursing hospital. He arrived and was put on a filthy dirty foam mattress. "You have to bring your own sheets," said the nurse. The heater was dead in his freezing cold room. "We don't have spare parts to mend it," said the nurse. "You have to bring your own." There were no bulbs in the light fixtures. "The patients take

Baghdad, January 1993. Baghdad residents buy food in anticipation of hard times following the West's warning that it will use force if Baghdad does not back down.

them," said the nurse. "You have to bring your own." At lunchtime, a large nurse comes around the ward swinging a big ladle in her hand. "Where's your plate?" she asked poor old Medhat. "You have to provide your own." "Why don't you tell us all this before we come in so that we come supplied?" answered Medhat, who loves eating. "Do you mean to say that I won't get anything to eat now?" "Well," she said, "this time I will give you your lunch on a tray." They got boiled rice with a bit of tomato sauce mixed with a few chickpeas, and for dinner boiled-rice soup. That night his neighbor got terrible cramps (something was wrong with his blood circulation), and he began ranting and raving. So Medhat had to go and search for a doctor. After much wandering he found a nurse who told him that there was no doctor on night duty, only the main hospital ten minutes walk away had an attending doctor, and added that no one would come out on such a freezing night as this. "Tell him to stand up and get the blood going, walk him a bit," she said. "He can't," answered Medhat. "Well, he will just have to wait till the morning," she replied. "He could die," said Medhat. She shrugged her shoulders.

All the handles on the toilet stall doors had been stolen—round empty holes face you when you sit on the toilet. He got better soon, and left after two days to recuperate at home.

Yayladere, Turkey, April 7, 1991. Iraqi Kurdish refugees gather bread crumbs from a dirt road to feed family members in the Isikveren refugee camp. The crumbs were dumped from a truck after all the loaves were distributed to the refugees.

February 17 Medhat's daughter Maysa said there is too much talk these days about Gulf War Syndrome. It's the norm now in Bags. But we are also dealing with basic diseases like cholera, polio, TB—major stuff, she continued. Gulf War Syndrome talk is for those who don't know what's happening in the hospitals. Gynecologists are reusing disposable gloves, just dipping them in Dettol; it's the same with disposable syringes. The anesthetic that is used has come as a gift from various countries, different brands, and no one knows the strengths or what dosage to give to patients. One woman took fifteen hours to wake up from an anesthetic injection after a cesarean operation. Surgical thread is some old-fashioned stuff from Pakistan that takes five to eight months to dissolve and causes infections and complications. Anyone over fifty years old is told that there are no medicines. Doctors want to keep what little there is for younger patients. That's the level we've reached. I asked her what has really increased since the war. "Depression," she answered, "more than anything else." "What do you give them?" I asked. "Electric shocks," she said. "It's faster, leaves no after-effects and is available." Everyone who was present said *ooh . . . ahh . . . how awful*, etc. "No," she said, "it's only Egyptian movies that have made out that electric-shock treatment is evil and only for loonies." "Are there more women than men?" I asked. "Far more," she answered. "They carry all the responsibilities of caring for the house and children on virtually nothing while the men disappear or stay home and sleep." There is a story circulating around Bags about a father who could no longer support his family. He bought a big fish in the market, poisoned it, and fed it to his family. They all died together—a caring father?

February 26 Apparently we returned thirty-six kilos of uranium to the Russians in partial payment for our debt. It had been hidden in a cement bunker. Imagine if that had received a direct hit!

March 2 Everyone is talking about the UN delivering rations to the masses. Ma insists that there is a ship in Basra full of apples and bananas. By the time they sort out the distribution, the bananas will have rotted. Those who receive UN rations will have their Iraqi rations cut, or so say the rumors. Zuhair came today and said that France, the U.K., and the U.S.A. will distribute the rations, twenty-one items per person including cans and chocolates. No one knows anything. I think it is all talk. I am selling everything I don't need and spending the money as quickly as it comes in. I buy truffles or anything else that I want. There is no point in keeping the money—valueless photocopied stuff.

I think I might get a cow. Our guard Majeed knows how to milk it and his wife Hamdiya can make yogurt, and we have plenty of greeneries to feed it. I thought of goats but they are so destructive and we can't keep them tied up all day. Cows just sort of muck around, and we would not have to buy any more manure for the orchard.

March 3 Just returned from a long day of visitings. Since we still have a few die-hard Ottomans left in Bags, I went to check on their memories. Attaturk had taken my fancy, so I asked my aunt Abla Jalila whether she had ever met him. "No," she said, but her friend Nahida, who was visiting her, said that she had met him twice when she was a student. He was good-looking, with piercing blue eyes. He remembered her when they met again at a function for Reza Shah of Iran and singled her out. All eyes were turned on her and, as she bent to take her first sip of champagne, a great big strawberry hit her and splashed all over the front of her dress. Perturbation all around until the Shah's aide came to her side and said to her, "In our society when someone gets too much attention a fruit is thrown at them to ward off the evil eye," so everyone relaxed and laughed.

There was a Swiss epidemiologist at lunch and I told him that I hoped epidemics didn't follow him around, and he said, "No, only work epidemics." This country is being used as a lab with all of us as guinea pigs. They are taking count of the last six years and what diseases have increased. He says it is an utter disaster and that they will lift the embargo when they read his report. I told him that this embargo was a political one and would not end until the U.S. decided so. I asked him whether there was an increase in cancer and he said he did not know, he only does contagious diseases. I told him that he should advise the outside authorities to send a cancer specialist to check whether the pollution of the war (all the chemicals that were thrown at us and that will remain in the soil, acting as a slow poison) has increased that disease. But then I remembered that the U.S. experimented on its own soldiers, so why should they care if we survive or not? In fact, it is useful for them. They can check results in total freedom and unhampered by any legal constraints.

Maybe I should start the family biography that I am supposed to be writing by listing all the firsts of the family in the early years of the newly independent Iraq. My grandfather founded the first Agricultural Bank, my great-uncle Sa'ib was the first surgeon, my father the first agriculturist/horticulturalist—he began all the experimental farms in Iraq. Even in our generation, my sister Sol was the first woman archaeologist and I was the first woman potter. However, there is no place for us members of the old society in this new one. We don't speak the same language.

A lot of kidnapping is taking place around Bags. Here's how it happens. A car stops at a traffic light, someone points a gun through the window and says, "Give me your car keys." While the driver is concentrating on getting the keys, a second person is busy hustling out his woman passenger. She is taken out, raped, beaten, shorn of her hair, and finally thrown out naked on the street. The government is apparently worried because they don't know who is responsible for this latest crime wave. It is not limited to a particular area of Bags but happens in different districts.

March 18 Saw Wissam, who is our ambassador to the Vatican, on the news with the Pope. Looked in his element with all that wonderful granite and marble at the Vatican. The Pope said the embargo was wrong and only hurt the people—that embargoes should be used for short and restricted periods only. Tariq Aziz is going to spend the next two months doing an Albright—touring all the countries of the world that will have him. What are we going to offer them, I wonder.

The Red Cross had a luncheon in Amal's Beit al-Iraqi* and she took me along as a token Iraqi. Most were Swiss but there was an Irish lady who is in charge of spare limb parts, fitting them on and teaching the exercises. She says false limbs are the one thing that this country can do. They are cheap to make and not banned under the embargo. There are plenty of people with missing limbs, and many more every day from exploding mines. No one has bothered to de-mine the country—not like Kuwait which had the whole world helping to clear its minefields. Another Red Cross delegate was in charge of missing people, Kuwaitis and Iraqis. I asked her how many and she said about ninety. "Well, that's not too many," I said. Perhaps they are dead and buried as happens in war—so few compared to our killed count. Peanuts. They have made only one positive identification—a man who came back and did not bother to inform the Red Cross. When they phoned up his family, he answered and said, "Oh, I've been back for two years!" They keep the names on their list for nine months. I asked about the Iranians, but the Red Cross is not responsible for their count. None of their officials are allowed into Iran. No wonder so many of the Iranian prisoners have not returned or been heard of in years.

Two Americans strayed into Iraq unknowingly,

* A local crafts center run by a friend of Al-Radi's family.

or so they said, and there is a great commotion because they have been held in custody for a week. Well, no sympathy will be lost on those two, sorry.

March 29 My old friend Issam came to visit today and raved about the smell of orange blossoms. I have gotten used to it. We had a long talk about sewage: he's worried that, if there were another attempt to wipe us out, they might hit the sewage plants instead of the electricity, then we really would be up to our noses in shit. I told him that he should worry about the shit that we are in now, rather than worry about what may or may not happen. I took him to my studio to show him my latest madness. I will call this exhibition *Embargo Art*. All the sculptures, whole families of people made of stone and car parts—busted exhausts and mufflers that I collected when I went to mend my muffler—quite funny. The heads are painted stones and come off easily. A recognition of the reality that is present-day Iraq?

Nuha Al-Radi, *Embargo Person*, 1995.

April 11 One is at a loss for words in this most hypocritical of situations. How can the U.S. justify bringing in the UN to protect the Iraqi Kurds when they sanction the Turks killing the Turkish Kurds? What makes a Turkish Kurd any different from an Iraqi one and how the hell can they tell the difference between them?

April 16 We have not agreed to the UN resolution allowing for a partial lifting of the sanctions. The dollar is going up and down, and with it the price of sugar, rice, etc. People must be making and losing fortunes overnight. Isabel, a French scientist, says that parents are beating up their children because they can be hospitalized for up to three weeks. There, they can be fed.

June 6 Isabel said it is the bad environment that is making the oranges fall off the tree, a result of bombs (with barium) dropped during the war. She said that we need to plant four million bombex, ficus, and other large trees to improve the quality of the air. The government can import them from Pakistan, which has a similar climate, at the price of one dollar per tree. Otherwise all our trees will die. What about us? Will we die too? And where are we going to get four million dollars?

Went to Saddam Centre and saw a fellow artist, Ali Jabiri. We had a great conversation about who was dead or alive and who has left or will leave the country. . . . People seem to be dying like flies. Ali says that, if we ask for a permit to die, they will say, "Come back in a week and bring all your papers with you." We would have to pay and then they might refuse our request!

June 11 Gave a big dinner last night and again never managed to have a proper conversation with anyone. Amal came in very fancy high-heeled shoes that looked like perspex pyramids. Halfway through dinner, one of the heels came apart so I told her that I would glue it for her and gave her a pair of slippers to go home in. She was wearing an embroidered Palestinian dress and she said, "Don't you remember this dress? It was eaten by rats when I was staying at your house during the war." Amal gave it to some Palestinian lady to repair and she cut out the eaten pieces and patched it. It has no back now (presumably that went to patch up the front), so she wears it with a jacket.

Dr. Dhafir has a story that he has told us many times but which seems to be more true every day. The time is February 1993, when Dhafir was in Somalia working as a doctor for the UN forces. His wife Mutaza, in Bags, was driving to a dinner at Sahira's house (it was Ramadan). A horrific storm blew up and turned everything orange and black. By the time they left to go back home, the car was covered with black dust and mud that they had to wipe off to be able to see. . . . It was also difficult to breathe. A couple of weeks later, Dhafir was sitting with his fellow workers in the dark in Somalia (no electricity) and each was telling a story. One of the senior field officers told them about how he had been exploding warheads that day. Apparently they have to dig a huge, deep hole, line the interior with a steel and concrete frame, put in the stuff that has to be exploded, and then seal it with cement so that the dust of the explosion stays buried for generations. In Iraq, he continued to tell them, we had a similar assignment—to blow up war materials. When he went to the site, he noticed that there was no concrete bunker or even a built structure, just a hole in the ground. So he radioed to his superiors and informed them of this. They told him not to bother with safety measures and just to explode the material regardless. Everyone knew that there was a big storm coming from the south, but they blew up the warheads anyway. He wrote up a report and sent it to headquarters, so presumably it is part of the sea of unread files in the UN. He then went on to tell them that in the next two to four years there will be a terrible increase in cancer, leukemia, glaucoma, bone and joint problems in Iraq. Trees and plants will suffer too, although a few may flourish. Fruit will fall off the trees and it will be an environmental disaster. Dhafir could not remember the man's name, but says he has it somewhere among his papers and will look it up. Well, aren't we living that scenario right now, blow by blow, and who gives the orders to the UN? The U.S., of course.

The UN will keep the embargo going until all Iraqis are dead. But we will not die. Civilization started here and it will end here.

June 14 The UN man in Somalia was a senior field officer in the UN Department for Humanitarian Affairs. Dhafir looked him up. He had not known that Dhafir was only out of Iraq for a short while and would return, and, when he found out, he said, "Gosh, I should not have told you that. Now you will tell everyone." And Dhafir said he would not tell.

Isabel says a lot of the embassies are being harassed. The French have had rocks thrown at them and at their windows. I can't blame people too much if there is resentment.

AMMAN, JORDAN

June 23 I now have a thumbprint on my passport instead of a signature. . . . I came out as an illiterate—that way one can leave without paying an extra million. They took $150 from me at the border. I was given a receipt for it—supposedly one gets refunded upon return. Every time one leaves Iraq, it involves melodrama and endless humiliation. One wonders why one ever returns. Memory playing tricks again.

The first thing all Iraqis do on arrival in Amman is to make a beeline to various doctors' waiting rooms—each to their own particular ailments. Once that has been taken care of they queue up for visas. Any embassy will do.

August 12 The BBC is comparing Suds to King Lear and his daughters.* I like that.

Every other person working at the Darat** is an Iraqi on the way out, waiting for the clearance of papers to Sweden, Australia, Canada, New Zealand, Malaysia, or Holland. It's tragic. They are all young and want to make a new life for themselves elsewhere. I sit here like a old crony, giving advice, filling out forms for them, and writing petitions. I can't tell them not to go—everyone needs a chance in this life. What chance have they in Iraq? It will be centuries before the country is normal again.

BEIRUT, LEBANON

November 17 Ma came across an Iraqi who works in a bakery and he gave her a letter to take to his family in Bags when she goes back. When he tried to call them from Beirut, they refused to take the call or even to acknowledge his existence. Apparently, he had already been declared a war hero and his family has taken (and spent?) the cash bonus for a war martyr. They did not want to know him anymore. He wants Ma to talk to his sister because she may be more sympathetic to his plight. Poor man, he ran away from the army and has been cut off from family and friends for six years. He cannot even be put on an immigration or amnesty list. It's too late.

* On August 8, 1995, Saddam Hussein's two daughters and their husbands, brothers Lieutenant General Hussein Kamel and Colonel Saddam Kamel, both top-level Iraqi government officials, defected to Jordan, along with their children.

** Darat al-Funun, part of the Shoman Foundation, a Jordanian arts organization.

December 20 My friend Mini told us the following story: During the civil war in Beirut a Tarzan film was showing to a packed movie house when in walked a fundamentalist-looking type with a loaded gun. When Tarzan put his hand on Jane's thighs, this guy stood up and yelled, "Take your hands off the girl." Of course, Tarzan paid no attention, so the fundamentalist took up his gun, aimed, and started shooting at Tarzan. Everyone in the cinema was terrified and hid under their seats. The film stopped, and the place slowly emptied. I said, "That's a beautiful story, but it must be apocryphal." "No," she said, "my cousin was in the audience."

Beirut is much safer these days, there has been much improvement since I was here last year. It may even be the safest place to live in the Muddled East. Instead of guns, everyone carries mobile phones . . . *le cellulaire*, as they are called here. They ring in cinemas, at funerals, in handbags. . . . The streets echo to the sound of "*allô, allô.*"

1996

January 22 Rifat, a relative, said, "Iraq is the source of my inspiration, yes, I would go back. I would live nine months of the year there and the rest abroad. Because I write, I can rely on myself, it has been okay." When Rifat was in prison in Bags, a security guard asked him to come with him for questioning. Rifat told him to come back after eleven o'clock (he never talks before that time, just works). The guard did not persist. Rifat is rather imperious and can get away with such behavior. When they finally let him out of prison his response was, "Too bad, I needed another three months to finish my book. . . ."

AMMAN, JORDAN

February 15 There is hardly an Iraqi who has come to Jordan who has relaxed or felt as if he or she were here to stay. Getting a residence or work permit is nearly impossible. It is not really Jordan's fault. They are a small country and have overstretched their capacity. Even if one gets a job here, it's for low pay and not much prospect. Insecurity and vulnerability are permanent

North of Safwan, Occupied Iraq, April 14, 1991. Two Iraqi soldiers walk barefoot.

conditions; most Iraqis would return if things were right again in Iraq.

More stories from Bags: Chaos ensued when the dinar suddenly soared in value. People went on crazy buying sprees as food prices plummeted. The banks remained open all night long so that people could exchange their hoarded dollars for the dreaded dinars that they had not been keeping. I smell a rat—the government was the clear winner. People rushed to the market and bought sheep, thousands of them . . . so many slaughtered, a grizzly sight. There may not be enough lambs born next spring. On top of that, not enough farmers planted grain this year because the dinar had plummeted at seed-buying time and the government did not lower the prices. Most farmers could not afford to buy expensive seeds so they left their fields fallow. Apparently there is little cash left in the banks; they give out pieces of paper, like IOUs . . . People bringing their grain to government depots are getting free fridges and washing machines instead of cash!

February 19 A lovely story that was published in the *Hayat** newspaper today: Apparently, an Iraqi had agreed with his parents on a special code that he would use when he made good his escape from Iraq. The code went as follows: Once he was out he would phone and say that he had arrived in Iran. This meant that he was safely out. If he said that he had moved to a new house it meant that he had managed to get to Sweden as an immigrant. They also decided that he should have a new name, Zuhair (his real name was Qais). So when he got to Sweden, he phoned his mother and said, "Hello, this is Zuhair speaking." "What Zuhair?" she said. "Just Zuhair," he answered. "Oh," she replied, "you think I can't recognize your voice. You're Qais. Where are you?" So he said, "I've gone away." "I know," she says, "you left Iran." So he thought quickly and decided that if he said he had moved

* An Arabic daily published in London.

to a new house she might remember that this conversation was supposed to be in code. So he said, "I've moved to a new home." "I know," she said, "you've gone to Sweden." By then the father had realized what was happening and grabbed the telephone from his wife's hand, and she suddenly remembered that it was supposed to be their code—she had forgotten.

The latest story of hardship from Bags: the shortages have now hit the zoo. Bananas were never cheap in Bags, even at the best of times, but now their price is so prohibitive that the zoo can't afford them, so monkeys are being fed with carrots instead. They do not like carrots and fling them one by one at passersby. Lions won't eat carrots, so old donkeys are being killed and their meat given to the lions.

February 21 I can't believe it. It seems that Suds's two sons-in-law have returned to Bags. We were amazed when they left Baghdad with wives and kids in the first place—but to return seems suicidal. I have come to the conclusion that Iraqis must be the most unpredictable people in the world.

February 24 I knew that the brothers would be knocked off, but I did not think it would be quite so soon.* Suds said that he would treat them like ordinary Iraqis. Well, wasn't that an appropriate description of what happened to them. It is obvious that H.K. just could not bear to live in exile. But to the extent that he was willing to chance going back to his father-in-law?

March 4 So what is exile? My father died in exile in Beirut in 1971 and Ma thought to take him back and bury him in Bags. Does it make a difference? I myself want to be buried wherever I die. I dislike the West temporarily for making us suffer more than we already have, and so will keep myself and my travels limited to the East . . . not that the West is dying for my company. It is a kind of self-imposed embargo—a little gesture. There is a purpose and a pride that you lose when you don't have a country. That purpose means you are acknowledged, recognized. In the outside world you are nothing. You have to constantly introduce and reintroduce yourself. You start from scratch every time.

---

* Promised pardons by Saddam Hussein, Hussein and Saddam Kamel returned to Baghdad in February 1996 and were killed, according to *The Boston Globe*, by Saddam Hussein's son Uday's personal hit team.

CHRISTOPHER MIDDLETON

Loom Is Being Granular

This room, too thin, nothing hot in it,
A thousand books, carpets nomad women wove

And daybreak when, splendid on a piece of ham,
Enormous light diagonally slices in—

Still I make my exit, eyesight eases up
And down the book spines, nose takes comfort,

Off I careen, down the steps, a tumult
For scattering cats, how graceful, them,

Though it happens I am long gone to Berlin,
Haunting whose saloons, destination Belgrade,

Pretend dead, play possum beneath bullets
If only I could burrow through the flagstones

For Istanbul is next and means choosing
Free speech in a certain torture chamber,

Only in Antioch, more precisely Daphne,
Am I released, for dumping in the sea

Still at the foot of my steps, still here,
Not along the continuum, O no, the elastic

Broke, groove split, creamy voice knocked it off,
And reconsider the room and me, liar, in it

And the sea crashing through it, thoughts
Loom, purple, and tastes fade into cheese,

Sensation as on a quivering ship of wood
When it turns about, into the wave's whack,

And if it crests, hot slit, matters not one bit
To the moon. So my orbit, back up and home,

Draws out threads and rams them forward in,
The while, archaic, cloud cools my head:

What's to do out there, this music lacking?
I marvel then that shipwrights, long ago,

Fitted their pine planks and braced them
With mortice orthogonal and tenon, tight;

As masons might pitch a temple roof
Foursquare on tenuous illusions of oval,

Dancers danced to it, in a ring their muscle
Wove to contain, 'confusedly regular,

The moving maze' or to transform the season
Their twin rows with a shriek of flutes meet

Spinning, in, out, for their pomegranate housed
A thousand pips, soon apart, soon again together.

Adagio in the Shipyard

Traits there are,
Traits you happen to follow, in earth
Ravines cloven by the ploughshare,
Wet, and wedged in the earth
Pressure-flaked in a flint tool,
A skin scraper.

A smell of coal, how it curdled
In that backyard the air around you.
And Hector Llewellyn, scrum half,
Plucked out and flung the ball, his body
Flew full-stretch and still, as he did so,
Is suspended in the middle air.

The traces, which way do they go
Back or on? Up, too. Never quite
Levitating, the dancers. Not knowing why,
You took to the darkening theater. Distant
Arms, all at once they cleft the air
And with light feet that made no sound
How come their flesh folds into a rose?

Around the disc of bronze, magic letters:
Rare, the sestertius of Pertinax,
Rarer the silver horses galloping right
And Syracusan Arethusa, her
Streaming hair and ghost of a dimple.

None of this had to lead anywhere. Each
Instant of uplift
Secretes (does it?) a church bell. Recalled
Or prospective time, incised in it
Every trace of there and then, here and now
Might have pronounced the note,
Conspired the sign from another world.

But no melody selects itself.
Even your dead do not lie still.
Everything sickens the heart,
For it has chosen not to stop beating;
Back and forth its bellnotes
Swing, take their toll, so modulate,
But the swirl of the world, its offing,
They do map it.

A haze constellates, the new ships
Hoist orange sails, happening to loom
Through: sharper prows, lighter poops, masts,
Look, they balance broadening day,
Dancers need no decks,
Their arms reach out, embrace, as if
It were nothing, the wind.

Anatolian Horses

As we drove up in the old Mercedes, twelve years ago now, up to the plateau, we were absorbed in our thoughts, but they stopped and then we looked: round the clock an ocean of grass. Horses far off. We were seeing whole herds of horses, left and right, between the low horizons and the road we were still traveling southward on. No fences. No fields. No trees. Sunlight burnishing grass as it surged in the wind. High sierra, this was it. And the weight of single horses, of their throngs, balancing on every surface.

But you horses are far off and would not understand an old man wanting to set this down, to be speaking to you, before he can say no more. The grass luminous, luminous horses. Standing singly or on the move in clusters randomly variable to us, but to you, at pasture in your Anatolian silence, natural and necessary clusters, substance of horse. Battles and migrations, men and women, served by you, Anatolian horses.

To tell the truth, there was no astonishment; that came later. No way to hear you talk. Had we closed in on you, you would have melted into air. We would only have seen miles of horse between the distant yurts; their tilted roofs, their pinnacles. We would have smelled you, perhaps; the air filled our lungs and you were absorbed in it, the serene blue mass of air, all horse.

Then we were on the way elsewhere, and still we are. Ghosts, still elsewhere, and on the way, Anatolian horses. Of you I had nothing to say then, but say this to you, this, as I touch on the image an old man might have wanted to speak of, now and then.

VIVAN SUNDARAM THE SHER-GIL ARCHIVE

LEFT
Four Black Boxes for the Family (detail), 1995.

ABOVE
Box Five: Family Album, 1995.

Portraits of self and daughter Amrita taken by Umrao Singh Sher-Gil (1870–1954) between 1930 and 1940 in Paris and Shimla.

VIVAN SUNDARAM

Vivan Sundaram's grandfather, Umrao Singh Sher-Gil, was a Sikh of northern India, a man of letters and an early enthusiast of photography. During the first decade of our century, he met a Hungarian beauty called Marie Antoinette, who was traveling to India with the entourage of Princess Bamba, the daughter of the Maharaja Dalip Singh. Umrao and Marie Antoinette fell in love, married, and settled in Budapest, where they had two daughters, Amrita and Indira, Vivan's mother. In 1930, the family shifted to Paris, where Amrita studied painting and Indira European music. All but Amrita soon gravitated back to the Himalayan hills and this separation between father and daughter forms the center of Vivan Sundaram's *Sher-Gil Archive* project. Adding further weight to the project are Amrita's sudden, somewhat mysterious, death at the age of twenty-eight, and the importance that her paintings have been accorded in India, where they command a room of their own at New Delhi's National Gallery of Modern Art.

In *The Sher-Gil Archive*, Sundaram elaborates on the complexities of his family history through multiple portraits in a variety of forms and media. The letters Amrita wrote to her parents have been embroidered onto curtains: the words of the daughter grappling with modernism and her own identity drift homeward, eastward, her phrases billowing with both uncertainty and enthusiasm. The family's memorabilia have been assembled into boxes that resemble suitcases, the potential sentimentality tempered by the suggestion of mobility and rootlessness, of the Victorian era aggressively contained by the modern, of history "on the go."

In the black-and-white photographs taken by Umrao Singh Sher-Gil and edited and arranged by his grandson, the photographer portrays, explores, and ponders both his own visage and that of his daughter Amrita. Vivan Sundaram has coaxed the two into a pair of timelines, a sliding scale of honesty and disguise, of self-discovery and denial, the comfort of tradition and the anxiety of the modern world. This story could easily stand in for the high drama of India in the twentieth century—Umrao's and Amrita's struggles and passions played out against a backdrop of an ancient, implacable culture and an aloof, almost unconcerned "rest of the world."

From Salman Rushdie's *Midnight's Children* to, most recently, Arundhati Roy's *The God of Small Things*, the stories of Indian families of the twentieth century have become both relevant and illuminating to that "rest of the world." As this realism is now applauded on the world stage, it may prove to be just the tip of an iceberg, a slow-moving mass of a cultural paradigm, an Indian perception that will prove to be remarkably appropriate for the twenty-first century. If there is a "magic" to this realism, it comes from the simple awe of awakening to one's own history.

Peter A. Nagy

LEFT *Amrita Sher-Gil (1913–1941) in Front of Her Painting "Woman on Charpoy" (1941)*, 1997, and *Letter to Parents*, 1997, with 1934 text by Amrita Sher-Gil. Installation view, 1997 Havana Biennial.

A VOICE from DEATH ROW

TERESA ALLEN | ANDREA HICKS JACKSON

There are currently forty-seven women condemned to die in the United States. Working with a partner or alone, they have been convicted of killing their husbands, children, boyfriends, and strangers. A large percentage have documented histories of physical or sexual abuse, as well as drug and alcohol addictions. More than half are white. Many are mothers with school-age children. Few have murdered for monetary gain. The majority live in specially designed cellblocks, away from the mainline population, where movement is greatly curtailed, lifestyle is bleak, and days and years pass indistinguishably and uneventfully inside their locked prison cells.

Compared to their male counterparts, who number in the hundreds in many states, women comprise only about two percent of the nation's condemned. California, Florida, and Oklahoma have the largest numbers of women on death row. A handful of other states, such as Idaho, have only one condemned woman and must grapple with a unique problem. Most states are mandated by law to segregate condemned inmates from the regular prison population. Because of this, Idaho must require that its only female death-row inmate, who was sentenced to death in 1993, eat alone, exercise alone, and, until another woman joins her on death row, pass the years with virtually no human interaction.

A debate continues over why death sentences for women began to rise in the mid-1980s in many states, especially when the number of murders committed by women did not increase. There are those who speculate that women have rightfully lost a "privileged" status in the criminal justice system that has, until now, kept death-row numbers down and often allowed women inmates to serve shorter sentences—or even probation—for serious offenses. It is unclear whether this new apparent toughness toward female felons is in any way a feminist backlash, as some suggest, or simply society's new willingness to prosecute aggressively and punish all criminals, regardless of gender.

No woman has been put to death in the United States since 1984.

*

When Andrea Hicks Jackson arrived at Broward Correctional Institute in southern Florida in 1984, she was the state's only condemned woman and lived alone on a makeshift death row in a cell fortified with a steel door. Almost two years later she was joined by another condemned woman, nicknamed the "Black Widow," who was sentenced to death for poisoning her husband with arsenic. Today, the state's five condemned women live on a new death-row wing with cells that look like drum-tight submarine hatches, a shower room down the *hall, a caged outdoor exercise yard with a basketball hoop, and additional cell space for future residents. Also located on the "row" is a room designed as the "death-watch" cell where the women are housed twenty-four hours prior to their execution date. No woman has been put to death in Florida since 1848, when a slave was reportedly hanged for murdering her white master. Twice, however, Jackson has had her death warrant signed and once was en route to be executed at Florida State Prison in Starke (where serial killer Ted Bundy was electrocuted in the late 1980s), when word came that she had been granted a stay. The "death caravan," as she calls it, was forced to turn around.*

It was in 1983 that Jackson, then a twenty-five-year-old mother of two young boys with a history of drug and alcohol abuse, was convicted of shooting and killing a police officer in her hometown, Jacksonville, Florida. The officer had been called to the scene to investigate a vandalized car—which belonged to Jackson. According to Jackson's current attorney, the officer arrested her on a misdemeanor charge for making a false statement about the car in order to file a fraudulent insurance claim. (Jackson denies this.) When the officer placed her in his squad car, a struggle erupted and Jackson reportedly shot him four times in the head and twice in the chest with a .22-caliber handgun she had in her possession. He died instantly. Jackson, who says she was high at the time, claims not to remember shooting him. She also says that she was sexually assaulted as a child and repeatedly beaten by her husband, and she believes that, in her intoxicated state, she confused the officer with someone who had abused her in the past. Other than misdemeanor violations, Jackson did not have a criminal record prior to the shooting.

Strung out and a lean hundred and nineteen pounds when she entered the system, Jackson, now thirty-eight, weighs close to two hundred pounds—a condition she blames on little exercise and starchy prison foods. She has kicked her drug habit and was born again as a Christian several years ago. She spends her days reading the Bible, praying, weaving baskets out of old newspapers, and watching sporting events on the prison-regulation nine-inch, black-and-white television that is lashed to the wall above the toilet in her cell. Occasionally she receives a visit from her sons, but they live with their father, hundreds of miles away in Jacksonville, and seldom make the trip. Jackson, who continues to appeal her death sentence, has served the majority of her thirteen years at Broward, with occasional stints at the Jacksonville County Jail while awaiting resentencing.

The following text is taken from an interview with Jackson conducted in the prison interview room at Broward Correctional Institute and through the barred window of Jackson's cell door on February 20, 1997, and from earlier telephone conversations in 1994 and 1995, when Jackson was at the Jacksonville County Jail.

Teresa Allen

Even when I heard that they had signed my warrant, I wasn't scared. Christ has told me that I won't die here, and I have faith in Him. They let me call my mother, and that was . . . hard. Then they took all my property and guarded me twenty-four hours a day. They stripped me down and put me by myself in the death-watch room. They took me to Starke five days early for security reasons. I had this motorcade with two armed officers inside with me, and two cars in front of me. It was like I was the President. I tell you, they were really mad when they had to turn around that death caravan and bring me all the way back. Coming down, they were laughing and joking. They said I'd fit just right in the chair. . . . I was riding with an officer, and she was angry. She said to me, "It might not be today, and it might not be tomorrow. But we're going to fry your black ass." As soon as I saw the superintendent standing in the road, waving his arms around at us like a crazy man, I knew I was stayed. They looked so disappointed. I put my feet up. "Home, James," I said. Boy, that made them mad.

On the way back we commandeered a rest stop, a gas station, because I had to use the toilet. People were sitting around, you know, pumping gas, and in we all come. They had shotguns and stuff. They made people inside the mini-mart stand up against the wall. It was like a television movie or something. Then I walked in, shackled, handcuffed, and chained. I mean, I was chained up. The only place I didn't have a chain was around my neck. All this just so I could take a pee. I'm sure everyone was wondering, "God, what did she do?"

Mostly my lawyers didn't have a defense for me.* For a while, they thought they would say I had PMS. They were constantly doing tests, drawing enough blood out of me to make another person. My lawyer, he thought they was going to charge me with second-degree murder. When he found out it was murder in the first, well, he only had two months to prepare the case. He told the judge that I was competent to stand trial, that I understood the facts in my case. But I didn't. I admit that what I did was wrong. I don't think that anybody has the right to take another person's life. But it still remains that I did not have any control over the situation and I shouldn't be on death row. Do you think I would go out and kill somebody now? For what reason? I mean, I look like a sane person, right? I don't even know this man. And the state had the audacity to say that the reason I killed this man was because I didn't want to go to jail. If there's one sure way of going to jail, it's to kill a police officer.

It's a funny thing. The whole time I was in the county jail [awaiting trial], I had no idea what was going on around me. It was like I was in a play or watching a play. Later I got saved and I sobered up too. Want to hear my story about being saved? Because I love to tell it. All of a sudden I just felt a load of guilt and I started crying, and I was feeling so bad, and vomiting at the same time. I remember I was wearing a green dress and I pulled it up under my chin to catch the vomit, and I was vomiting my guts out and [the prison chaplain] is praying over me. I wish I had brought some pictures to show you because from then on, in every picture, there's a glow right here on the top of my head. It looks like a cross. And he was praying and speaking in tongues over me and the vomit was just coming out. I believe I am saved and I trust the Lord explicitly. If He says to me some day, "Andrea, it's time for you to come home," I expect I will wake up in His presence. . . . I remember when my death sentence was reinstated the last time. I came back to my cell and I wept. I said, "Lord, you know I didn't mean to do this." I was crying and crying. You know what He said to me: "Daughter, it is forgotten." He has told me that He has the last word on everything. And I trust that. If they take me to be executed, that's okay, too. I have that assurance that I am saved. I have a clean slate.

* Jackson went to trial with a public defender.

When I first got here in 1984 they didn't have a place for death-row women 'cause there weren't none. So they made a special room and locked me in there. There was this screen in front of my door and one day one of the girls helped me dig out a corner, helped me pull it out, so that she could sneak me cigarettes and matches. I was a smoker then. And sometimes the other girls would come over and talk. Later they built us a place of our own and I was moved there. Now I spend a lot of time just standing in my cell, looking out of the peephole. But there's not a lot to see. I tell you, and I don't like saying this, but I've gotten used to being locked inside after all these years. I can talk to the other girls when they take us out into the yard, but mostly I like to keep to myself. Sometimes I don't come out of my cell and I don't talk to people for days. You see, this has been my life for thirteen years now. I guess I've become institutionalized. I get along with me. I guess what I'm saying is, over the years, you adjust. But one thing you never adjust to is the lack of privacy. This is one of the hardest things. They check through the peephole every hour, or any time they want. You think you're sitting in there alone and in private, but, you see, this isn't always the case. And we're talking about men guards, too. I'm not supposed to, but when I use the bathroom I put a piece of paper over the window of my cell.

The way it is today in society with everybody screaming that prisons are not tough enough . . . people have no idea. Hell, I've had to fight for everything here, walk hours, ice cubes, even to shower more than three times a week. Over time I've learned to bathe in my sink, but can you imagine how hard it is to fit this big old body in the sink? They take you out in the yard for one hour a day, but not on Friday, Saturday, or Sunday. What if you are out in the yard on a Thursday on a hot summer day? You come back and you're sweaty, you're hot. And you can't take a shower until Monday. When I complained that there was nothing to do out there, they got us a jump rope. Once they bought us a basketball but it busted almost immediately. We beg and beg and beg to be given a cooler to take outside with ice in it, and to be able to bring just one little cup of ice back into our rooms in summer.

At first I tried to get things changed. I'd talk to the women. But I've gotten tired of writing stuff up, writing the ACLU. What's the point really? Anyway, I expect to be out of here soon. Why not just sit here in my cell and relax. . . . The thing is, we may be sentenced to death, but we are still human beings. We still need to have outlets, like educational programs, even jobs. But as far as they're concerned, you're already dead if you're on death row. Try getting an operation you need or proper medical help. Why bother, they say. You're dead anyway.

Life on death row is all about the hardest punishment. You can see for yourself. There's a bunk, a foot locker, a chair, a TV over the toilet. We can't keep nothing on the walls. It's a pretty monotonous life. I wake up around 5:30, and they come around at about 6:30 with breakfast that they serve through the slot. Lunch is at 11:30, dinner between 4:00 and 5:00. There are no programs. And we're not allowed to work. So I'm in my cell all of the time except for showers and when they let us out into the yard. One thing that I am is a basketball fan. I mean, passionate. I look forward to watching the games on TV. I read my Bible and I subscribe to *USA Today* for the sports section. And I do a lot of correspondence. I have sixty-five pen pals in the free world. The highlight of my day is getting my mail. When there's nothing, well, I just hate that.

You could give me a stereo, a color TV, a refrigerator, but the truth of it all is, I just want to go home. Nothing else matters. I want to be with my boys and family. They live with their father in Jacksonville and it's a long way to come. Last time? About a year ago. I don't let them come over the holidays because it's too dangerous on the roads. And on Christmas they have their own things going. . . . My boys are seventeen and eighteen now, but when I came in they were just little 'uns. And I know this sounds like a small thing, but I can't even tell you what size shoe my oldest wears. You know what I'm saying? I don't know what size shirts they wear or their favorite foods. And these are the kinds of things a mother wants to know. I just want to go home. Please understand what I'm saying. I could never do enough time to replace a human life. There's nothing I can do to bring him back. But I have given him thirteen years of my life now. What is the sense of keeping me here?

you island-meadow
you yourself
fogged in with
hope

Against
the
fence

of our
own
century

—too much
ash to
bless—

we follow
gray
thread

finger-
splitting

bits
of
bolt & barb

the furnace
stars downriver
to

another
song
the singer's

PETER SACKS

Kein Ander

hand caught
brighter
than a red rag in

the wire

*

loosestrife
forget-me-nots
cut

& bound to
wheat
shocks

your body
thrown
between

the blind
man at the mill
enslaved

& a thawing
gutterful
of vowels

half-ground
against
the end—

one black one
reddening
one red

*

out of
the battering
wheel

each spoke
another
rivulet

sheared off
between
high stone

hedges
of the Seine

the knife
resharpened
bodies

stacked
the
threshing

stone
your chest
ripped

shivering
from
depths

*

the rose

of wire
knotted
sharp enough

to memorize
the hand for
once

as once
the bird
leaned all

night long
against
the thorn—

*

behind
the hanging
veil

each last
child swept
downriver

looking back—

the mother
muttering
but listen

listen
too afraid
to hide is

taken out
& shot

a bullet
in the neck

*

& he
that singeth
hard against

the wire
sang
he sang

*

all-spending
river

we too
drag him
through folds

of feldspar
metagraywacke
gneiss

plutonic magma
buckled
to our own

horizon
riven past
invention

& remade

*

the bridge
falls upward
splinters

in the mind
—it is the
force

beneath
the words
that drives

through death
the stiffened
silence

travels
past the river
mouth

the white-
lipped
sea rebuffs

& crushes in
the old
salt quarry

where
the words
whirl out

*

implacable

brought near
engraved
volcanic

schist
stripped
back to

stone bees
in the flint
the wings

unbroken
barely
tarnished

nibs
of pollen
glimmering

*

one for
many

none

the early
vessel crazed
by images

of earthly
fire
the almond

blossom
strung
ignited by

our thirst
word after
pouring

word thrust
further
downward

—*you*
wedged
headlong

deep into
the crown
of roots

no other

seed no
scratch
of light

*

your throat

torn through
the soiled
waters

*

torn away

KALPA

Lewis deSoto

This work, made of human and coyote bones linked end to end on a platform of redwood
planks, is based on the *kalpa*, the measure of an eon in Hindu and Buddhist literature.
This time period is sometimes described as the interval it takes for a *deva* or angel,
descending from heaven once a year,
to wear down a mile-high iron mountain with a silk scarf.
In the beginning of *kalpa*, order reigns and time unfolds slowly.
Toward the end, however, events pass more rapidly,
until there is a burst of chaos and an interminable void takes its place.

COSÌ FAN TUTTE AT THE LIMITS

Peter Sellars's production of *Così fan tutte*,
PepsiCo Summerfare, Purchase, New York, 1986.

EDWARD W. SAID

Così fan tutte was the first opera I saw when I came to the United States as a schoolboy in the early 1950s. The 1951 Metropolitan Opera production was directed by renowned theater figure Alfred Lunt, and, as I recall, much celebrated as a brilliant yet faithful English-language rendition of an elegant opera that boasted an excellent cast —John Brownlee as Don Alfonso, Eleanor Steber and Blanche Thebom as the two sisters, Richard Tucker and Frank Guarrera as the young men, Patrice Munsel as Despina—and a fastidiously executed conception as an eighteenth-century court comedy. I remember a lot of curtseying, many lace hankies, elaborate wigs, and acres of beauty spots, much chuckling and all-round good fun, all of which seemed to go well with the very polished, indeed even superb singing by the ensemble. So powerful was the impression made on me by this *Così fan tutte* that most of the many subsequent performances of the work that I saw or listened to seemed simply variations on that quintessentially classical production. When I saw the 1958 Salzburg production with Karl Böhm conducting and Elisabeth Schwarzkopf, Christa Ludwig, Rolando Panerai, Luigi Alva, and Graziella Sciutti in the cast, I took it to be an elaboration of the Metropolitan realization.

Although I am neither a professional musicologist nor a Mozart scholar, it has seemed to me that most, if not all, interpretations of the opera stress the aspects that Lunt picked up on: the work's effervescent, rollicking, courtly fun, the apparent triviality of its plot and its characters, who verge on silliness, and the astonishing beauty of its music. Although I have never been completely convinced that that particular mode was the right one for this superb yet elusive and somewhat mysterious opera, I have also resigned myself to performances that are firmly grooved within it.

The only real departure from the pattern was, of course, Peter Sellars's production, staged along with the two other Mozart–Da Ponte collaborations at the now defunct PepsiCo Summerfare in Purchase, New York, in the late 1980s. The great virtue of those productions was that Sellars managed to sweep away all of the eighteenth-century clichés. As Mozart had written the operas while the ancient régime was crumbling, Sellars argued, they should be set by contemporary directors at a similar moment in our own time—with the crumbling of the American empire alluded to by characters and settings, as well as by class deformations and personal histories that bore the marks of a society in crisis. Thus Sellars's version of *La Nozze di Figaro* takes place in the overblown luxury of Trump Tower, *Don Giovanni* on a poorly lit street in Spanish Harlem where dealers and junkies transact their business, *Così fan tutte* in Despina's Diner, where a group of Vietnam veterans and their girlfriends hang out, play tricky games, and get frighteningly embroiled in feelings and self-discoveries for which they are unprepared and with which they are largely incapable of dealing.

[ABOVE] Peter Sellars's production of *Così fan tutte*, 1986.
[RIGHT] Alfred Lunt's production of *Così fan tutte* at the Metropolitan Opera, New York, 1951.

To the best of my knowledge, no one but Sellars has attempted such a full-scale revisionist interpretation of the three Da Ponte operas, which remain in the repertory as essentially courtly, classical, eighteenth-century operas. Even Salzburg's recent Patrice Chéreau production of *Don Giovanni*—despite its striking savagery and relentlessly obsessive pace—functions within what we take to be Mozart's strictly conventional theatrical idiom. What makes Sellars's productions of the three operas so powerful is that they put the viewer directly in touch with what is most eccentric and opaque about Mozart: the obsessive patterning in the operas, patterning that finally has little to do with showing that crime doesn't pay or that the faithlessness inherent in all human beings must be overcome before true union can occur. Mozart's characters in *Don Giovanni* and *Così fan tutte* can indeed be interpreted not just as individuals with definable biographies and characteristics but as figures driven by forces outside themselves which they make no serious effort to comprehend. These operas, in fact, are much more about power and manipulation than most opera directors acknowledge; in them, individuality is reduced to a momentary identity in the impersonal rush of things. There is little room therefore for providence, or for the heroics of charismatic personalities, although Don Giovanni himself cuts a defiant and dashing figure within a very limited scope.

In comparison with the operas of Beethoven, Verdi, or even Rossini, the world that Mozart depicts is amoral and Lucretian, a world in which power has its own logic, undomesticated either by conditions of piety or verisimilitude. As much as he seems to have looked down on Mozart's lack of seriousness, Wagner shares a similar worldview, I think, and that is one of the reasons that his characters in *The Ring*, *Tristan und Isolde*, and *Parsifal* spend as much as time as they do going over, renarrating, and recomprehending the remorseless chain of actions in which they are imprisoned and from which there can be no significant escape. What is it that keeps Don Giovanni irrecusably bound to his licentiousness or *Così*'s Don Alfonso and Despina to their schemes and fixings? Little in the operas themselves provides an immediate answer.

Indeed, I think Mozart has tried to embody an abstract force that drives people by means of agents (in *Così fan tutte*) or sheer sexual energy (in *Don Giovanni*), without the reflective consent of their mind or will. As many commentators have noted, the plot of *Così fan tutte* has antecedents in various "test" plays and operas and, as scholar Charles Rosen says, it resembles the "demonstration" plays written by Marivaux among others. "They demonstrate—prove by acting out—psychological ideas and 'laws' that everyone accepted," Rosen adds, "and they are almost scientific in the way they show precisely how these laws work in practice." He goes on to speak of *Così fan tutte* as "a closed system," an interesting if insufficiently examined notion, which does in fact apply.

The intrigue in *Così fan tutte* is the result of a bet between Alfonso and his young friends Ferrando and Guglielmo that is inspired neither by a sense of moral purpose nor by ideological passion. Ferrando is in love with Dorabella, Guglielmo with Fiordiligi; Alfonso bets that the women will be unfaithful. A subterfuge is then enacted: the two men will pretend that they have been called off to war. Then they will come back in disguise and woo the girls. As Albanian (i.e. Oriental) men, the two attempt to seduce each other's fiancées: Guglielmo quickly succeeds with Dorabella. Ferrando needs more time, but he too is successful with Fiordiligi, who is clearly the more serious of the two sisters. Alfonso is helped in the plot by Despina, a cynical maid who assists in her mistresses' downfall, although she does not know of the bet between the men. Finally the plot is exposed, the women are furious, but return to their lovers even though Mozart does not specify whether the pairs will remain as they were at the outset.

We can learn much about *Così fan tutte* in the late-eighteenth-century cultural setting by looking at Beethoven's reactions to the Da Ponte operas, which he, as Mozart's younger contemporary and an Enlightenment enthusiast, seems always to have regarded with a certain amount of discomfort. Like many critics of Mozart's operas, Beethoven is—so far as I have been able to discover—curiously silent about *Così fan tutte*. To generations of Mozart admirers, including Beethoven, the opera does not seem to offer the kind of metaphysical or social or cultural significance found readily by Kierkegaard and other luminaries in *Don Giovanni*, *Die Zauberflöte*, and *Figaro*. Therefore, there seems to be very little to say about it. Significantly enough, Beethoven seems to have thought *Die Zauberflöte* the greatest of Mozart's works (mainly because it was a German work), and he has been quoted in several instances as expressing his dislike of *Don Giovanni* and *Figaro*; they were too trivial, too Italian, too scandalous for a serious composer. Once, however, he expressed pleasure at *Don Giovanni*'s success, although he was also said not to have wanted to attend Mozart's operas because they might make him forfeit his own originality.

These are the contradictory feelings of a composer who found Mozart's work as a whole unsettling and even disconcerting. Competitiveness is clearly a factor, but there is something else. It is Mozart's uncertain moral center, the absence in *Così fan tutte* of a specific humanistic message of the kind about which *Die Zauberflöte* is so laboriously explicit. What is still more significant about Beethoven's reactions to Mozart is that *Fidelio*, Beethoven's only opera, written fifteen years after *Così fan tutte*, can be interpreted as a direct and, in my opinion, somewhat desperate, response to the earlier opera. Take one small but certainly telling example: *Fidelio*'s heroine Leonore appears, at the beginning of the opera, disguised as a young man, "Fidelio," who comes to work as an assistant at the prison, where her husband, Florestan, is being held as a political prisoner by the tyrannical governor of Seville, Don Pizarro. In this guise, Leonore engages the amorous attentions of the jailer's daughter Marzelline. You could say that Beethoven has picked up the part of *Così*'s plot in which the disguised lovers return to Naples and proceed to advance on the wrong women. However, no sooner does the intrigue start up than Beethoven puts a stop to it, revealing to the audience that young Fidelio is really the ever faithful and constant Leonore, come to the prison in order to assert her fidelity and conjugal love to her imprisoned husband.

Still, Leonore's central aria, "*Komm Hoffnung*," is full of echoes of Fiordiligi's "*Per pietà, ben mio*" in Act Two of *Così*, which she sings as a last, forlorn plea to herself to remain constant and to drive away the dishonor she feels might be overcoming her as she suffers (and perhaps slightly enjoys) the impress of Ferrando's importuning: "*Svenerà quest'empia voglia, L'ardir mio, la mia costanza. Perderà la rimembranza Che vergogna e orror me fa.*" ("I'll rid myself of this terrible desire with my devotion and love. I'll blot out the memory that causes me shame and horror.") Memory is something to be banished, the memory she is ashamed of: her trifling with her real, but absent, lover Guglielmo. Yet memory is also what she must hold onto, the guarantee of her loyalty to her lover—for if she forgets, she loses the ability to judge her present, timidly flirtatious behavior for the shameful wavering it really is. Mozart gives her a noble, horn-accompanied figure for this avowal, a melody that is echoed in key (E major) and instrumentation (also horns) in Leonore's great appeal to hope, "*lass den letzen Stern de Müden nicht erbleicher*" ("let this last star for the weary not be extinguished"). But although, like Fiordiligi, Leonore has a secret, hers is an honorable one;

and she does not doubt love and hope, she depends on them. There is no wavering, no doubting or timidity in Leonore, and her powerful aria, with its battery of horns proclaiming her determination and resolve, seems almost like a reproach to Fiordiligi's rather more delicate and troubled musings.

Doubtless, in *Fidelio*, Beethoven wrestled with various issues that were important to him, fully

Alfred Lunt's production of *Così fan tutte*, 1951.

independently of *Così*, but I think we have to grant that something about Mozart's operatic world in his mature and greatest works (with the exception of *Die Zauberflöte*) kept bothering Beethoven. One aspect, of course, is their sunny, comic, and southern setting, which amplifies and makes more difficult to accept their underlying critique and implied rejection of the middle-class virtue that meant so much to Beethoven. Even *Don Giovanni*, the one Da Ponte opera whose twentieth-century reinterpretations have turned it into a "Northern" psychodrama of neurotic drives and transgressive passions, is essentially more unsettlingly powerful when enacted as a comedy of heedlessness and enjoyable insouciance. The style of famous twentieth-century Italian Dons like Ezio Pinza, Tito Gobbi, and Cesare Siepi prevailed until the 1970s, but their characterizations have given way to those of Thomas Allen, James Morris, Ferruccio Furlanetto, and Samuel Ramey, who represent the Don as a dark figure heavily influenced by his readings in Kierkegaard and Freud. *Così fan tutte* is even more aggressively "Southern," in that all of its Neapolitan characters are depicted as being shifty, pleasure-centered, and, with the exception of a brief moment here and there, selfish and relatively free of guilt, even though what they do is, by *Fidelio*'s standards, patently reprehensible.

Thus the earnest and deeply serious atmosphere of *Fidelio* can be seen as a reproach to *Così*, which, for all its irony and beauty, is grippingly without any kind of gravity at all. When the two pseudo-Oriental suitors are repulsed by Fiordiligi and Dorabella at the end of Act One, they drag the sisters into a broadly comic, false-suicide scene; what transpires is based on the ironic disparity between the women's earnest concern for the men, and the two suitors' amused playacting. Genuine emotion is thus undercut by the ridiculous. In Act Two, where the disguises and playacting advance quite significantly into the emotions of the four main characters, Mozart extends the joke even further. The result is that the four do fall in love again, though with the wrong partners, and this undermines something very dear to Beethoven: constancy of identity. Whereas Beethoven's Leonore takes on the mask of the boy Fidelio, her disguise is designed to get her closer to, not further away from, her real identity as faithful wife. Indeed, all the characters in *Fidelio* are rigorously circumscribed in their unvarying essence: Pizarro as unyielding villain, Florestan as champion of good, and so forth. This is at the opposite pole from *Così*, where disguises, and the wavering and wandering they foster, are the norm, and constancy and stability mocked as impossible.

Still *Così fan tutte* is an opera whose strange lightheartedness hides, or at least makes light of, an inner system that is quite severe and amoral in its workings. I do not at all want to say that the work must not be enjoyed as the brilliant romp that in many ways it is. The critic's role, however, is to try to lay bare what it is that Mozart and Da Ponte were intimating through their merry tale of deceit and displaced love. I shall therefore try to elucidate the way in which *Così fan tutte* is, at its concealed limits, a very different work than its rollicking exterior and sublime music suggest.

We now know that Mozart composed the ensembles of *Così* before he took on the arias or even the overture. This sequence corresponds to the opera's concentration on relationships between characters rather than on brilliant individuals as encountered in earlier operas such as *Figaro* or *Don Giovanni*. Of the three Da Ponte operas, *Così fan tutte* is not only the last and, in my opinion, the most complex and eccentric, but also the most internally well organized, the most full of echoes and references, and the most difficult to unlock—precisely because it goes further toward the limits of acceptable, ordinary experiences of love, life, and ideas than either of its two predecessors. The reasons for this, and indeed for *Così*'s opacity and even resistance to the kind of interpretive analysis that *Figaro* and *Don Giovanni* generally permit, are partly to be found in Mozart's life in 1789 and 1790, while he was at work on *Così*. But they are also to be found in the way Mozart and Da Ponte created the work together, without a well-known play or legendary figure to provide them with framework and directions. *Così* is the result of a collaboration, and its dynamics, the symmetrical structure of its plot, and the echoic quality of so much of its music are internal factors of its composition, not imposed on it by an outside source.

Many of the numbers of Act One, for example, are written to emphasize how the characters think, act, and sing in pairs; their lines generally imitate one another and recollect lines sung earlier. Mozart seems to want us to feel that we are inside a closed system in which melody, imitation, and parody are very difficult to separate from one another. This is superbly in evidence in the First Act sextet, which enacts a sort of mini-play in which Alfonso draws Despina, then the two disguised men, then the two women into his plot, while commenting on the action. The whole number is a dizzying maze of advance and expostulation, statement, echo, and inversion that rivals anything Mozart ever wrote for elegance, invention, and complexity. It simply sweeps aside the last trace of stability and gravity that we have so far been able to hold onto.

To come to terms with *Così* is first of all to be reminded that, when it premiered in Vienna on

January 26, 1790, it was a contemporary opera, not a classic, as it has become today. Mozart began to work on it in the first part of 1789, at a time when he had just passed through a period of great difficulty. Critic Andrew Steptoe points out that, after he had completed *Don Giovanni* in 1787, "Mozart's personal health and financial security deteriorated." Not only did a German tour he undertook fail, but he seems to have passed through "a loss in creative confidence," composing very few works and leaving an unusual number of fragments and unfinished pieces. We do not really know why he took up work on *Così fan tutte*, although Steptoe volunteers (correctly, I think) that the piece "was therefore located at a pivotal moment, and must have been seized upon by the composer both as an artistic challenge and a golden opportunity to recoup financially." The score that he finally did produce bears the marks, I believe, of other aspects of his life in 1789. One is his wife Constanze's absence for a rest cure in Baden while he worked on the opera. While there, she "displayed improprieties" that prompted a letter from Mozart which cast him as the constant one and his wife as the flighty, embarrassing partner who needed to be reminded of her position and domestic status:

Director/actor Alfred Lunt rehearsing with Eleanor Steber for her role as Fiordiligi in his legendary 1951 Metropolitan Opera production of *Così fan tutte.*

> Dear little wife! I want to talk to you quite frankly. You have no reason whatever to be unhappy. You have a husband who loves you and does all he possibly can for you. . . . I am glad indeed when you have some fun—of course I am—but I do wish that you would not sometimes make yourself so cheap. In my opinion you are far too free and easy with N.N. . . . Now please remember that N.N. are not half so familiar with other women, whom they perhaps know more intimately, as they are with you. Why, N.N. who is usually a well-conducted fellow and particularly respectful to women, must have been misled by your behavior into writing the most disgusting and most impertinent sottises which he put into his letter. A woman must always make herself respected, or else people will begin to talk about her. My love! Forgive me for being so frank, but my peace of mind demands it as well as our mutual happiness. Remember that you yourself once admitted to me that you were inclined to comply too easily. You know the consequences of that. Remember too the promises you gave to me. Oh, God, do try, my love!

How important Mozart's own almost Archimedean sense of stability and control was in dealing with Constanze is remarked by Steptoe, who argues that because Mozart did not believe in "blind romantic love" he went on to "satirize it mercilessly (most notably in *Così fan tutte*)." Yet the letters from the *Così* period tell a more complicated story. In one, Mozart tells Constanze how excited he is at the prospect of seeing her, and then adds, "If people could see into my heart, I should almost feel ashamed." We might then expect him to say something about seething passions and sensual thoughts. Instead he continues: "To me, everything is cold—cold as ice," and notes that "everything seems so empty." In a subsequent letter, Mozart speaks again of "feeling—a kind of emptiness, which hurts me dreadfully—a kind of longing, which is never satisfied, which never ceases, and which persists, nay rather increases daily." In Mozart's correspondence there are other letters of this sort that characterize his special combination of unstilled energy (expressed in the sense of ever increasing emptiness and unsatisfied longing) and cold control: these seem to me to have a particular relevance for the position of *Così fan tutte* in his life and oeuvre.

Just as the themes of memory and forgetting are imperative to *Così*'s plot, the opera itself looks back to earlier works and is full of "thematic reminiscences," as Andrew Steptoe calls them. In addition, at one point in Act One (Dorabella's accompanied recitative "*Ah, scostati*"), the orchestra suddenly plays the rapid scale passages associated with the Commendatore in *Don Giovanni*. Mozart's use of counterpoint gives the music added substance, so that in the E-flat Canon in the second act's finale one experiences not only a remarkable sense of rigor, but also a special ironic expressiveness well beyond the words and the situation. For, as the lovers have finally worked their way around to the new reversed pairing, three of them sing polyphonically of submerging all thought and memory in the wine they are about to drink, while only one, Guglielmo, remains disaffected—he had had greater faith in Fiordiligi's power to resist Ferrando, but he has been disproved—and he stands outside the canon; he wishes that the women ("*queste volpi senza onor*") would drink poison and end the whole thing. It is as if Mozart wanted the counterpoint to mirror the lovers' embarrassment in a closed polyphonic system, and also to show how even though they think of themselves as shedding all ties and memories, the music, by its circularity and echoic form, reveals them to be bound to each other in a new and logically consequent embrace.

Such a moment is unique to *Così fan tutte*: it depicts human desire and satisfaction in musical terms as essentially a matter of compositional control that directs feeling and appetite into a logical circuit allowing no escape and very little elevation. But the whole opera—plot, characters, situation, ensembles, and arias—tends toward such a cluster because it is derived from the movement of two intimate couples, two men and two women, plus two "outside" characters, coming together in various ways, and then pulling apart, then coming together again, with several changes along the way. The symmetries and repetitions are almost cloying, but they are the substance of the opera. We know very little about these figures; no traces of a former life adhere to them (unlike *Figaro* and *Don Giovanni*, both of which are steeped in earlier episodes, entanglements, intrigues); their identities exist in order to be tested and exercised as lovers, and once they have gone through one full turn and become the opposite of what they were, the opera ends. The overture, with its busy, clattering, round-like themes, catches the spirit of this movement quite perfectly. Remember that Mozart wrote it after he had finished most of the main body of the opera, that is, after the schematic character of what he was elaborating had impressed itself on his mind.

Only one figure, Don Alfonso, stands apart from all of this: his is the only activity that begins before the opera opens, and it continues uninterruptedly to the very end. Who is he really? He certainly belongs to a line of senior authority figures that extends through Mozart's life and works. Remember the Commendatore in *Giovanni*, or Sarastro in *Die Zauberflöte*, or even Bartolo and Almaviva in *Figaro*. Yet Alfonso's role is different from the others in that he seeks to prove not the underlying moral fiber but the inconstancy and unfaithfulness of women—and he succeeds. In the final ensemble, when he is denounced by the women as the man who misled them and staged their fall, Alfonso responds without a trace of regret: what he has done, he says, is to have *undeceived* the lovers, and this, he adds, puts them more under his command. "*V'ingannai, ma fu l'inganno Disinganno ai vostri amanti, Che piú saggi ormai saranno, Che faranquel chi'io vorró*" ("I deceived you, but my deception was to undeceive your lovers. From now on they'll both be wiser, and they'll do just as I say"). "Join hands," he says, "so that all four of you can laugh, as I have laughed and will laugh again." It is interesting and not entirely a coincidence that what he sings contains striking anticipations of *Die Zauberflöte*, an opera that Mozart perhaps wrote as a more morally acceptable version of the plot used in *Così fan tutte*. Whereas constancy doesn't win out in *Così*, in *Die Zauberflöte* it does.

Like Sarastro, Don Alfonso is a manager and controller of behavior—although, unlike Sarastro, he acts with neither solemnity nor high moral purpose. Most accounts of *Così* scarcely pay attention to him, and yet in the unguardedly amoral world of the opera he is not only a crucial or pivotal figure but a fascinating one as well. His many references to himself—as actor, teacher, scholar, plotter, courtier—do not directly allude to the one thing he seems above all others to be—that is, a mature libertine, someone who has had much worldly sexual experience and now wishes to direct, control, and manipulate the experiences of others. In this he resembles a schoolmaster, military strategist, and philosopher: he has seen much in the world and is more than able to stage another drama of the sort he has presumably lived through himself. He knows in advance what conclusion he will come to, so the action of the opera furnishes him with few surprises, least of all about the behavior of women. Plowing the sea, sowing on sand, trying to ensnare the wind in a net: these impossibilities (to which he refers) define the limits of Alfonso's reality, and they accentuate the element of radical instability in which, as a teacher of lovers and a practiced lover himself, he lives. But this does not apparently prevent him from enjoying both the experience of loving and the opportunity to prove his ideas.

I do not want to suggest that Don Alfonso is anything other than a comic figure. But I do want to argue that he stands very close to a number of cultural and psychological actualities that were very important to Mozart, as well as to other relatively advanced thinkers and artists of the time. Consider first the unmistakable progression in Mozart's operatic invention from Figaro, to Don Giovanni, to Don Alfonso. Each in his own way is unconventional and iconoclastic, although only Don Alfonso is neither punished, like Don Giovanni, nor in effect domesticated, as Figaro is. The discovery that the stabilities of marriage and the social norms habitually governing human life are inapplicable because life itself is elusive and inconstant has placed Don Alfonso in a new, more turbulent and troubling realm, one in which experience repeats the same disillusioning patterns without relief. What he devises for the two pairs of lovers is a game in which human identity is shown to be as protean, unstable, undifferentiated as anything in the actual world. Not surprisingly, then, one of the main motifs in *Così fan tutte* is the elimination of memory in favor of the present. The structure of the plot, with its play-within-a-play abstractions, enforces that: Alfonso sets up a test that separates the lovers from their past and their loyalties. Then the men assume new identities, entering into their roles as much as the women, taking seriously their charge as lovers, and, in the process, prove what Alfonso knew all along. Yet Guglielmo is not so easily resigned to Fiordiligi's apparent fickleness and therefore remains for a time outside Alfonso's circle of happy and deceived lovers; despite his bitterness, however, he eventually rallies round to Alfonso's thesis, given full articulation in the opera now for the first time. This is a late moment in the opera. Alfonso has been biding his time before putting things as flatly, in as unadorned and reductive a manner as this. It is as if he, and Mozart, needed Act One to set up the demonstration and Act Two to let it spin itself out, before he could come forward with this conclusion, which is also the musical root, finally revealed, of the opera.

In this respect, Don Alfonso represents the standpoint not only of a jaded, illusionless man of the world, but also of an indefatigable practitioner and teacher of his views, a figure who needs subjects and space for his demonstrations, even though he knows in advance that the pleasures he sets up are far from new. Alfonso resembles an understated version of his near contemporary the Marquis de Sade, a libertine who, as Foucault describes him memorably:

> is he who, while yielding to all the fantasies of desire and to each of its furies, can, but also must, illumine their slightest movement with a lucid and deliberately elucidated representation. There is a strict order governing the life of the libertine: every representation must be immediately endowed with life in the living body of desire, every desire must be expressed in the pure light of representative discourse. Hence the rigid sequence of "scenes" . . . and, within the scenes, the meticulous balance between the conjugation of bodies and the concentration of reasons.*

We recall that in the first number, when Alfonso speaks, he calls himself "*ex cathedro*," a man with gray hair and long experience: we are to assume, I think, that having yielded to desire in the past he is now ready to illuminate his ideas

* *The Order of Things*, pp. 209–10.

"with a lucid and deliberately elucidated representation." The plot of *Così* is a rigid sequence of scenes, all of them manipulated by Alfonso and Despina, his equally cynical helper, in which sexual desire is, as Foucault suggests, profligacy subjected to the order of representation—that is, the enacted tale of lovers being schooled in an illusionless, yet exciting love. When the game is revealed to Fiordiligi and Dorabella, they accept the truth of what they have experienced and, in a conclusion that has troubled interpreters and directors with its coy ambiguity, they sing of reason and mirth without any specific indication at all from Mozart that the two women and two men will return to their original lovers.

Such a conclusion opens up a troubling vista of numerous further substitutions, with no ties, no identity, no idea of stability or constancy left undisturbed. Foucault speaks of this cultural moment as one in which language retains the capacity to name, but can only do so in a "ceremony reduced to the utmost precision," and "extends it to infinity": the lovers will go on finding other partners, since the rhetoric of love and the representation of desire have lost their anchors in a fundamentally unchanging order of Being.

Responsible for this is Don Alfonso, a parodic Virgil leading young, inexperienced men and women into a world stripped of standards, norms, certainties. He speaks the language of wisdom and sagacity, allied to an admittedly small-scaled and limited vision of his power and control. There are plenty of classical references in the libretto: none of them refers to the Christian or Masonic deities that Mozart seems to have venerated elsewhere (he became a Mason in 1784). Don Alfonso's natural world is in part Rousseau's, stripped of sanctimonious piety, volatile with fancy and caprice, made rigorous with the need to experience desire without palliatives or conclusion. Even more significantly for Mozart, Don Alfonso is only the second authority figure to appear in his operas after the death of Mozart's father, Leopold, in 1787; given some urgency by Leopold's death, the terrifying Commendatore in *Don Giovanni* embodies the stern, judgmental aspect of Leopold's relationship with his son—an aspect that is not at all present in Alfonso, who is not easily provoked, gives every appearance of wanting to play the game with his young friends, and seems completely untroubled by the pervasive faithlessness his "scenes" uncover.

Alfonso, I believe, is an irreverent and later portrait of the senior patron, someone quite audaciously presented not as a moral instructor but as an amorous virtuoso, a libertine or retired rake whose influence is exerted through hoaxes, disguises, charades, and finally a philosophy of inconstancy as norm. Because he is an older man, Alfonso intimates a sense of mortality that is very far from the concerns of the young lovers. A famous letter written by Mozart to his father in the final period of the latter's life, on April 4, 1787, expresses a mood of illusionless fatalism: "As death," he says, "is the true goal of our existence I have formed during the first few years such close relations with this best and truest friend of mankind, that his image is not only no longer terrifying to me, but is indeed very soothing and consoling! . . . Death is the key that unlocks the door to our true happiness. I never lie down at night without reflecting that—young as I am—I may not live to see another day." In the opera, death is rendered less intimidating and formidable than it is for most people. This is not the usual, conventionally Christian sentiment, however, but a naturalist one: death as something familiar and even dear, a door to other experiences. Yet its prospect also induces a sense of fatalism and lateness—that is, the feeling that one is late in life and the end is near.

So the father figure has become the friend and cheerful, tyrannical mentor, a person to be obeyed who is somehow neither paternalistic nor minatory. And this status is confirmed in Mozart's style, in which posturing characters are displayed in such a way as to permit Alfonso to enter into a game with them, not as hectoring senior presence nor as admonishing pedagogue, but as an actor in the common entertainment. Alfonso predicts the conclusion or end of the comedy but here, according to musicologist Donald Mitchell,

> we stumble . . . on the most uncomfortable aspect of the opera's factuality. What we yearn for is the possibility of a fairy-tale reconciliation. But Mozart was far too truthful an artist to disguise the fact that a healing forgiveness is impossible where all the parties [Alfonso included] are not only equally "guilty" but share to the full the knowledge of each other's guilt. In *Così*, the best that can be done is to present as brave a front as one may to the fact of life [and, I could add, of death]. The coda that succeeds the *dénouement* does exactly that and no more.*

The conclusion of *Così* is really twofold: this is the way things are because that is what *they* do—*così fan tutte*—and, second, they will be like that, one situation, one substitution, succeeding another, until, it is implied, the process is stopped by death. All are the same, *così fan tutte*, in the meantime. As Fiordiligi says, "*e potra la morte sola far che cangi affetto il cor*" ("only death can affect the heart"). Death takes the place of Christian reconciliation and redemption, the key to our true, if unknown and indescribable, hope of rest and stability, soothing and consoling without providing anything more than a theoretical intimation of final repose. But like nearly every serious subject with which the opera flirts, death is kept at bay, indeed is mostly left out of *Così fan tutte*.

Within its carefully circumscribed limits, *Così fan tutte* allows itself only a number of gestures toward what stands just beyond it, or to vary the metaphor a bit, through what stands just inside it. Mozart never ventured so close to the potentially terrifying view he and Da Ponte seem to have uncovered of a universe shorn of any redemptive or palliative scheme, whose one law is motion and instability expressed as the power of libertinage and manipulation, and whose only conclusion is the terminal repose provided by death. That so astonishingly satisfying a musical score should be joined to so heedless and insignificant a tale is what *Così fan tutte* accomplishes with such a unique virtuosity. But I think we should not believe that the candid fun of the work does any more than hold its ominous vision in abeyance—that is, for as long as *Così fan tutte*'s limits are not permitted to invade the stage.

* *Cradles of the New*, p. 132.

Like an Old Elephant

MARCELLO MASTROIANNI

I remember a great medlar tree.
I remember my astonishment with New York City skyscrapers and the sunset on Park Avenue.
I remember the aluminum pan with a missing handle in which my mother fried eggs.
I remember Rabagliati's voice emanating from a huge record player, singing: *E tic e tac—cos'è che batte—è l'orologio del cuor.*
I remember a very young Clark Gable, in black and white, his back to the screen; then he turned and smiled. An irresistibly likable scoundrel. What film was it? *It Happened One Night*, I think.
I remember my grandfather's and father's workshop. My grandfather had made a chair.
I remember the odor of the wood. Yes, the odor of the wood.
I remember the German uniforms. I remember the evacuees.
Once, I remember, I dreamed I lived in an airship. Or maybe it was a spaceship.
I remember H. G. Wells, Simenon, Ray Bradbury.
I remember the color illustrations in *La Domenica del Corriere*. And I also remember Flash Gordon.
I remember that Fellini used to call me "Snaporaz."
I remember my first camping trip.
I remember Chekhov: especially Captain Soliony who goes *Pio-pio-pio-pio* in *Three Sisters*.
I remember the first time that I saw the mountains and the snow, and the emotions I felt.
I remember the music of *Star Dust*. It was before the War. I used to dance with a girl in a flowered dress.
I remember perfectly the flavor and smell of chickpea soup. And I remember we used to play bingo on Christmas Eve.
I remember the frightening roar of the "Liberators," the U.S. airplanes in the first bombing over Rome.
I remember watching the first man touch the moon in slow motion; but where was I?
I remember that I saw my first film in Turin. *Ben-Hur* with Ramon Novarro. I was six years old.
I remember Paris, where my first daughter Chiara was born.
I remember the rice croquettes. But you couldn't buy them every day. They cost forty cents.
I remember my first adult hat. It was a Saratoga model.
I remember Charlot's jokes.
I remember my brother Ruggero.
I remember that Cicero was born in 106 B.C., 2030 years before me, but only a few feet from my house in Arpino. My grandfather was proud of that. *Vitam regit fortuna, non sapientia*, he used to say, quoting our fellow countryman. Then he

Rome, 1944.

Clark Gable, 1934.

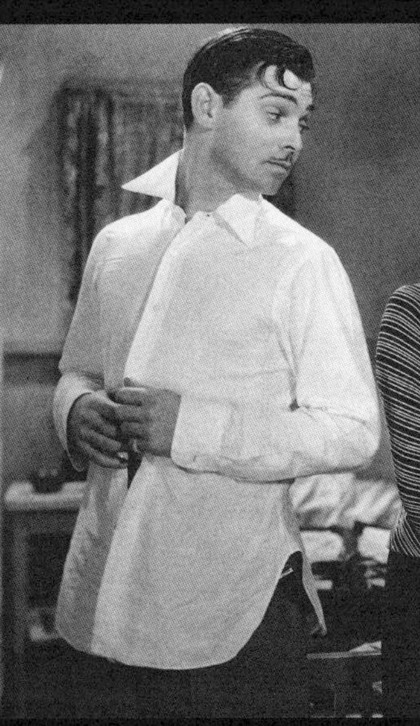

Flash Gordon, 1936.

Ramon Novarro
in *Ben-Hur*, 1926

Federico Fellini.

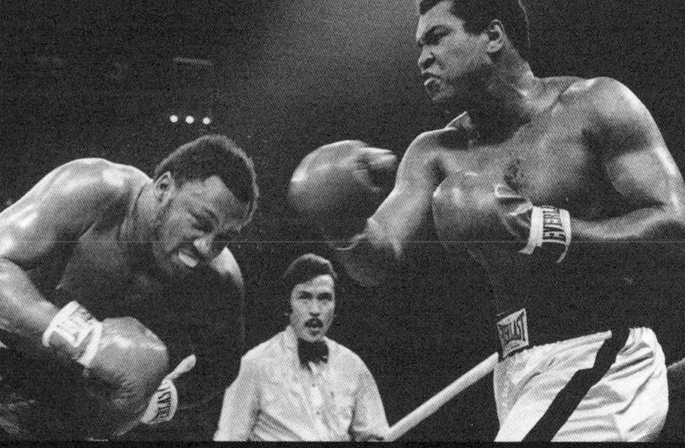

Muhammad Ali vs.
Joe Frazier, 1975.

Gary Cooper, 1957.

Greta Garbo.

The Kremlin,
Moscow, 1947.

Marilyn Monroe.

Moon Landing,
1969.

would sigh, "Oh yes, it's luck that sustains life, not wisdom."
I remember a summer evening smelling of rain.
I remember Ulysses's adventures: "Musa, that man of many-sided genius."
I remember Cassius Clay (nicknamed "The Mouth") in New York, against Frazier.
I remember the beautiful white hair of the architect Ridolfi, my professor of Architectonic Design.
I remember my daughter Barbara's first drawings.
I remember my project to raise the Tiber by building a road under it.
I remember Greta Garbo who stared at my feet, and asked me: "Italian shoes?"
I remember my first cigarette. It was made, I remember, with ear-of-corn hairs.
I remember my uncle Umberto's hands, hands as strong as pliers, hands of a sculptor.
I remember the silence that enveloped Maxim's, when Gary Cooper appeared in a white tuxedo.
I remember Marilyn Monroe.
I remember my first automobile; it was a Topolino station wagon.
I don't know why I remember this stupid rigmarole: "Oh, so many beautiful girls, Madama Doré, so many beautiful girls."
I remember the fireflies that you don't see anymore.
I remember the snow in Red Square in Moscow.
I remember a dream where somebody told me always to remember my parents' house.
I remember a train trip during the war. The train entered a tunnel. There was total darkness, and then, in the silence, a stranger kissed me on the lips.
I remember the Kurds gathered together in a biblical exodus. I remember that I must not forget the violence of many absurdly violent scenes.
I also remember the sensation of silence and of light, suspended like a mystic vapor in the city of Jerusalem.
I remember the desire to see what this world will do, what will happen in the year 2000, and to be there and remember everything, like an old elephant, yes, because—I remember—I have always been curious. So curious!
And then, I remember when we used to catch lizards. My slingshot!
I remember my first night of lovemaking.
I remember, yes, I remember.

Translated from the Italian by Vicki Satlow

Pepón Osorio

Más is More

[PAGE 113]
El Chandelier, 1988.

[RIGHT]
Scene of the Crime (Whose Crime?), 1993.

Denorex

La Cama, 1987.

Pepón Osorio

For the past eleven years, Pepón Osorio has been creating artwork and installations marked by their visual overload of tourist and religious kitsch objects, tchotchkas, flags, and plastic toys that represent a visually potent engagement with Puerto Rican popular culture in mainland U.S.A., as well as Osorio's own experiences in the barrios of New York City.

La Bicicleta or *The Bicycle* (1985) is one of the first works Osorio created using his particular vernacular of the dislocated Puerto Rican immigrant experience. A nostalgic tribute to his childhood in the 1950s and 1960s, Osorio's bicycle is covered with ribbons, flowers, plastic swans and palm trees, Kewpie dolls, a crucifix, a Chiclets box, beads, and pieces of reflective metallic tape. The decoration is so excessive that it renders the object basically nonfunctional—a personal shrine and an intensely private object.

Like most artists who work with kitsch, Osorio is also deeply concerned with domestic imagery. In *La Cama* or *The Bed* (1987), the domestic sphere becomes a liberated space of self-expression. With its bedspread made of hundreds of stitched *recuerdos**, and a pillowcase covered with popular religious iconography, the bed details various rites of passage.

In 1988, Osorio was inspired to create *El Chandelier*, after catching glimpses of ornate chandeliers inside New York Loisaida* housing projects—self-fashioned creations of abundance in otherwise impoverished settings.

While all of these objects appear to deal in surface decoration, they also reveal a harsher political message. Hoarding and overbuying became common practice in Puerto Rico in the 1940s and 1950s, in the wake of a serious depression after the main source of revenue for the island, the sugar market, had plummeted. The practice of hoarding continued and was carried over into the general culture of the middle class. In much of his work, Osorio uses the overabundance of collected objects to represent a general fear of not having—and the common American phenomenon of aspiring to a higher class than one's own.

Osorio's use of the kitsch aesthetic to disrupt the common definitions of taste and high art, as well as to employ a conscious strategy of cultural resistance, has prompted one critic, Joan Ross Acocella, to call his work "plastic heaven." New York's El Museo del Barrio titled his 1991 retrospective simply *Con to' los hierros*: a Puerto Rican expression loosely translated as "giving it all you've got."

Anna Indych

* Puerto Rican party favors given at birthdays, weddings, and baptisms.

* The Lower East Side of Manhattan, particularly parts of the East Village with strong Latino communities.

THE KARNAU TAPES

MARCEL BEYER

I can't hear a thing, not a thing, the sounds are indistinguishable, everything is drowned by this roar, this ear-numbing roar that has taken possession of the air and my trembling body. Is this the end—is this the roar in which all sounds become reduced to a final, fiendish cacophony? Is this the descent into death? No, the plane levels off once more and the stutter of its engines gives way to the whistle of the slipstream as we spiral down toward our destination, a sea of flames. No one knows exactly how far the enemy has advanced, so there's a constant threat of gunfire from the ruins below. We're coming in to land on a runway flanked by shattered buildings. Not the Kurfürstendamm, surely? But it must be, it's the only runway left. Every tree in the avenue has been felled and the tram lines are obscured by a layer of bulldozed, steamrollered rubble. As the makeshift landing strip draws steadily nearer, one detail after another flashes past at lightning speed: a burned-out tramcar, a wrecked vehicle sprawled across the pavement, mounds of debris, splintered wooden doors, bathtubs doing duty as antitank barriers, a legless cripple humping himself along on his hands, a string of refugees, the remains of a family, a perambulator piled high with household effects. I can even make out sunken cheeks, bloodshot eyes, a child's runny nose. The images vanish in a cloud of dust as we touch down with a jolt. Are my arms trembling or merely taking on the movements of our plane as it judders to a halt?

Armed men come sprinting out of a ruined store and start unloading the aircraft almost before it comes to a halt. They stand guard, rifles at the ready, while the freight compartment is emptied of its crates of foodstuffs. The whole city is rationed. Everyone is dependent on rapeseed cakes, turnips, and molasses. The inhabitants are being encouraged to gather roots and acorns, mushrooms, and clover. Any living creature that can still be found among the gutted ruins is fair game—the authorities have even issued instructions on how to catch frogs. All available warm-blooded animals are to be devoured without delay. Conditions at the zoo are disastrous. Two days ago, on Friday, April 20, it was compelled to close for the first time in its history. Lack of power has immobilized the pumps and reduced the aquatic animals' pools to turbid soup, with the result that cracks have begun to appear in the dolphins' skin.

Cigarette lighter flickering, I make my way down into the cellar reserved for nocturnal creatures. This is evidently where members of the zoo staff sheltered during air raids. A flying fox flutters toward me through the gloom, skims my head, and makes for the exit, where, bewildered by the bright spring sunlight, it circles in an untidy, haphazard way and quickly disappears from view. Someone has opened the cage, it seems, and as the lighter's feeble flame approaches the spot I'm overcome by a terrible presentiment. Another step, a faint splintering sound. Crouching down, I make out a tiny thorax and spinal column, both picked clean. I examine the floor, singe scraps of fur and surface hair with my lighter flame. A severed, membranous wing, residues of black and inedible matter. Not far away lies a peeled head with the eyes still open. Then darkness. The lighter has run out of fuel.

So one form of darkness has absorbed the other: black is immersed in black, in a darkness unconnected with the night-and-morning world where safety resides. Such darkness fails to act as a shield against glaring light because it does not recognize light as its counterpart: in such darkness, light is inconceivable.

Dr. Stumpfecker stands facing me in uniform. It was he who ordered me to report to him forthwith, here in this sunless, subterranean world, in order to record the voice of his very last patient. He puts a finger to his lips. We have to be as quiet as possible in the Bunker, especially here on the lowest level, because one never knows, at any time of the day or night, whether the patient is asleep, presiding over a secret meeting, or simply sitting in his quarters, saying nothing but intolerant of any sound, however faint, in the corridor outside his door.

The patient is far more sensitive to disturbances of human origin than to the thunder of the guns overhead. Stumpfecker believes that the patient's sensitivity extends to his own vocalizations: the voice that used to be so loud and clear is growing steadily fainter. "You've yet to see this for yourself, Karnau, but what really dismays me is the fact that sometimes, in the last few days, the patient has been incapable of making any sound at all. It's happening more and more often, too. He'll bid a wordless farewell to subordinates who are leaving the Bunker for good, and his only response if they say something while shaking hands is a silent movement of the lips."

There's a whole set of blank wax discs on the table in my cubicle, and a portable recording machine is permanently at the ready. Stumpfecker has gone off to see how his patient is. All that mitigates the oppressive silence is the hum of the overtaxed air-conditioning system. The telephone rings. It's Stumpfecker: "Come quickly, Karnau, it's the patient, a very serious situation, he's been yelling at his subordinates in conference, hasn't strained his voice so badly for a long time. It'll give out at any moment, so get your equipment down here fast."

The stairs and the narrow corridor are thronged with people listening with expressions of alarm. The patient is clearly audible now, even though all the doors are closed. It's possible to hear every word he bellows in that maltreated voice, which does indeed sound on the point of giving out. I can already detect rents in his vocal cords, laryngeal lesions, but the eavesdroppers seem unaware of this; their whole attention is focused on the wording of his furious accusations and invocations of doom.

Stumpfecker, crouching outside the door of the room from which the noise is coming, nervously fidgets with his medical bag. We continue to wait, unable as yet to enter the room but poised to do so once the tantrum has run its course.

"He'll be slumped in his chair, utterly exhausted," Stumpfecker murmurs. "Stay in the background to begin with. Then, when I've checked his blood pressure and given him his medication, hold the microphone to his lips. You must start recording at once. It'll be my job to coax a few words out of him. You can't afford any slipups, Karnau. We don't know if he'll ever get his voice back. This could be our very last chance to record it."

But the red, raw, worn-out throat fails to emit another sound. We sit in

Stumpfecker's consulting room on the lower level and listen to the recorded silence. Stumpfecker tries hard to retain his composure. "Let's hope this difficult phase will soon be over," he says. "There may be light at the end of the tunnel. After all, he's undergone several polypectomies—for instance, in May 1935, on the advice of the doctors at the Charité Hospital. Having listened to one of his speeches on the radio, they inferred from his raucous voice that someone who could bellow so loudly for two solid hours must either have a larynx made of steel or be doomed to vocal paralysis. To the best of my knowledge, the last operation took place in October last year, shortly before my posting to East Prussia. It entailed the removal of another growth on the vocal cords.

"Many people regard the situation as hopeless," Stumpfecker goes on. "They think we're all condemned to look on idly at close quarters while the patient's physical condition deteriorates. Medical men have mistakenly believed that he was suffering from Parkinson's, but mark my words, Karnau: once the war is over—and it won't be long now—the patient's constitution will soon be restored by doses of fresh air, prolonged exposure to glorious summer sunlight, and rigorous detoxification."

It's only two days since Stumpfecker was promoted to the position of personal physician to the patient, in succession to the man who could silently insert cannulas into any vein he chose. Dr. Morell, renowned for his miracle pills, quit the Bunker in a hurry, and no one reckoned with the possibility that Stumpfecker, of all the numerous doctors present, would replace him—least of all Stumpfecker himself. The truth is that the end of our joint research had cast a shadow over his career. Although the authorities tolerated the failure of his transplant experiments at Hohenlychen, where he attempted to graft slivers of bone taken from inmates of the Ravensbrück concentration camp onto patients in the SS hospital—a procedure that resulted in the growth of proud flesh, gangrene, and, ultimately, death—they did not feel able, in the light of military developments, to fund our research any longer. Having embarked on it with the aim of exploring the foundations of a radical form of speech therapy, we had ended up with a collection of mutes.

Instead of purposefully eradicating vocal defects, we had erased whole voices. This meant, in the end, that all our efforts were expended on reversing the process, on trying to adjust and repair damaged voices—on conducting futile breathing exercises and clearing asthmatic tubes, on directing the course of these only moderately successful experiments, when there was no real hope of repairing organs already given up for lost. This fact was, of course, concealed from our guinea pigs, who would only have panicked and rent the air with countless aberrant sound waves.

Our work was finally terminated when a special SS unit herded the unresisting test subjects into a corner of their ward, doused them in surgical spirit, and set fire to them, destroying the entire building as well. Stumpfecker felt sure he would be demoted several ranks in consequence. He owed it to his teacher and patron, Professor Gebhardt, that the opposite happened. Not long afterward, in October of last year, he was appointed surgeon at HQ Eastern Front, where he often accompanied the patient on his daily walks.

And now, within the space of a few hours, he has had to familiarize himself with his patient's medical history by consulting the notes which Morell, in a very slapdash fashion, had kept over the years. Under present circumstances, however, the professional competence of his new personal physician matters less to the patient than his physical stature. Almost six foot six, Stumpfecker is known here as "the Giant." Although he may not be able to administer injections as neatly and painlessly as Morell—Stumpfecker's own staff informed him of the patient's misgivings in this respect—his titanic physique would readily permit him, in the event of a dangerous bombardment, to carry the patient on his back to a place of safety. Laden with a rigid figure whose straining arms threatened to squeeze the air from his lungs, he could, if need be, hasten from room to room, dodging the chunks of concrete and steel girders that rained down on them both. His reserves of energy would enable him to scramble over rubble for a considerable period, upturned eyes forever focused on the crumbling Bunker ceiling and ears ignoring his human burden's stertorous breathing in favor of sounds indicative of where the concrete would be rent asunder or the next shell would land.

At our session the next day Stumpfecker is once more filled with optimism. The patient has fully recovered from the exhaustion induced by yesterday's interminable tirade. He seems cheerful, relaxed, and in excellent voice. The needle quivers restlessly, leaving a silvery groove in the disc's matte wax surface. Every now and then the patient helps himself to a chocolate from a salver, a habit that struck me yesterday. It probably serves to lubricate his voice in a routine, unobtrusive manner.

I find it a trial, the lighting here below ground. There's no dawn light in the morning, no twilight in the evening, none of the gradual blurring of outlines that precedes the nocturnal evanescence of objects and human figures. Colors don't graduate from purple to the red of coagulated blood, from pale to dark blue, until, little by little, they're all reduced to shades of gray that eventually turn a blackish blue and envelop the whole world. There's not a glimmer now, no faint glow from the night sky, just an abrupt transition when I turn the light in my cubicle on or off. There are no light switches at all in the corridors and communal rooms. The lights out there burn twenty-four hours a day. They must consume a lot of power—the generators on the lower level can barely cope. Strange that precious electricity should be wasted in this way, but I suppose it's official policy that every space apart from our sleeping quarters should be illuminated. No shadowy figures must encounter each other in the gloom and no one can be allowed to withdraw into even temporary seclusion. What kind of life do we lead in our ever-illuminated surroundings?

The artificial light in which we have now been living for so many days is not particularly bright. It flickers or even goes out under the effect of gunfire, thereby seeming to imitate nature, but it burns and stings the skin as soon as it comes on. In time you perceive it less as a condition than as a substance. It diffuses an oily yellow glow over everything and defies removal, no matter how hard you scrub. Even our acoustics here are affected by the light. It suppresses natural sonic conditions: all voices sound a full tone lower, all noises muffled and indistinct. The brighter the light and the sharper the outlines, the more muffled the voices. This is an unreal acoustic environment, one in which everything loud and shrill stands out like a sore thumb. Does the wind still whistle? Do doves still coo? Do blackbirds still twitter as they hop from branch to branch? Is the air still alive with almost imperceptible stirrings whose origin cannot be located? Down here, everything can be traced to its source with ease: a change of pressure simply denotes that someone has closed the heavy steel door at the end of the corridor.

It's hard on the constitution, a daily routine no longer governed by the sun: never to bed before three in the morning, up at noon, straight off to a recording session. Still tired out, I manipulate the controls in a kind of dream, observe my movements like a stranger: my hand, the rippling tendons, the curious way my forefinger bends when I extend it, and the half-moons I've never noticed before, the pronounced half-moons at the base of my fingernails.

The Bunker's entire ventilation system is on the verge of collapse. The stale air is no longer being fully extracted, so we filter the remaining oxygen from it by breathing faster than normal. Fainting fits are becoming more frequent. The ventilators themselves may be clogged with swarms of fruit flies sucked in from the kitchen. The cook can no longer hold the little insects at bay, there's too much food lying around: ration packs of rusks and crisp bread, honey by the bucketful, ketchup—comestibles for which no use can be found now that most of the staff are getting their meals from a big kitchen elsewhere in the Bunker.

"Look at this," says the cook. "Everything's going bad: fresh vegetables, cottage cheese, yogurt, mushrooms. It hasn't occurred to anyone to cancel them—they're still being flown in daily from Bavaria, even though the Führer won't touch them any longer. I've never known a sadder day in all my time as his personal diet cook. For years I cooked him vegetarian meals on doctor's instructions, meals that took account of his weak stomach and his digestive problems, and now what? All my good work is undone in a matter of days because he abandons his diet and refuses to eat anything but pastries and chocolates.

"On getting up, he has a bowl of chocolate-flavored gruel or blancmange made from bars of bitter chocolate, but without milk. Vegetable matter only—that at least I can make sure of, being his diet cook. The Führer can't tolerate milk, unlike yogurt or cream, so I use agar instead. Regular works of art in agar I turn out. The main thing is to make them creamy and very chocolaty. He gorges himself on chocolates and chocolate-flavored pastries all day long. The squares of nougat he mostly eats at night, during those tiring conferences of his: very sweet, good for the nerves. I'll see he goes on getting them to the last, provided our supplies don't run out.

"We've just lost a whole roomful of milk chocolate—without nuts, of course. It was blown to bits, plus sentry, off a corridor on the top floor of the Chancellery—a risky location for a secret storeroom, but ingenious. I mean, who would have dared to go looting on the top floor with all those shells falling?

"We're all fervently hoping that fresh supplies will continue to arrive from Switzerland every morning. Red Cross flights are still getting through, but the situation is critical. The members of the chocolate guard detail are scared of becoming embroiled in the fighting outside when they have to leave here and escort the daily chocolate consignment. As for the confectioner, who's working around the clock, he's afraid it'll be his neck if the day ever comes when he can't produce a salverful of chocolates."

Tuesday, April 24. An absolute disaster: the patient is refusing chocolate-flavored dishes of any kind. He won't touch chocolate in adulterated form, even in pastries or gâteaux; he now insists on straight chocolate—milk chocolate, to be precise, and nothing else will do. The kind of very fine chocolate that melts in your mouth without having to be chewed or sucked or rolled around your tongue: it dissolves of its own accord, diffuses itself throughout the oral cavity, and coats the teeth and gums with a thin film of creamy cocoa butter. Nougat, too, is out from now on. Stumpfecker, who has closely examined the patient's gums and tongue, diagnoses nervous irritation of the taste buds. There's no hope now, everyone can sense it: this is the beginning of the end.

Today, after all the recordings I've made that picked up virtually nothing, all the well-nigh wasted discs on which the grooves incised by the cutting stylus are almost devoid of oscillations, we're treated to another session at full volume. His nerves at breaking point, a state of affairs that may be attributable partly to the precarious chocolate situation, the patient flies into one of the notorious tantrums that can easily fill a whole set of discs. Every stirring of emotion vents itself in bellows of rage and wild, inarticulate sounds. We have just arrived for our routine recording session, and Stumpfecker signals to me to switch on the machine without the patient noticing.

Afterward, Stumpfecker follows me into his consulting room for a trial playback: a perfect, crystal-clear recording, its only drawback being that the patient's voice periodically swells and fades as his restless perambulations take him nearer or further from the microphone: "Betrayed, I've been betrayed . . . surrounded by nothing but traitors . . ." Similar snatches recur on several of the discs I've cut in the last few days.

Apart from carefully eking out his stock of morphine, Stumpfecker has for some days been responsible less for his patient's health and well-being than for devising a suitable way for him to die. It was at first taken for granted—not that the patient himself was privy to such conjectures—that his bodyguard would solve this problem by assassinating him. Although the possibility of apoplexy cannot be discounted, a natural death due to chronic malnutrition and nervous exhaustion must, in view of the patient's exceptionally robust constitution, be ruled out.

Consequently, on the night of April 29, Stumpfecker successfully tries out one possible way of causing death by external means on the patient's Alsatian bitch: he doctors her food with cyanide trickled into her bowl from an ampoule and stirred into the mush. For some unknown reason the animal spurns this offering and backs away from the bowl. She then has to be lured into the guards' washroom, where her jaws are prized apart and the contents of another ampoule, which has been crushed with a pair of pliers, emptied onto her tongue. Death supervenes within seconds.

Death by poisoning would necessitate the patient's consent, however, because he no longer partakes of any food whose consistency would enable it to be mixed with cyanide, and one could hardly lever his jaws open and force him to swallow the ampoule.

Mouth liberally smeared with chocolate, the patient dictates his last will and testament, leafing through dictionaries and thesauruses in search of apt words and telling phrases. If one reference book fails to yield what he seeks at first glance, he hurls the heavy volume across the room and reaches for another. He dictates while lying on the sofa, cramming square after square of chocolate into his mouth. Much to the secretary's annoyance, he indicates any passages to be altered with fingers that anoint her shorthand pad with chocolate and leave greasy brown blotches in the midst of his momentous last words, which are then fair-copied on a typewriter with characters three times the normal size and submitted to him for signature. The characters are uneven because the typewriter has a mechanical defect that obstructs the carriage as it glides from right to left, and the ribbon's inferior quality is such that it disfigures the paper with smudges and black fluff. The nib of the fountain pen splutters across the foot of the final sheet. The patient's signature is less neat than usual, not only because of his agitated state but also, quite possibly, because the pen is so bedaubed with chocolate that it slips through his fingers.

Meanwhile, the patient's chauffeur has been instructed to retrieve and replace the dictionaries littering the carpet. Before putting them back on the shelf, he smoothes out the innumerable dog-ears that mark the places where his lord and master has discovered words and definitions of interest. Another of his allotted tasks is to stem the water trickling down the stairs into the rooms on the lower level, so much of which has already been absorbed by the carpets that every footstep is accompanied by a sound like someone smacking his lips. In this the chauffeur fails because the Bunker lacks sufficient caulking material to seal the cracks in the water pipes and concrete walls occasioned by incessant detonations in the immediate vicinity.

We've been recording the patient every hour, on the hour, since the night before last. The phone rings: Stumpfecker. Surely it can't be a whole hour since the last session? One loses all sense of time down here. What's the date today?

Monday, April 30. A gramophone starts blaring in the passage. Most of the staff have gathered in the open space outside my door, which usually serves as a canteen, and are holding an impromptu dance. SS men, bodyguards, and domestic staff are sitting around on the benches tapping their feet. An SS officer unbuttons his tunic, loosens his tie, and, with a bow, invites the cook to dance. She gives him her arm, and the two of them thread their way through the tables and chairs that have been pushed aside for the occasion. Once on the dance floor they traverse it with élan from end to end.

Down below, Stumpfecker stops me at the entrance to the patient's quarters: "No, Karnau, no more recordings, the patient's voice has given out. He can't speak anymore, not that it matters now. Fetch your things from the consulting room and get those wax discs out of here. They're the only means anyone will ever have of hearing his voice in the future, so take the utmost care of them. To be on the safe side, better make some copies right away."

I hear a familiar cough in the background just as Stumpfecker closes the door behind him and locks it from the inside. So this is the end. The water in the stairwell is now ankle-deep, and there are hand grenades, medals, and peaked caps strewn everywhere. I climb the spiral stairs to the emergency exit and step out into the garden. A bright, sunny afternoon. I haven't seen the sky since my arrival. If it weren't for the infernal din, the incessant explosions, I could almost believe the war was over.

It isn't, though, so I have to take cover. Here in the lee of a ruined wall my bronchial tubes relax for the first time in a long time and my lungs, having expelled the stale, subterranean air of recent days and nights, replace it with the balmy air of springtime. A sudden flicker of flame elsewhere in the garden. Are they burning the last telling documents? There's Stumpfecker, but he isn't carrying any folders under his arm, just holding a single sheet of paper. He bends over a body lying on the ground. More men are standing near the flames with shadows dancing across their faces. A sudden, ear-splitting crash, and the figures jump back: a shell has landed nearby. They're out of sight when the gasoline-soaked uniform on the ground finally catches fire, ignited by a blazing page from a dictionary. Looking more closely, I make out the burning cadaver's gaping, blood-smeared mouth and the hole in the back of its head. A moment later it's enveloped in dense, dark smoke. Now a second corpse lands beside it and promptly catches fire too. The flames fan out from the center, upward to the swelling bosom and downward to the black suede shoes.

It's all settled: we're taking everyone along. Our intention is to break out of the Bunker piecemeal and make our way out of the city in small, inconspicuous groups. The Bunker's occupants are packing the last of their possessions, and the prevailing commotion is incredible: boots clumping along the corridors, pots and pans clattering, a crash of broken china followed not by silence but by loud laughter. Not as loud as all that, though: it's the sheer contrast with the whispering and tiptoeing of the last few days that makes every noise seem so violent and protracted. None of us feels exultant, however. We're all too drained and exhausted for that.

While awaiting the breakout I sit in my cubicle and work. There are two copies to be made of our most recent recordings. One set of discs will be sent on ahead, the other Stumpfecker will take with him when he heads south. I, who intend to head west, have been entrusted with the originals.

Everyone is smoking. The whole Bunker is suddenly thick with smoke after a nonsmoking eternity. We all fish out the cigarettes we've been hiding for weeks in expectation of this moment, when we can at last light up again because the master of the house is no longer in a position to maintain his ban on smoking. We make up for lost time with a vengeance. Clouds of tobacco smoke fill the air day and night. It won't be long before the walls and furniture are blotted out: indeed, I can barely see my own hand, which itself is holding a cigarette.

Just before ten P.M. on May 1. It must be getting dark outside, and that's how we propose to make our final exit, under cover of darkness. Where's Stumpfecker? It's time he came to collect his box of discs. Maybe he's down below in the SS guardroom. No, not here, the place is deserted. The concrete walls are covered with crudely executed pornographic murals: grinning women with massive breasts and sporrans of hair between their legs. One of the SS troopers comes hurrying along the passage with an empty jerrican. He has just set fire to the conference room, so we'd better get out before the smoke asphyxiates us. The members of our group have already assembled in the entrance upstairs, complete with their belongings. Stumpfecker is standing guard over the two boxes of records.

He turns to me before we set off. "As long as there's any risk of our being picked up by the invaders," he says, "get this straight: your first priority is to learn to speak like a victim. Summon up a precise recollection of the words, sentence structure, and intonation of your own test subjects. Recall them, imitate them, repeat them slowly, at first in your head, then in a low voice. Speak with downcast eyes, keep breaking off in midstream to convey that you've undergone some atrocious experiences but can't bring yourself to describe them. Say nothing of those alleged atrocities. Gloss over your doings in recent years by inserting judicious pauses. Draw a veil over your activities by stopping short just in time. Contort your face, develop a stutter, learn to make your eyes grow moist by an effort of the will, seem helpful and communicative, affect a willingness to describe the terrible things that have happened to you, coupled with heartfelt regret at your inability to do so.

Break down and they'll exempt you from further questioning—in fact, they'll end by commiserating with you. You'll be taken for a victim, the victim of some nameless and indescribable atrocity. In other words, you'll have changed sides. As your interrogation proceeds, you'll imperceptibly turn into one of those whose treatment at your hands formed the basis of the interrogators' original, accusations. You must learn to do precisely what always revolted you in others and inspired the disgust that motivated your activities in the first place: you must stammer, dry up, pretend to be at a loss for words. For a while, alas, we're destined to play the inarticulate."

*

In July 1992, during a routine inspection of Dresden's municipal orphanage, workmen removed some boards nailed over a hole in the cellar wall. Beyond it lay a secret sound archive. Despite its age and provenance, which the nature of the material stored there proved beyond doubt, no one had previously known as its existence.

The sound archive was found to be connected with the nearby Museum of Hygiene by a series of underground passages. From this it could be inferred that members of the museum staff had once had access to the premises, and that exchanges of information and personnel may even have taken place. None of the museum's current employees knew about the archive, however, so only privileged personnel could have been aware of the connecting passages, whose existence was kept strictly confidential. Very few details of the sound archive's staff had survived. The only name definitely listed in the card index, the bulk of which had been destroyed, was that of a retired security man: Hermann Karnau.

While attending a preliminary, on-the-spot inspection by a committee of inquiry, Karnau made the following statement:

"Here, gentlemen, if you can spare the time to confirm this for yourselves, you will find every conceivable aid to research into the relevant field, including, of course, a whole library of recordings representative of every leading figure in politics and public life since the invention of the phonograph. It even includes that supposedly long-lost series of recordings entitled *The Führer Coughs*, shellac, seventy-eight rpm."

Karnau was then asked what purpose the establishment had served. His explanation:

"Weekly recordings on wax were made of the Führer's pulse rate while he was subjected to stress, in motion, or delivering a speech, so that regular comparisons could be made by playing back different weekly results in parallel. Were his blood vessels dilated? Had his blood pressure gone down? Did his heart take an appropriate time to regain its normal rhythm after a speech delivered *con brio*? Those were some of the aspects in which these cylinders, shellac discs, and tapes were evaluated.

"The approaches were doubly secured by grilles and massive steel doors. Anyone working in the brick-lined vault beyond them had to crouch a little. The recording studio was more luxuriously appointed: a comfortable armchair behind the microphone, wall-to-wall carpet, and cloth-lined walls, not only for soundproofing purposes but because the important persons who frequented the studio were accustomed to a certain degree of comfort. Nothing could be heard of the children running around two floors above."

A shelf laden with tapes, some of them partially unwound, bore witness to sundry attempts to transfer all the recordings to the latest type of recording medium—attempts that had never progressed far because the influx of material to be evaluated and filed was far too voluminous. Although strict attention had always been paid to cleanliness (the entire archive could so easily have been destroyed by vermin), the innumerable cardboard boxes had built up a layer of fine dust over the years. This had to be brushed off with the back of the hand before the lids could be lifted and the documents inside, discs in paper sleeves, removed. Standing in one corner of the ill-lit room was a gramophone on which these discs, many of whose white labels bore no inscription, could be played. Technological developments notwithstanding, this obsolete equipment had not been discarded because of the continuing need to play historic recordings for purposes of comparison. Winding up the gramophone was a strenuous business. While doing so, a committee member knocked some 1930s sapphire needles off the table. Karnau's statement went on:

"Germany was far ahead of other countries in the field of sound recording. The portable tape recorders we developed for use at the front continued to be one of the enemy's favorite acquisitions until the war ended, and here at the archive only the very finest equipment and materials were employed. On one occasion our entire collection of wax discs almost melted because the heating system malfunctioned. However, discs have one advantage over tapes, in that contact with a magnet cannot obliterate their contents. That was another reason why security was so important. Imagine if saboteurs had installed an electromagnet here and wiped out the entire archive!

"One of our tasks was to optimize vocal conditions by technological means—for instance, the public-address systems used at mass rallies. Sophisticated forms of speech therapy enabled glottal stops to be suppressed, thereby avoiding overmodulation in large halls. Salivation was controlled during loud, rapid speech and glandular activity brought into balance with the aid of medication, the object being to render every last spoken word intelligible. One or two experiments were conducted into breathing under stress and its potentially disruptive effects. Amplification by loudspeakers renders such questions extremely important."

Another series of experiments which defied complete elucidation, but which, to judge by the medical technology employed, could not have been carried out so very long ago, included the introduction of probes into the pharynx and the bloodstream for the purpose of recording various unidentifiable bodily noises. As for the human guinea pigs from whom this data was obtained, sometimes in an extremely painful manner, the committee of inquiry could not discover whence they were recruited.

"The Museum of Hygiene concerned itself with man in his visible form," Karnau explained, "whereas we dealt with his audible manifestations. We were united by our attention to detail, and pathologists of one discipline were often of service to those of the other, for instance when ascribing our clients' articulatory changes to changes of a physiological nature."

Karnau proved to be extremely talkative; more than that, he possessed a knowledge of technical matters that was wholly at odds with his status as a security guard. On examining Karnau's statements more closely, the committee members began to entertain certain doubts about them. His detailed knowledge of the archive's procedures and research projects aroused a suspicion that he had not merely been in charge of security, as he steadfastly maintained, but must have held a far more responsible position.

It also transpired that the underground complex was more extensive than

Karnau, outwardly so eager to be helpful, had at first disclosed: a second recording studio came to light. Far less comfortably appointed than the first, this took the form of a tiled, neon-lit chamber whose bleak decor bespoke an operating theater. A full set of surgical instruments reposed on a stainless steel trolley, and the microphone assembly overhung an operating table from which blood-encrusted straps were dangling.

Forensic analysis of the blood on the straps revealed that the most recent operation had taken place only a few weeks before. This seemed to disprove Karnau's assertion that work at the archive had ceased before the end of World War II. On the contrary, the obvious inference was that plans had been made to continue the medical research of which the committee had gained certain intimations. Having learned by some unknown means that the orphanage was about to be inspected, the person or persons engaged in these obscure experiments had hurriedly moved out with the intention of pursuing them elsewhere. Unfortunately, no information on this subject could be gleaned from Karnau. He left the city the next morning, destination unknown.

Translated from the German by John Brownjohn

Sticks and Stones

The Irish Identity

ROBERT McLIAM WILSON

I am five foot eleven. I weigh around 170 pounds. I have brown hair, green eyes, and no real distinguishing marks. I'm heterosexual, atheist, liberal, and white. I don't shave as often as I should and I have pale, Irish skin. I smoke and I always wear a suit. I drive a small black car and I don't drink much alcohol. I prefer cats to dogs.

I don't know what that makes me, but I suspect that it makes me what I am.

When I was seventeen, I decided that I wanted to be Jewish. Like most Roman Catholics, I had only the vaguest notion of what this might entail. I stopped being good at sports and frequented the only kosher butcher in the city. (How he blushed for me, the poor man). I could never understand why no one took me seriously. I could never understand why I should not simply decide such questions for myself. Why was I such a goy? Who had decided that this should be so?

Like that of most citizens of Belfast, my identity is the subject of some local dispute. Some say I'm British, some say I'm Irish, some even say that there's no way I'm five foot eleven and that I'm five ten at best. In many ways I'm not permitted to contribute to this debate. If the controversy is ever satisfactorily concluded, I will be whatever the majority of people tell me I am.

As a quotidian absolute, nationality is almost meaningless. For an Italian living in Italy, Italianness is patently not much of a distinction. What really gives nationality its chiaroscuro, its flavor, is a little dash of hatred and fear. Nobody really knows or cares what they are until they meet what they don't want to be. Then it's time for the flags and guns to come out.

So when the airport cops ask me what I am, how do I explain that I live in the northeastern segment of an island sliced like a cheap pizza and with as many titles as a bar full of yuppie cocktails—Ireland, Northern Ireland, Britain, Eire, Ulster, etc. How do I explain how little that would tell them?

I suppose I could tell them that I live in a place where people have killed and died in an interminable fight over the names they should call themselves and each other. (In Belfast, sticks and stones may break your bones but names will blow you to pieces on a regular basis.) I could tell them about the self-defeating eugenic templates of racial purity by which no human being still living on the island can be properly deemed Irish. That the English and the

Scottish have been here a long time and that we're all smudged by now—café au lait, mulattoes, half-breeds, spicks, wops, and dagos. I could tell them that I don't really understand the question.

Irishness is unique amongst the self-conscious nationalisms. A self-conscious Frenchman bores everyone. A self-conscious American is a nightmare. And a self-conscious Englishman makes you want to lie down in a darkened room. But a self-conscious Irishman is a friend to the world and the world listens attentively. The reviews are always good. There's a global appetite for Irishness that is almost without parallel.

Nationalistic self-obsession is corrupt, corrosive, and bogus enough without this extra angle. When well-received, this fake concoction of myth and bullshit is reflected in the mirror of imprecise good will and sentimental foolishness. This in itself produces further distortions which are then seamlessly incorporated into the "genuine" article. Over the years I've watched the fundamental concepts of what it is to be Irish being altered by common-currency American errors. Here in the "old country," when we hear that New Yorkers are marching in green-kilted bagpipe bands (an entirely Scottish phenomenon) on St. Patrick's Day, we immediately look around for somewhere to buy green kilts and bagpipes. Our racial authenticity is an extremely negotiable commodity.

Yet I've always believed that such Americans have it just about right. Their ideas of Irishness are as fake as a hooker's tit, but then so are ours.

To understand all things Irish, you must understand something fundamental. Everyone knows that Ireland is the land of myth. And myth is a beautiful and resonant word. It sounds so profound, so spiritual. There is something visceral in it. Our mythmaking is vital to the self-imposed standardized norms of nationality that are current here at home. Catholics are Irish, so Irish, and Protestants are British, poor things. The common assumption that the Irish language, Irish music, and Irish history are pure Catholic monoliths, and the oft-suppressed expression of the indigenous culture, ignores the truth that the Irish linguistic, musical, and cultural revivals were the product of nineteenth-century Protestant historicism. Everything we say is myth. The lies are old and dusty. The waters are muddy and the truth long gone.

Even our understanding of our own history—you know the kind of thing, perfidious Albion, eight hundred years of oppression, etc.—teems with bullshit. King William of Orange waged war in seventeenth-century Ireland and is still a Catholic-baiting Protestant icon who causes trouble here. No one remembers that he was blessed by the Pope. Wolfe Tone is a much-loved historical rebel leader who sailed with a French army to liberate Catholic Ireland. No one mentions that he was defeated by a Catholic militia. The President of Ireland called on a German minister to express his official condolences after Hitler's suicide at the end of World War II. Nobody wrote any songs about that.

In some ways, the Irish tendency for romancing can be seen as harmless, almost charming. It is, after all, what produces our leprechauns, our fairy rings, all our beguiling fakery. But it also produces people who will murder for lies they only half-believe and certainly never understand—for the Irish have always armed their ideas. We don't have any white lies here anymore. We only have the deadly barbaric type.

Given the wildest differences in latitude and climate, it is remarkable how countries can remind you of one another. In cold March Manhattan, the air is as thick, dark, and injurious as any Berlin winter. In Paris, the rain falls and stains the pale stone with the same dispiriting grace you find in Cambridge on most days of the year. London can look and feel like everywhere.

If true of the places, how much truer of the people. *Quod erat demonstrandum* and then some.

We are a pretty poor species. Even the most gifted of us, the wisest and most studious of us, are weak-minded. We toss aside our Pushkin and read Judith Krantz. We watch goofy TV shows and asinine movies. We can't help liking big noises, colored lights, and pictures of naked people.

Our beliefs are often fantastic alloys of fear, self-interest, prejudice, and ignorance. As Tolstoy gloriously demonstrates, our finest moments of heroism, selflessness, and grandeur are usually founded on the meanest egotisms and vanities. Our notion of the sublime is laughable. In acts of worship, many of us pay homage to some form of invisible man who mimics us in the pettiest detail. Apart from our uncharacteristic capacity for love (a mistake, a design flaw), we're a shambles.

It is the things we say that most prove what monkeys we still are. We are driven to generalize, to sweep on through, to prognosticate, to diagnose. Typically male, we say, typically female. That's the problem with rich people, we opine. The poor were ever so. Gentlemen prefer blondes. Fuck right off, I can't help thinking.

Our most outrageous banalities are reserved for questions of race and nationality. This is how the French behave, we say. How do we know? Have we met them all? Have we asked any of them? Millions of people are summoned and dismissed in a few moments of robust fatuousness.

I'm five foot eleven. I weigh around 170 pounds. I have brown hair, green eyes, and so on. Irish or British is very far down on my list—somewhere below my favorite color. Nonetheless, I must concede that nationality is tenacious. People have real stamina when it comes to this business. I must further concede that Irishness is a great arena for disquisitions on national identity. Because the Irish conflict is internecine (it has nothing to do with the English anymore), definitions of Irishness have particular charm. Nationalities primarily define themselves by what they're not. The Swiss are not German, the Scottish are not English, and the Canadians are definitely not American. But the Irish make internal distinctions as well. Some of the Irish aren't properly Irish. Some of the Irish aren't even vaguely Irish. In pursuit of the mantle of absolute Irishness, brother kills brother and sisters look on and applaud.

A few years ago I had an apartment on a leafy South Belfast street called Adelaide Park. A police station was being rebuilt across the street from my building (the original had been flattened by a bomb a few years before). It was a controversial building site, naturally. Apart from their well-known attacks on the policemen, soldiers, prison officers, and almost everyone else, the IRA liked to target construction workers who helped build police stations. Thus, the site was guarded round the clock by the police. For nearly six months there were always a couple of cops standing in my driveway, all peaked caps, submachine guns, and high anxiety. This was okay in the spring. It was fine in the summer, and manageable in the fall. But as winter set in, the position of these guys became more and more unpleasant. It was windy and cold, and it rained for months. As night fell, I would look out my apartment window and watch the damp rozzers. It was obviously not a good gig.

For weeks I debated whether or not I should take them cups of coffee. It was more complicated than it might sound. Policemen and soldiers here are very unlikely to accept such things from the public now. Twenty-five years of ground glass, rat poison, and Drano in friendly cups of tea discouraged them from accepting such largesse. Not long before, a woman had handed some soldiers a bomb in a biscuit tin in a charming incident near Derry. Additionally, of course, there might have been swathes of people willing to do me grief for being nice to the police.

Policemen are usually Protestant and I myself am customarily Catholic. They couldn't have known that I was a Catholic, but they would have been suspicious. (In this country, the big haters can't really tell each other apart. How we envy those who hate black or white people—that obvious difference, that demonstrable objection.)

It was a small thing, a minor transaction, an unimportant detail. The weeks passed, the wind blew, and the rain rained. I didn't hand out any coffee.

—July 1997

زنان خدا : هویت مخفی

WOMEN OF ALLAH : SECRET IDENTITIES

SHIRIN NESHAT

[PAGE 141] *Whispers*, 1997.

[ABOVE] *Birthmark*, 1997. | [RIGHT] *Identified*, 1997.

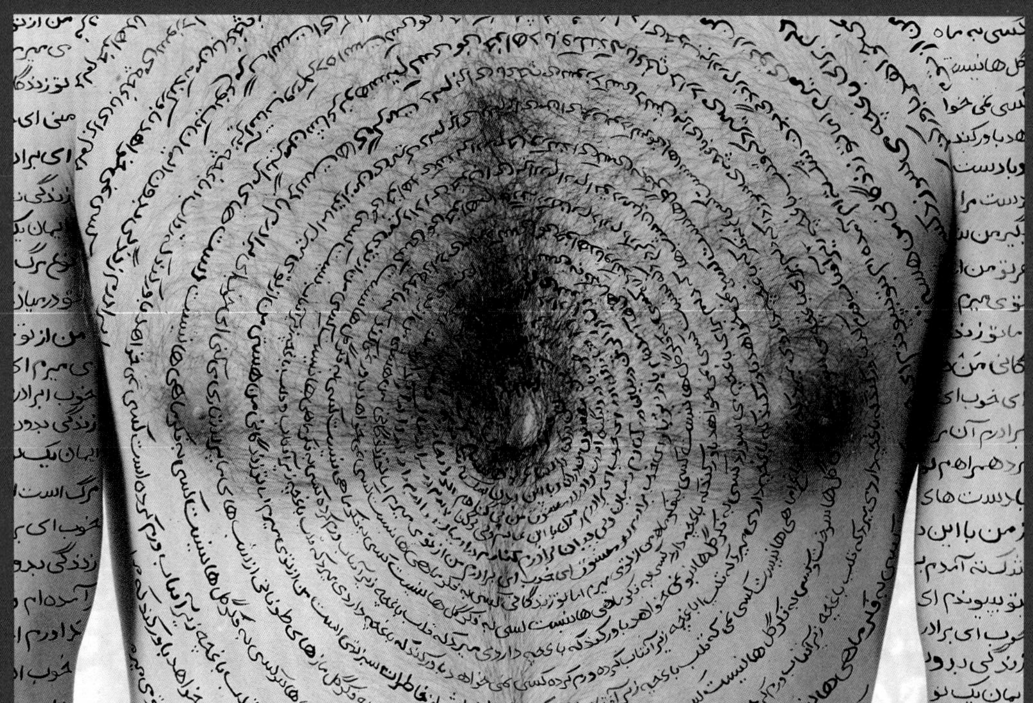

Careless, 1997.

SHIRIN NESHAT

The following is taken from an interview with Shirin Neshat conducted by Anne Doran on July 2, 1997.

I began to focus on the issue of Islam in my work because, after the revolution, everything was transformed and, living in the United States, I felt as though I had no connection to home anymore. So, in a way, this work is my way of discovering and re-identifying with the new Iran. On a more philosophical level, I am very interested in the lives of the women I characterize, particularly in how they survive within that pure ideological existence that is so controlled. The fundamental question for me is how you can find liberation and strength in a situation that is so limited by authority, where the focus is on the collective and not the individual, and the ultimate struggle is simply to be yourself.

In any Islamic country, the women on the street are almost completely hidden behind their veils, and yet they can communicate so much with the little they have exposed. Direct eye contact is one of the most important elements in my work. I like to use the combination of different forces—what the woman is holding, how she is dressed, and so on—to show the conflicting references within her identity. In some images I use guns or bullets to suggest terrorism and how that idea can raise so much fear about Arab identity in the West. Those props shatter our stereotype of the typical Muslim woman as a passive and submissive victim. Islamic women have actually always been very active in the military—in some ways that is one area in which they are equal to men.

I use Farsi script to give the woman's date of birth, the name of the saint she believes in, the names of her father and her mother, her habits, and so on. On the larger images, I often use expressions or lines of poetry. I don't think it matters that the writing can't be understood in the West. So much of it is written within the context of Islamic religion, politics, and the history of feminism in Iran that it would not have the same meaning for someone who was not from Iran as it would for an Iranian.

A lot of Iranians have asked me what I think my work would be like if I lived in Iran now. Obviously an artist who lives in Iran and is concerned about the same issues might have a totally different reading of the state of women or the ideology of Muslim fundamentalism. So I'm very aware of my limitations. I don't take any responsibility for answering questions. I just try to raise a few from my own perspective.

ROBIN ROBERTSON

After the Overdose

What surprised me most?
Coming home to an open door,
rose petals everywhere, the bed
incongruous with blood?
The paramedic's satchel
left behind in all the rush?

Or you in the hospital,
the crusted corners of your mouth,
the gown they'd put you in?
You never wore short sleeves,
not since you burned a name
into your arm with cigarettes.

Or, finally, that you weren't dead?
That surprised me. That regret.

Navigating North

He'd hitched out of Frankfurt
till the fog and the dark
turned the road to a loud ocean,
its headlights ropes of pearl.
He got out here—four hundred kilometers
from the sea—reminded of Aberdeen.

Three hours ago he'd been
fucking the chambermaid:
making her show the white of her teeth.
Then she fucked him;
the schnapps in the shot glass
shivering by the bed.

The adult channel had the room
flickering as she finished him off.
Swallowing his pride, he might have
glossed ten years ago,
tossing back his drink,
crashing it at the wall.

But here was a car graveyard in a pool
of sodium and glass. He'd cut himself
opening up the Audi he sat in now,
watching the lit sea
rock the light,
the night-fishers spilling their nets.

Stars fall from his hands,
his cut hands full of splinters
and herring-scales; his shirt slaked red.
He is navigating north
in a beached car; his hands shake
constellations on the floor.

Static

The storm shakes out its sheets
against the darkening window:
the glass flinches under thrown hail.
Unhinged, the television slips its hold,
streams into black and white
then silence, as the lines go down.
Her postcards stir on the shelf, tip over;
the lights of Calais trip out one by one.

He cannot tell her
how the geese scull back at twilight,
how the lighthouse walks its beam
across the trenches of the sea.
He cannot tell her how the open night
swings like a door without her,
how he is the lock
and she is the key.

Retreat

In the abandoned house
the chairs are tipped,
the coffee cups thick with spoor;
rolled mattresses shift and sound
as the springs return
to the shape of the sleeper.
I have carried the cold in from outside
so find sticks for the grate
and throw in my diaries,
one by one,
'86 to '74.
The years burn well, the wood roaring;
the fire turns the pages,
reads each book backwards.

Outside, the trees stand like smoke;
the moon declines
behind a scarf of cloud.
I want to go where I am not known,
where there are no signs,
where the snow squeaks like polystyrene
on a discontinued path to the dark
knot of the forest.
I want to go somewhere
to let out this life like warm water
and lie there
clean and cold:
the steady heart's diminuendo,
a bag of pipes' diminishing drone.

Ludic

She felt like liver
in the spilling dark
and I was hard as an arm,

lopped at the wrist,
raw and rich still
with the lucid milt.

We gape and we are healed:
her mouth on me
like wind on an open wound.

Blowing out the Light

After fourteen gins, the end
of this night's slipway
is an unmarked door, and this:
postcards and photographs tipped in
to the mirror's frame,
a few choice icons propped amongst ash,
cosmetics, spent matches;
the teddy bear is there
as if to cancel out the blister-pack of pills.
A poster of Paris, Doisneau's lovers;
a candle on the window sill.
Closing my eyes
I stitch the sheet with seed,
subside, and head for home.

Lithium

After the arc of ECT
and the blunt concussion of pills,
they gave him lithium to cling to—
the psychiatrist's stone.
A metal that floats on water,
must be kept in kerosene,
can be drawn into wire.
(He who had jumped in the harbor,
burnt his hair off,
been caught hanging from the light.)
He'd heard it was once used
to make hydrogen bombs,
but now was a coolant for nuclear reactors,
so he broke out of hospital barefoot
and walked ten miles to meet me in the snow.

FROM *Apple Tree in the Corridor*

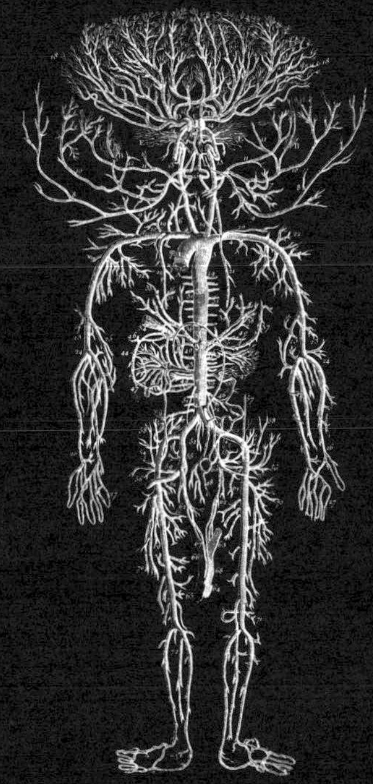

"What are the long-legged mosquitoes humming about? It's so ridiculous," Mother's voice came unexpectedly from the shadow behind the bed. She had been hiding in that corner since the last rain. She wanted people to think she had disappeared. Excitedly, she found a big umbrella and covered herself completely with it. "My body is puffed up like an oxygen pillow." In the drawer, she had found a five-headed needle, and she was punching it into her skin. With her teeth clenched, she punched and pressed, saying, "I've got to get rid of some water, or I'll be dead."

I wanted to tell her something about the summer. Hesitantly, I opened my mouth: "The hornet's nest was humming on the bare branch. Something was swinging in the air . . . Once I lost a wallet. Obviously you remember the accident. It was stolen by a guy with a beard. The streets at the time were covered with white bed sheets that shone in the sun. Children were running around carrying torches. Don't you feel that the needles are pushing against rotting meat?"

All my family members had undivulged secrets. They must have seemed like frightening people. My father, for instance, was a very unusual person. I never understood him. To me, he was analogous to insects, because he always gave me a feeling of beetle shells. He would sneak in every night after supper had already started. Darting to the table, he would fill his bowl with rice, while scanning the other dishes. He chewed and swallowed all the good dishes before banging his bowl down on the table and fleeing.

"Father is suffering some internal agony," my third sister would say, showing the whites of her eyes. Her voice resembled a noodle hanging in the damp air. She always gnawed at the rims of bowls at mealtime. As a result, all of our blue china bowls had chipped edges. I saw with my own eyes that she swallowed the chips with her rice. For a cure to her asthma, she had, up to that time, eaten more than a thousand earthworms. Actually, she drank them after melting them down in sugar. "Isn't that miraculous!" Panting, she would put on an expression of wonder.

"Your third sister, it's hard to say," Mother commented in a sarcastic tone. "Did you hear her thumping the bed? The doctors think she is having endocrinopathy. It's a subtle ailment."

I was about to reply when I heard a deafening noise from the upstairs neighbor. According to my reconnoitering, the guy had been fooling around with an iron drilling rod. The cement floor of his apartment was covered with small holes like a honeycomb. Mother continued indifferently, turning a deaf ear to the noise from upstairs: "I can see through anybody's tricks. I have become so ingeniously skillful that I am a master of magic. Day after day, I sit in this corner, puncturing myself with needles in my fight against the fluids. Sometimes I forget you are my children. Whenever I recall the past, the wild mountains and deserted forests appear in my mind's eye, stars fall down like fireworks, and the black figure of your father hangs from a branch of the tree. Quickly he has turned into what he is now. It's just too fast."

At the windowpane appeared a huge pair of sunglasses. That was the guy from upstairs coming down to spy on our reaction to his dirty trick. He never forgot to put on his sunglasses, believing that no one could recognize him this way.

"This guy is suffering from ringworm on his feet," Mother turned her small, flat head distractedly. Every time the back of her head brushed her shoulders, wisps of dry, broken hair drifted into the air. "Can't you smell the liquid for ringworms? Nearly everyone has some subtle ailment. But everyone racks their brains for ways to appear healthy."

Sunglasses entered the room. Dressed in a white coverall and with a stethoscope hanging at his chest, he appeared full of dignity and dash. To show off, he raised the stethoscope solemnly to listen to the wall for a long time. Then, with an air of pretended wisdom, he said in a lowered voice: "I am a medical doctor. I live at No. 65 on Thirteenth Avenue. Your family has some serious problems."

"Medical doctor? Perfect, doctor!" Mother shrilled from the shadow. "I'd like you to have a look at my ears! My ears are so sensitive. Is there any way to cure them, like giving them anesthesia?"

He bounced up and down several times on the spot, before disappearing completely.

"This is called the invisible method," Mother told me quietly.

"A horse in heat, a tragic reality?" My third sister drifted into the room. Softly, she descended on the bed. Supporting her chin with her fine, vinelike fingers, she was spellbound, staring into the air. "Such people have a special kind of organ," she added, her eyes filled with rheumy tears. "All disasters are caused by this unlucky smell!" She dashed into her bedroom and started sobbing heavily. In fact, she would have felt much better if she had set herself down to crochet lace. When she was young, she used to sit quietly by the window, crocheting her lace. A slight touch by others would cause her nose to bleed. I was quite surprised to see her becoming so forward.

After dark every day, I started looking for my family members. From this room to that, I found that they had disappeared totally. The wind swayed the little electric bulb, making the light turn bloody red all of a sudden. The west wind was blowing hard. I was feeling uneasy at not being able to figure out where they were hiding.

Then I formulated a plan. After supper one day, I asked Mother to lend me her needles. "What for?" Her eyes looked like billiard balls ready to roll.

"You always abandon me, thinking I am useless. But on the contrary, I have my own skill. It may well be that I am more nimble than you are." While talking, I grabbed her sleeve tightly, afraid that she might suddenly disappear.

"*I'm-sleeping-in-the-trunk*," she said enunciating word by word and glaring at me. "Every time you pace around in my room, as anxious as an ant in a hot pot. Once you even stepped on my eyeball. Didn't you feel it? I just can't sleep. See the two huge dark rings under my eyes. They're caused by insomnia."

At night, I did notice there was a worn-out trunk, on which hung a rusty bronze lock. So I entered her room to look for the trunk, but there was nothing in the corner.

"You're wasting your energy," she chuckled dryly. "Very often you remember something, but you won't know that there is no such thing until you try to look for it. Once upon a time, there was some dough in our cupboard and it was all moldy. Last year, I was digging in the cupboard in our attic, looking for that dough. I had been searching for a year when finally the stairs collapsed and I fell. Your third sister told me that the cupboard was not the original one, I had remembered wrong. Your third sister has her mind stuffed with fantasies about men. I know that's the source of her disease. There's no hope for a cure." She shrugged in resignation. "How do you feel about our apartment?" Her triangular eyes gazed at me with interest.

"I've been searching for you. My legs are so sore that I can no longer raise them. I pitch stones on the ground. You have heard it, haven't you?"

"What trunk are you talking about? It's just a story I told you before. I warned you that it's a waste of energy. It's so stupid for you to search everywhere. You also mentioned three-needle acupuncture. You sound like a snake player. Are you really so afraid? Wait until you reach my age, then you won't be afraid anymore. In your arrogant memory there must be many types of broken trunks. They are hidden here and there. You believe they contain something. It's a phenomenon of youth, in fact . . ." She stopped short, impatiently examining the window behind me.

During the day I kept telling myself that I shouldn't forget to pay attention to those trunks at night. I wondered why I always forgot, and thought I should make a mark at those spots. Yet as soon as night arrived, my memory was befuddled. I turned this way and that, passing a trunk, a broom, a wallet, etc. But I just couldn't remember anything. Where were my family members? They should at least have left some clue. Rats started a fight in the light fixture. The rats in this house were as big as cats. I covered the bulb with my pale hands to avoid attracting moths. The light was cold, and its rays penetrated to the depths of my heart. I intended to tell Mother about the summer. Suddenly all the kidney beans she had salted melted into stinking water and the Boston ivy drooped over. In the shadow, the bronze kettle rattled angrily. A cat climbed over the wall, at the foot of which there grew castor-oil plants. My third sister came by whistling. She had two bamboo leaves stuck in her nostrils. They had red spots on them and resembled dominoes.

There was nobody in Father's room, either. The air smelled of sweat. There was a banana peel on the stool. During the day, he told me in secret that he had recently been engaged in catching locusts. With his own eyes he saw Mother kill five flowery moths and dump them into the dried-up well at the back of the house. "Tomorrow I will climb the green mountain," he said, twisting his hips and tapping the earthenware pot that he held against his chest like a little kid. "The locusts are flourishing there." He was enjoying the verb he used, his face glowing with health.

"I'd like to tell Mother something," I said.

"Your mother," he rolled his huge eyeballs with difficulty, trying to recall something. "She is not a reliable thing. Don't trust such a thing easily." He jumped high on one foot, spilling all of the sand out of the pot. "I've been sleeping in the cotton fiber. It's so quiet there, and no rats, too. How long have you been suffering from sleepwalking? It's certainly a painful ailment. I once had it, too. Now about Sunglasses, you don't need to guard against him, but treat him nicely. That guy is my friend. When dawn comes, we wander around and, at night, we sleep in the cotton fiber. One day when the Chinese scholar tree blossomed all in white, I squatted down at the corner of the street. Taking off my vest, I scratched myself as much as I could—I hadn't had a bath for the whole winter. Later on, I noticed somebody else squatting there. That was him, he was scratching also. Together we listened to the humming of the mosquitoes, and our bodies felt all warmed up."

The door banged open. "I just can't wash my hair." My third sister stood between Father and me, with her hands on her hips, and her hair down. "Every time I wash my hair, my head gets light and drifty, like a balloon, and floats away from my neck. You simply cannot experience such a thing, no way! I'm just wasting my time." She sat heavily on the bed, a hook from her bra strap unfastened. "Who understands my sorrow? In the blue sky, there flies a yellow weasel! Ah? Ah? . . ." She sang and panted in an odd tone and spat on the floor.

"She has an enlarged cervical vertebra." Father's nose wrinkled up. He threw something at the foot of the bed.

"Father?"

"Your mother will come and eat it. Do you know why your mother hides herself? She's trying to avoid rats. Last time I threw down a piece of cooked meat with maggots in it, but she ate it happily. Her stomach is rumbling with hunger. She eats everything I throw down. You may try, too!" Tightening his pants, he let out the aged, shrunken, smooth left leg. Then he threw his canvas bag onto his shoulder. With high spirits, he said, "I'm going to the green mountains today!"

I could hear him whistling outside the window.

Finally, I told Mother the story about the summer. I repeated it again and again, my face turning purple. Mother appeared half-listening, smiling indulgently. With a bare foot she scratched her tightened calf muscle.

"That's right, when the sun rises, I will turn into a fat hen." In that instant, her pupils seemed to be melting. "The whole day, I squat in the woodpile under the eaves. Little children come and throw cobblestones at me. Eventually, one of them will break my spine." She suddenly stood up, her eyes turned left and right in an equivocal way. "Now I need to change my approach completely. I have displayed fortitude and resolution. Just now I have broken a window. You all believe that I've been kept in the dark, don't you? You, every one of you, what are you crying for underneath your quilts? Every day—just look at your swollen eyelids. I'm also making my own plans. You can't see through me, but you think you can do everything your own way now! That's why you are jabbering such nonsense to me."

Since a certain day, Mother had started to frighten us. She hid herself on purpose, yet she was present everywhere—underneath the bed, on top of the cupboard, behind the kitchen door, inside the cistern. Her deformed shadow drifted all over the place. The shadow was fat, swollen, purple in color, and smelled moldy. As a result, we walked quietly and spoke in whispers. Often when I was talking in Father's ear, she screamed, as if she were about to jump out. It scared the wits out of us. Yet when we looked around, she was nowhere to be found. And the scream was coming from the radio. At other times, she giggled in the shadows instead of screaming. The sound raised goose bumps on our bodies. My third sister was the first to burn out. Struggling out of her fits of hysteria, she searched for our missing mother with a spade on her shoulder. At those moments, her face was purple, her neck stiff—she looked valiant and spirited. The base of the walls inside the house, the stove, and everything else had been dug into a mess.

The day I suddenly realized that Mother had disappeared from the house forever, Father was putting on his leg wrappings. "I'm going to the green mountains to fish for two months," he told me in high spirits. His cheeks were flushed with excitement.

"What shall we do about Mother?" I asked abruptly.

"I've raised a poisonous snake in the bushes. It comes out whenever I call it. Are you interested? We can catch locusts together."

"There's a poisonous snake I raised right under my bed," Mother's sharp voice resounded in the shadows.

Taking up his canvas bag, Father dashed out of the house like a young boy, his bag flopping against his skinny hips. "Two months!" he shouted back to me, raising two fingers while running away.

I heard a suspicious sound behind me. When I turned around, I saw my third sister smashing her spade down on the dark spot where Mother's voice had been heard. A string of yellow sparks leapt from the cement.

"The buttons on that thing must be almost all gone, am I right?" I suddenly remembered.

My third sister never took me seriously. Dripping with black sweat, she was digging enthusiastically at the cement, her nostrils flared. "I've been sleeping too long. So I need to stretch my body a little," she defended herself. "You've been imagining that the house is collapsing. It's so vague. Why can't you think of something else? I can't understand how you've become such a misanthrope. Such people make me sick, sick." At noon, she took her nap half naked. She lay on her bed convulsing, stinking saliva dripping from her mouth. She usually slept like this until dusk and refused to have supper. When Father was home, he would peep into her open door, poke out his tongue, and say, "What a miracle and wonder inheritance can play! Following the rule, what kind of decisive turning point will occur?" After such a remark, he felt he had somehow qualified himself to grab all the food in the house and take it away in his travel bag.

One rainy day, a soaking wet man staggered in. Wiping rainwater from his face, he bawled down to Mother's shadow in the corner, addressing her in a shrill voice: "Hi, Mom!" Like a gust of wind, my third sister dashed over, and wrapped him in a huge bath towel that had black spots on it. She rubbed and rubbed until his lips turned red and his eyeballs bloodstained. Then she fell to the floor and cried out, "It's awful to have a fiancé!" Then she suddenly became so muscular that she could carry the whole bundle wrapped inside the towel all the way to the bed. Carefully she put the bundle down, covered it with a quilt, and patted him to sleep.

"It's so uncomfortable to have a doctor at home." Mother's head stretched out like that of a snake.

"Who's that?"

"Sunglasses, of course. I knew long ago that Sunglasses was her fiancé. Now her illness will be healed. Such an awkward illness. Such things are totally strange." She drifted back beneath the bed.

"How could it be that the fence turns green? I've lost my stethoscope." The fiancé was groaning inside a bath towel. "The room is high in temperature. That's good. I feel sleepy when it's hot."

After the heavy rain, our house was full of spiderwebs. The slightest move would cause them to billow into one's eyes. My third sister was jumping about chasing spiders. Torn webs wafted all over the place.

"Oh, her youthful vitality." The fiancé opened one eye to enjoy the scene. "In my place, I have all sorts of insects. In the full of the night, when I was wandering around outside, one of the insects must have sneaked into my bedding. This has occupied my mind, and I cry my heart out for that."

"But why did you make such a startling noise above us?" I asked him curiously. "Because of some inner fear?"

He hesitated. "The illness of your third sister bothers me day and night. It must be a very complicated syndrome."

All of a sudden, I had a desire to chat with him. Tugging his ear, I told him: "Every night this apartment turns empty. Everybody hides. Even the doors and windows disappear. It simply turns into a sealed iron box. I wander about, bumping into all kinds of things. In anxiety, I kick the wall until my toenails swell up. My third sister, she must have hinted to you. She believes that I never get up at night. She points out that it is my scattered quilt that proves this. It seems you are not hearing me. Tell me, is there any sound from my mouth?"

"The room is awfully hot." He was squint-eyed, his head hanging down, and he started to snore.

"You always tangle up everyone you meet like a beggar." My third sister slapped my hand and blew on the reddened ear of her fiancé. She gave me an angry stare, while rubbing his hair, and then yelled, "Scram!"

For the next several days, she and her fiancé occupied the whole house. Early every morning, they drove me out. Closing the door behind me, they simply turned the house into a lunatic asylum. A broom came flying out of the window facing the street, then a bag of plum pits. Once the thing flying out was Sunglasses himself. He was all black and blue and cried, "Acute changes are going on in your sister's body. Where did she get all that strength? Endocrinopathy is not a curable disease. The first time I saw her, she had bamboo leaves in her nostrils. That peddler selling popsicles yelled and yelled. It was so disgusting. My back was soaked with sweat, and my socks smelled . . ."

"It was summer," I reminded him.

"True. It was summer. My affliction of foul-smelling feet was cured. Your third sister ordered me to wash with soda water every day. But now I feel nothing is meaningful." Finally he observed me carefully. "Why can't a serious person like you involve yourself in some business, such as collecting snakeskins? Every time you approach me, I feel uncertain about you. Your existence is a problem. It seems that you have made up your mind that you are stuck here, and you never think of getting into something positive, for instance, snakeskins. You are just too much at ease. After all, this is a disease of the reproductive system. Your family . . ."

Once I saw my father while I was wandering around. He dashed out from behind a big tree and ran across the street. He tossed his canvas bag into the air, scattering little fish and tiny shrimps all over the ground. With just one flash of his army-green leg wrapping, he disappeared completely. I ran over and picked up the fish and shrimp, but then I realized that the little creatures in my hands were actually green worms and ants.

"Have you discovered that Father is completely done?" My third sister bent her two short legs, and leaned on a lamppost. She continued: "He pretends that nothing has happened. Wandering around the street, he appears talented and unconventional, but it's a false image. I've experienced the disease of blockage in the urethra, so I know he is in great pain. We shake with laughter when we see him chatting with you in dead earnest about something like the green mountains. Every time he leaves the house, he sleeps in that run-down temple. There's some straw in the corner, and other people also sleep there. In fact, at the moment when I first communicated my love to the doctor, he was staying there, too. Once when I went there, Father jabbered to me all day about a dog-skin vest. Over and over he explained that the vest had fallen beneath the floor of our original house. It fell through a hole in the floor. He also said some kind of dog-shit mold grew there as big as a fist. The reason he was wandering about was to look for that vest. That green mountain, I can see, is only a symptom of urethra blockage."

I walked into the collapsing temple and saw several feral cats scurry away. Two black faces emerging from the straw pile told me that Father was no longer there. I understood that he had become too ashamed when he realized that I'd seen through his lies. I left the place in a hurry so he wouldn't feel too embarrassed. When I turned my head, to my surprise, I found him making faces at me through the window. "I've been in the green mountains all the time!" He pointed two fingers at me. I was at such a loss that I felt deeply disheartened.

"You traitor!" My third sister dashed over from across the street and blocked my way. "Why did you go to that old temple? Huh? Who gave you the right to act on your own? You've degraded all of us! Now that old guy is chuckling behind the window. He thought that we instructed you to go there, you fool. So now we have all become the laughingstock of others!" She punched me angrily, and all the seams of her blouse burst open.

I'd hidden a hammer at the corner of the house. When everybody was in their hiding places and everything had quieted down, I felt my way to the window by the dim light from the street. Opening the window, I spat ferociously into the darkness. I saw my sputum flash in a ray of light, until my mouth became numb. My hammer clanged against the brick wall, and made a dull, muffled echo. A light from some house flashed once. Who couldn't hear such deafening noise? Or could it be that my hand could never produce real sound? I hammered the whole night through, in vain. In the morning, I hid the hammer away in shame. My body ached all over. My third sister walked out of her bedroom, yawning. Her mouth smelled. She glared at me sneeringly, shrugged, and spat on the floor.

"Where has Mother gone?" I asked her with a straight face, wondering where she had emerged from.

My third sister jumped up with a scream in the middle of the room: "Stop your dirty tricks! You're an odd one to put on the face of savior. It's disgusting! You're the one who's sick! And you mistake me for the one! Who's not clear about such things? In this corridor of ours, this disastrous passage, such soul-stirring changes are taking place, don't you feel it? We'd be overjoyed if you left us! Yet you never leave: you're stuck here . . ."

It was obvious that Mother had disappeared. Why should they remain so straight-faced and deny it? A living being should be seen and touched, yet Mother could be neither of these. But whenever I raised the issue, they blew up. Their tempers were definitely getting worse.

When I stepped into the kitchen, a large black figure emerged from the cistern. The soaking creature howled at me: "Look out!" It turned out to be the fiancé. How could he hide in the cistern? And what a coincidence that he rose up to threaten me just at the moment when I entered the kitchen. There must have been some ulterior motive there. "I'm a doctor." Dripping wet, he stood erect and continued. At the same time, he kept poking my cheeks with his wet finger: "Your whole family has that complicated syndrome. Without my care, God knows what misery you would be living in. People in dire straits all want to save face, and they pretend that nothing has happened. When I was living above you, I could hear your third sister hit her head against the bed frame in pain. The reason I stamped on the floor so hard was to reduce her pain, in fear that she might run upstairs and have a fit. You're the sickest of all your family. I've been watching your behavior all the time. I had been hidden in the water for more than two hours when you entered the kitchen. I'm shivering with cold." His eyes grew dim, and he started sneezing repeatedly, until my third sister rushed in and carried him off like a gust of wind blowing away a fallen leaf.

Father had been spreading the rumor that he left home because of unbearable oppression. He also said he had been living on fish and shrimps, but it wasn't true, because he sneaked back home to steal food. It wasn't even subtle stealing, but brazen robbery. But, at every theft, they all pretended not to notice. They played their roles so well that I was tempted to think they had trouble with their eyesight. Maybe they were able not to see something—for instance, Father pilfering food—if they didn't want to see it. On the other hand, they could always see something—for instance, our disappeared mother—if they wanted to see it. Therefore, they discriminated against people with eyes like mine. Sunglasses once said about me: "It's horrifying for a person to develop such an unfortunate temperament as his."

For several days, I'd felt terribly dizzy. I dared not look at people or even out the window. Wrapping my head in a cotton-padded quilt, I had lain in bed for three days and three nights. The fourth day, I supported myself by leaning against the wall and moved the door muddle-headedly. I stood there clutching the door frame. In the wind, everything was tilted and had several silhouettes. It was impossible to see anything clearly. Under that dead tree sat my mother. She had her nylons peeled down and was scratching her swollen feet. Because of the wind, her white hair stood toward the sky. She looked like a primitive figure. "Mo-ma!" I called out in a funny way. She turned her head toward me. I saw an unfamiliar, vague face. This was a young woman. "Your illness is serious. You've had that disease for a long time. It started from the inside, and hope for recovery is slim. You should keep this fact covered up." She made a resolute gesture with a sneer.

My mouth felt very heavy, and the wind was so noisy I couldn't hear my own voice. So I shouted, "I can't see anything clearly! My head has a bellowing inside! You are so young, so why is your hair all white?"

"That's the problem with your eyes," she sneered viciously. "From now on, just don't use your eyes anymore. It's much better that way. Your dizziness is caused solely by the eyes. I have a relative who is suffering from the same disease. He used his eyes so much that eventually his eyeballs fell out. Since you can't see things anymore, you have to admit it as a defect. Ambition will lead to no good ending."

I remembered that red snake berries once grew along the wall. Bending low and closing my eyes, I could feel them with my trembling fingers.

The sky was dim; everything underneath it looked like some kind of fluid. Three white geese flew through the mist like swimmers, then in one white flash they all disappeared. My finger touched a snail. My heart quivered, and my body was covered by goose bumps. Forcing my eyes open, I saw the woman fall back, farther and farther away. My eyeballs expanded so fast that I felt they might drop out of their sockets.

"I've also been sick," she waved her hand at last. "You've seen that my feet are swollen like carrots. I feel terrible every time I touch them . . . I've been taking extra precautions to hide it."

"You, go lie down." My third sister jabbed my back and said with boredom, "Your spine is like a snake in puberty."

Half-conscious, I felt my way back to bed and covered myself with the quilt. Even inside the quilt, I could still hear the noise of my sister rummaging through chests and cupboards and also the howling and crying of her fiancé being chased and beaten. My third sister was getting more and more unbridled daily. She let down her hair and wore shorts and T-shirts. She beat my quilt with a broom. I had never thought she possessed such strength. In fact, her asthma was only one of her little dramas made up out of nowhere. She always succeeded at whatever she involved herself in. I curled up inside the quilt, soaking with sweat, waiting for the fit to die down.

It was getting dark, and I still couldn't get up. I dug out a broken mirror and looked into it. I saw a vague lump of a face, with two reddened balls rolling around in it. They must have been my eyeballs. I tossed the mirror aside. It crashed onto the concrete floor with an irritating sound.

In the dim red light, the fiancé's round face appeared. It had a gray lining. His tongue flickered in and out, as if playing a new trick. I listened carefully and heard his voice.

"Why are you lying down? The situation in the family is very complicated. You must be aware of pine moths. I'm surprised that when I was living in the temple with your father, I felt much more relaxed. Now I'm shaking with fright, in fear of stepping on a pine moth. They are crawling everywhere. Often when you are about to fall asleep, you'll find one hidden in your quilt. When the old fellow brought back that pine branch, I anticipated such an unsolvable problem today. It's been one week that your third sister has been eliminating those poisonous insects. Our quilt has been ruined completely by the beatings. She is never merciful, and she has a stony heart . . ." As he spoke, he lost his concentration.

"Do you think I have glaucoma?" Breathing with difficulty, I saw him melt into a shadow.

"Ahmm, in the temple, one heard the seeds of the Chinese parasol tree drop to the ground every night. Your father will never come back. He's got what he wanted, and now he's boasting about himself to the proprietress."

The very night that the fiancé had warned me about the pine moths, I was attacked by them. They crawled into my quilt and nestled close to my legs, waist, arms—like a carpet full of needles. Turning on the light, I peeled them away and threw them out the window. Yet hardly had I lain down than they were with me again. They rustled; they pricked. I felt dizzy with pain. So I turned the light on again and peeled them off and threw them out, again and again. I was exhausted, but still couldn't sleep. In the morning I found no pine moths but only skin made raw from scratching.

"It's tragic to be attacked by pine moths." My third sister was staring at me. "There's no use trying to hide. You have to be whipped severely. When I'm in the mood, I often rip the whole quilt with my whip. Yesterday, I almost whipped the doctor's eyeballs out. He was in my way. Serves him right, whoever tries to block me." Her T-shirt had dark wrinkles under the armpits. She was standing in the middle of the room with her hands on her hips. Her face had a murderous look. "In the temple, pine moths swarm out of the rotten floorboards every time the mountain wind blows. The day before yesterday, I found that Father's hair was filled with such insects. He was sleeping on the floor, and the moths were making nests in his hair. *Jingle-jingle*, a little lamb was eating grass. When the wind stopped, the lamb would run very fast. Tiny pebbles rattled down . . . Ha, our father, it's extremely difficult to figure out his attitude toward life."

"I'd like to consult with others about our obstacles in verbal expression." My mind was working, yet my mouth was motionless. My lips had turned into a pair of iron clips.

"Hush." My third sister stopped me. Apparently she had heard the sentence in my mind. "Wild flights of fancy can only worsen your sickness. Let me tell you the cause of the asthma. It was caused by the medicine that the doctor prescribed. He was making fun of my emotions. What a fool I was to believe him. My heart breaks now that I think of it! Don't you take any medicine. It can only cause a neurosis. Never believe the doctor in this family. When you think about it, you won't be surprised to find that he is not a doctor at all. I believed it just because I wanted to. These days Mother chats with me about wild bees every night and about her lost wallet. I was moved to tears. In one stretch, I find myself walking on that stone path. When dawn comes, I realize that there is no wallet. She made up the whole story to get my sympathy. Our mother squats in the corner making up such stories for others. She is immensely proud of herself whenever somebody is taken in."

One morning, my legs swelled terribly, but my dizziness stopped unexpectedly. I listened intently. The house was dead quiet. Getting up, I circled through the house, supported by a stick, but not a soul was to be seen.

I walked out the door and limped down the street. The sun was hot, glaring down from the branch of a tree. All the joining parts of the walls were puffing out dust. My T-shirt stuck to my back. Raising my head, I saw numerous blue and purple circles.

"Isn't that Ah-wen?" An old man stopped blankly. "Good, come and have a stroll. Good!" While talking, he scratched his armpit with force, and then spat heavily at my feet. I walked away, and could still hear him chasing me and shouting, "Very good! Good sun, good . . ."

"Be on guard with such people. . . ." The old man's voice entered my ears like a gust of wind. "He sneaks into a python's cage whenever he feels like it."

Blood surged into my brain. In a hurry, I complained to the shadow beside the road: "I've been thinking of bestirring myself. I think so very hard. Every day, I hear the leaves rustle in the old camphor tree at the doorway. Just count how many blisters on my lips and you will understand me. Only if . . . I've met so many people. I tug at their sleeves, and mean to tell every one of them, but there is a great obstacle preventing me from expressing myself in words."

The shadow turned its back on me and remained silent. I could see the sun move to the top of the lamppost. The walls continued to puff dust.

"Good, good sun, good!" The old man was chasing after me. He ran a few steps, and then bent down to roll up his extremely long trousers, which were dragging on the ground.

The shadow turned back all of a sudden. His vague face was now turned toward me. He spoke each word separately through his teeth: "As a youth, you once had a food phobia."

On top of my third sister's bed lay a mountain of cotton fiber she had torn into shreds. Somewhere outside, a black hand was scratching on the wall: *scrtch, scrtch. . .*

"It's a wire brush." The pale little face of my third sister peeped out from inside the cotton pile. "It's like this every night. It has aroused in me an unfounded melancholy."

"You?"

Translated from the Chinese by Ronald R. Janssen and Jian Zhang

Juan Rulfo

Nothing of This is a Dream

Juan Rulfo

p. 169
Judas para el sábado de gloria (*Judas for the Glorious Saturday*), Mexico City, circa 1955.

p. 170
Bardas tiradas a la calle (*Walls Lying on the Street*), circa 1950.

p. 171
Untitled, circa 1950.

p. 172
Untitled, Capilla Real, Cholula, Puebla, circa 1955.

p. 173
Untitled, Popocatepetl Volcano, circa 1955.

p. 174
Casa en llamas (*Burning House*), circa 1955.

p. 175
El Paricutín (*The Paricutín Volcano*), Michoacán, circa 1950.

p. 176
Untitled, circa 1945.

My father died when I was six years old, and my mother when I was eight. When my parents died, I was still scribbling little zeros, nothing but little balls, in my school notebook. I was born the 16th of May, 1918, in Sayula, but they took me later to San Gabriel. I am the son of Juan Nepomuceno Pérez and María Vizcaíno. I have many names: Juan Nepomuceno Carlos Pérez Rulfo Vizcaíno. My mother was named Vizcaíno and in Spain there is a province called Vizcaya, but no one, no Spaniard is named Vizcaíno. That name doesn't exist, which means that it was invented in Mexico.

My parents were hacendados. *One had a* hacienda, *San Pedro Toxin, and the other a place called Apulco, which was where we spent vacations. Apulco is on a cliff and San Pedro is on the shores of the Armería River. In the story,* The Burning Plain*, *that river of my youth reappears. That's where the highwaymen holed up. A gang of highway thieves that hung around there killed my father when he was thirty-three. It was filled with bandits over there, pockets of men who had joined the Revolution** and who later felt like keeping up the fighting and the looting. Our* hacienda *San Pedro was burned four times while my father was still alive. They murdered my uncle, and they hung my grandfather by his thumbs, which he lost; there was*

* Juan Rulfo's *The Burning Plain* was included in his 1953 collection *El llano en llamas*.

** The Mexican Revolution, which began after President Porfirio Díaz fixed the 1910 election results, was led by Francisco Madero, and sparked several subsequent revolts, including those led by Pancho Villa and Emiliano Zapata.

much violence and everyone died at the age of thirty-three. Like Christ. Thus I am the son of moneyed people who lost everything in the Revolution. . . .

When he went to fight in the Cristero Revolt, the priest of my town left his library in our house because we lived across the street from the rectory converted into barracks, and, before leaving, the priest moved everything. He had a lot of books because he passed himself off as an ecclesiastical censor and he gathered volumes from people's houses. He had the Papal Index and with that he would officially ban the books, but what he really did was keep them because in his library there were many more profane books than religious ones, all of which I sat myself down to read—the novels of Dumas, Victor Hugo, Dick Turpin, books about Buffalo Bill and Sitting Bull. All of that I read when I was ten years old. I spent all the time reading because you couldn't go out for fear of getting shot. I heard a lot of shooting, and after some confrontation between Cristeros and Federales, there were men hung on all the posts. That's for sure, the Federales looted as much as the Cristeros. It was rare that we didn't see one of our own people hung by the feet on some post on whatever road. They stayed there until they became old and they curled up like untanned leather. The vultures would eat their insides, leaving only a shell. And since they hung them very high, there they would sway in the breeze for many days, sometimes months, sometimes only the tatters of their pants billowing out with the wind as if someone had put them out to dry there. And you felt that things were really serious when you saw that.*

* The Cristero Revolt, in which the Cristeros, a rebel army made up largely of peasants, fought in defense of their faith and the power of the Catholic Church in Mexico, erupted in 1926, after the archbishop of Mexico declared that the clergy would not recognize certain anti-clerical articles of the 1917 Constitution.

*

Rulfo always seems possessed, and at times one notes in him the lethargy characteristic of mediums: he goes through daily life like a sleepwalker reluctantly fulfilling the vulgar tasks of waking existence. With his ear tuned, he lets the worldly noises go by, waiting for the precise message that will set him writing again, like a telegrapher waiting for a code. In his stories, many individual souls have spoken, but in his novel, *Pedro Páramo*, he made a whole people talk. The voices mix with one another and you can't tell who is who, but it doesn't matter. The connected souls form one: alive or dead, Rulfo's men come in and out of our own souls as if they were in their own houses.

It would not be rash to say that the literature of Juan Rulfo is based on rancor. Or rancors. The land surrenders only its leathery surface; the sun bakes, bald plains and hallucinating heads, the women burning pestles, their flesh quickly warmed by the heat of the earth. Rulfo's men, or rather, his souls in limbo travel across the burning plains looking for a father who disinherited them at the moment of conception. They are the just sons of a mother who left them with the onus of avenging her and who died on time, because otherwise they would have been the butt of jokes for the others, for those who drink beer that is as warm as burro piss in the cantinas.

—1980

Elena Poniatowska

Translated from the Spanish by Frank Janney

MATTHEW SWEENEY

The Mules

One of them was lame when they bought him
but a rest and a bandage saw to that,
then a week of parsnips and sugar
had him whinnying for the valley,
up which his comrades would canter
at least once daily, carrying panniers
of lemons and olives, newspapers, bread,
goat's milk for the allergic, medicines,
incense, wine for the doctors,
and once a consignment of used Amstrads
that the mules would never forget.
They didn't mind the twisting narrow lanes
that rose from the valley. Even when snow
kept the postman at sea level,
they slithered down to the village,
and all three of them got used to the hands
of the gentler patients, stroking them
as they stood there chomping daffodils,
or peeing on flagstones, or sleeping
standing up, oblivious to problems
with striking nurses, ward revolts,
doctor burn-outs, or the RAF maneuvers
that exploded the sky above them.
There were worse outposts for a mule.

Reading

Yes, I was reading on the M1.
Yes, I was driving, and reading, too—
a book of poems by Paul Durcan,
The Berlin Wall Café, left by my wife
when she walked out. It wasn't
a twisty cliff-top road I was reading on,
it was a motorway, and anybody
with one good eye in their head
could drive on that. Didn't I,
as a hitchhiking student, get asked
to drive a car for thirty miles
while the driver slept in the back?
I can't drive, I remember saying.
It's a motorway, he said. Just keep
in the slow lane, and bring her in
at the second next services.
And it wasn't a novel I was reading—
the thing about poems, your Honor,
is they're mostly short. You can look up
between them, or between stanzas,
and see what's happening ahead.
Would you prefer if I'd been swigging
from a hip flask, or sucking on a joint,
or canoodling . . . ? Never mind that.
And what about that blind driver
whose dog barked at red lights?
I refute the charge of swaying
from lane to lane. I stayed in
the slow lane, did a steady 65.
It was 3 A.M., your Honor, the motorway
was as quiet as it ever gets,
I had no one to hurry home to,
so I took out my Durcan and opened it.
It didn't seem a wrong thing at all.

Chinese Opera

She lit the sky with her own fireworks show
at 4 A.M. Up there on her roof garden,
in her moon & stars dressing gown
she drained the last of the champagne
then struck the first match. Downstairs,
in the living room, Chinese opera was playing—
the last gift he'd given her with a grin.
She'd played that tape nonstop since then.

He'd laughed until she'd started joining in
with thin quivery vowels stretched and bent,
sobs and cymbal bashes, and dialogue
spoken in English—her own translations
which varied every time but always
had broken or sacrificed men—and laments
sung in her improvised Chinese, like now
on the roof as she sent the rockets high.

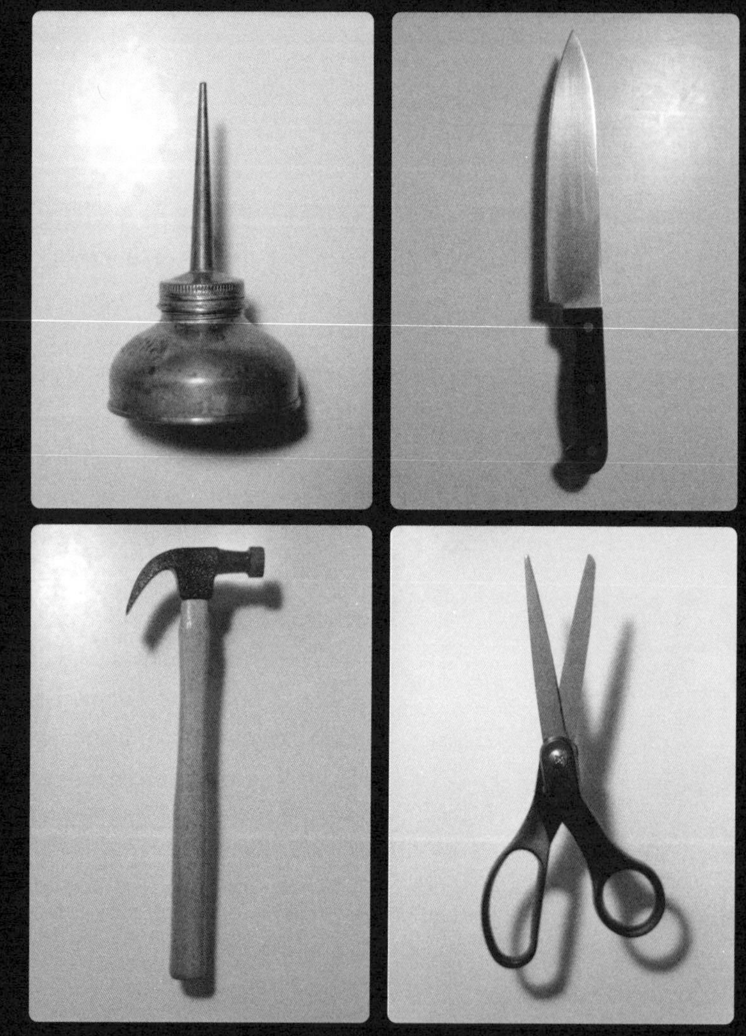

TOOLBOX

FABIO MORÁBITO

Oil

Oil is water that has lost its get-up-and-go, its insolent forward drive. Having exhausted all of its routes, it's caught treading over ground it trod before. It is water that has turned its back on the world. It is *de trop*. It has forfeited its old rights of way across the floor and now has to step to one side in favor of younger and grander fluids. It is luxury water, which after so much flowing has felt the weight of experience, maybe bitter experience. It's as if it had other water at its service; hence its sumptuousness, not far from prostration, for where there is sumptuousness, there's always somebody on his knees, tied with bonds.

So oil is a form of water that needs to prop itself up on another form, one hand placed over another hand—that's the fundamental nature of oil—and this disability makes it uneasy. It's water clogged with sand, a water that went astray on a hairpin bend that cut down its progress and couldn't shake off the sand, so it said good-bye to foam and withdrew into itself, taciturn, choked with grit. It is water that is weak at the knees.

Incapable of running, of instinctively shaking off hazards, of stepping warmly on every stone, of producing a crystal-clear diction, oil has turned snooty, calculating, sedentary. Having used up all its routes, it became reflexive. It ruminates and shilly-shallies like somebody who cautiously returns to his home ground and, rather than walk further, occupies it, seizes possession. All possessive forces keep going over the same ground, and oil is back at home again.

It is water with a predatory air. While young waters disinterestedly investigate the earth, oils get on their high horse, develop ambitions. They are water on the up and up. Their sandiness lets them climb upward slowly but steadily. Without oils, in fact, our world would lack surprises, would be constantly heading downhill, tyrannized by gravity, a place of limitless flatness.

In the long run, a world without oil would become geometric. But oil puts a stop to that possibility by being antidoctrinaire. It proves this by its cautious progress, its sounding out of things. It is water with its hopes shattered. It forms around objects a zone of confusion that saves them from being brutally scrubbed by the world. It encloses them in a hypnotic state. That's how lubrication works. Any piece that is lubricated subtly washes its hands of other pieces;

it achieves autonomy, and, within the mechanism as a whole, it recaptures the rhythms of its own will, or at least the illusion of them.

Oil really does project an individual temperament; it comprehends and knows how to listen. Hence where water, distracted and gullible, charges ahead, oil turns back, full of guile, holds itself in check, and takes in its surroundings. It neither tosses things away nor draws conclusions. Instead, it discerningly imprints a face and an age on whatever it touches. Everything oily has a name.

Without oil, there would be no culture, no commerce, no transportation. Oil is water with a burden to carry. Thanks to oil, our world has different hues, things swap postures and places, and open themselves up to unsuspected uses. Oil, if we may put it this way, acts like a butler; it's the bridge or the mattress which makes possible affable contact between things. It legitimates relationships and bestows a lasting stamp on them. It doesn't throw its weight around; it applies pressure with finesse, gets chatty, reanimates, civilizes.

Deprived of oil, we'd be subject to water's monastic lifestyle and forever uncouth. Kinkiness and hope would be taboo. We'd live without cunning, but also without grace. Water searches for channels and always finds them. It loves order and repetition. Oil, which travels at one or two gears lower than water, has a multitude of eyes that induce it to spill over and not exclude. It has community spirit and is inventive. Where water settles disputes and gives each his own, oil mixes things up in a utopian fashion. Every mixture contains a trace of utopia and puts rumors and spirited efforts to the test. It is a circus strongman.

Its job involves rigmarole. The oil that covers a certain material—a pipe or whatever—and lubricates it is subtly duplicating it, like an echo. It extends it microscopically in order to take away its claws and to help it relax. Oiled materials collide with no more than a shrug. The curtain of oil functions like an evangelizing fire and individual points of friction lose their gleaming sharpness. A sense of overall enthusiasm prevails, for oil is like the pump that vitalizes the whole contraption, getting the parts to pass from a state of sleepiness to excitement, and then to humility, setting aside their private concerns, as they pitch in together on the main job, whose whole purpose is mutual contact.

Oil, therefore, is the speediest of messengers, leaving nobody uninformed or confused. Its masterpiece, or rather its whole raison d'être, is hugging things, mixing them together, cooking them, rounding them out to perfection. Unlike water which heads toward the sea, oil takes any route it can to produce a stew, a sense of communion.

Knife

A knife is an end point plus a sensation of cold. It settles accounts. It disheartens and sends into exile. Never ever, for any reason, does it glance backward. Its whole being is forward motion, and yet it doesn't explore, investigate, make progress, or learn things. It's an interjection.

Why are other things so different from knives? Because, at some moment, even if it's only casually, momentarily, other things double back, twist around, take a fancy to something, and forfeit a fraction of time. This brief moment is enough to allow the approach of a turned back, a shadow, a stoutness of body, and a chance to become something. And that's enough to put an end to a knife, the pure knife point. (What's known as the blade is simply a carousel of such points.)

The point of a knife is radically void of memory and of bonds; it knows nothing at all; it is indebted to no one for anything; it casts no shadow. In a certain sense it is dead; it is a ruination, a cyst. It is what remains at the end, a thing that scorches, an ineluctable force, an enemy of skin and of reason—the skin and reason that do their jobs by wavelike motion, by absolution, by collective effort.

A knife point is pure discord. It is the end result of a grievous distillation. Behind each point stand thousands of years. Its ability to wound comes from the enormous weight that, bruised and disciplined, crouched on all fours, is encased in it.

The logic behind every sharpened object consists in arranging a situation in which *one*, pushed forward by *many*, sullies himself and cracks up on behalf of all.

It's as if everyone ran forward toward a point and then, suddenly, at a given signal, went into reverse. There will always be somebody who is last to get into line; and this is the one who, to be frank, is prevented from getting into line. That somebody is the knife point, the sacrificial victim. The others thrust him away, so that he doesn't get mixed up with them; they treat him like a stinking pariah.

The victim, in short, is the one whom the others push away, the one who has no fun. Every push he receives sets him farther from the tribe. Hence the gradualness with which things get sharpened to a point. It takes a lot of pushing for *a* victim to be finally transformed into *the* victim, for him to stand there all alone and accursed before the tribe, for him to reach the point of never again being able to assimilate.

It's as if the tribe were painfully evacuating its bowels. To make the point clear, imagine a group of men clambering down a slope. Before long, one of those at the rear hangs back and dodges behind a tree. Then another hangs back and dodges behind a boulder, then another behind a bush. Those up at the front aren't aware of this and carry on downhill; but the desertions continue. All of them, as soon as they sense they are dawdling slightly, take advantage of any chance feature of the landscape to find a hiding place. Until only one of the men remains on his feet, with no place to hide, exposed in broad daylight. He turns back but he can't see anybody. They've left him all alone. He is stuck. He is the knife point. And he can't scurry back up the slope to find cover, because all the hiding places are now occupied. He is the fall guy, the excrement.

This ironlike gradualness, this crafty advancing, constitutes the essence of a knife. Just look at the hardness and stubbornness of its blade. It is a brotherhood of the deaf. Nobody knows anything; nobody hears anything. They all push because they are pushed by others who are, in their turn, pushed by others. Nobody wants to be the last one left on the downhill trip, so they all push to get somebody ahead of them, and thanks to their pushing the closer they get to the abyss, the more brutal they become, until the last one turns into the knife point.

They all ought to go home and forget the whole business, but in order to do that they'd have to climb back up the slope—which would take some doing. They prefer to see the business finished, to run a slight risk, and stay to see who ends up exposed as the knife point. They want a close-up view; they want to see him with their own eyes. They need personal proof that the game has been played out, that the victim is someone else. That's why they're so pushy.

But what do they mean by "victim"? They realize too late in the day that they've been tricked. There is no victim. The victim is going to be delivered up right now, in his sleepwalking progress toward the fire. The victim is the one who gets too far ahead, the one who wants to check things out more than he should, the one who doesn't brake in time and stands out from the mass, who turns into an undesirable excrescence, the lousy piece of shit, the knife point. He, then, is the one who gets burnt, the one who immolates himself, and in so doing enjoys the secret triumph, that mystic exaltation which in due time overtakes every victim.

This blending of repulsion and desire, of advancing and retreating, this holding back without ever actually stopping—a characteristic of those who descend slopes—determines the nature of knives and everything else sharpened to a point.

The shape of a knife evokes the image of an impulse not checked in time and recalls a slippery world where things abruptly escape our control and achieve a dangerously nasty autonomy. It's as if a troop of cavalry, after routing the enemy forces, were to insist on pursuing them out of sheer momentum (or an excess of gallantry) until they found themselves deep in hostile territory, surrounded and besieged on all sides. The pig-headed cavalry troop with its exaggerated forward drive and its feeble braking capacity perfectly represents a knife's equivocal nature, its tendency to backfire, to spill blood without intending to, and it also explains, incidentally, quarrels, the sudden, treacherous stabbing, the sordid slashing with a blade, the drunken knifing, misery, and flight.

Hammer

A hammer is at once the easiest of our tools and the most profound. No other tool fills the hand as much as a hammer does; none inspires the same degree of dedication to the job and such total acceptance of the task.

With a hammer in hand, our body acquires its proper tension, a classic tension. Every statue ought to have a hammer, visible or invisible, like a second heart or a counterweight to offset the weight of its limbs. Wielding a hammer, we get rounded out, more integrated; it is exactly the one extra thing we need to feel ourselves permanent.

Grasped by the hand, obtuse, cyclopean, childlike, with its weight and its feel, it gives us once again that sensation of freshness in a tool, of a satisfying extension to our bodies, of an effort directed without waste or frustration.

O, first-rate hammer! Willing brother! Few things are as straightforward as you!

It acts like an epic poem; it's bilious, goatish, and eagle-like. The force of a juicy anger has been attached to a wooden handle and has been left to ferment and toughen there. That's how we get hammers—from a slow drip-drip of rage, which finally forms a scab at the end of the handle, an amalgam of wrath. Shape it and polish it, and your hammer is ready to go.

Passivity and power coexist in a hammer. In

fact, a hammer works by surprise, by nasty surprises, and its bruising strength is indebted not so much to its force as to its laconic delivery. It doesn't affirm, it skewers. All of a hammer's rage, slowly absorbed by the handle, slowly fermented, slowly assimilated, is expressed in one sharp bang! There's no time for anyone else.

A man who hammers, it would seem, combines in the hammer head the best of himself and his forefathers. The man himself, as a particular individual, is symbolized by the handle, which determines the willingness and direction of the blow, but the impact itself is entirely indebted to his past, a past heavy with the weight of the dead. A horde of the dead are packed into every hammer blow, your own dead, all that has been distilled in times before yours, everything tough that preceded you, and it's that toughness you hammer with, along with all your dead kin, whose purpose is to serve the living as a final hardness, as their sharpened steel, their armor plating. Anyone who tries to live without the dead, without a family tree, is barely alive and won't last long.

Thus a hammer never says anything that hasn't been said before; no novel emotion ever changes its tone. The dead always produce the same response. Their productions get weaker with the passing of time; vast areas of memory crumble away, and their vocabulary gets continually smaller until at last it is reduced to a single syllable, hard and obdurate.

Upon reaching the kingdom of the dead, every dead person loses definition and his faltering voice is erased by the voices of others. Every hammer blow is like that, a flowing lava of voices that has been reduced to one lone syllable. Every hammer blow raises to the surface our lowest depths, which are often close to a petrified inertia, their connections with the here-and-now shrunk to a few dreams, a few pangs of conscience, a few blows from a hammer.

That's why one man's hammer blows are vastly different from those of another; they glue together parts that are peculiar to the individual, matters that defy translation. Maybe at some point, in the farthest distance, they do touch each other and mingle, but even so they retain their separateness. Only the most sensitive of instruments could sort out those crude bangings into all their strata of voices that have been lost in the passage of time. But it would be a hellish instrument. We'd hear the swarm of our dead speaking one by one, in a terrifying whirlwind of sound.

We have to bring the dead together and confuse them, to stop them from frightening us, so that they'll let us live. We have to amalgamate them, squash them together, rub out their features and voices, until they linger on only as a choir, a distant clay pit, a half-shadow.

That's the reason behind the invention of the hammer, its unified force. With a single blow it binds us to our dead and at the same time plunges them deep into the past. It buries them, gets them out from under our feet. When we talk to the dead through a hammer, we liberate ourselves from them. We can then go forward. The hammer flattens out, opens up a pathway, crushes down bumps in the road, levels off the track, heads toward tomorrow. A hammer is a prow, no more no less.

But like every prow, it leaves behind a large wake, a choir of voices that are our dead, echoing in every blow. To move ahead is to move toward the dead. With every blow those who went before and those who are coming after, our yesterdays and our tomorrows, our liberty and our origins, touch each other and fuse. With every blow we are nailed to the earth, redefined in a burst of bright flame, as if we were statues, not wholly alive, not wholly here, mildly classical and forever.

Scissors

Scissors are ambassadors of cold. They bring us notice of the brilliant cruelties of which cold is capable when it's concentrated into a tool.

While heat spreads out and fuses things together, concentrated cold does the opposite: it contracts and divides; it opens up gaps and reduces morale. Along with water, it possesses the power to reduce us, time after time, to the simplicity of ground-level existence and simultaneously to free us from the grubbiness of fruitless illusions. That's why we take baths, of course. Not merely to get cleaner, but to grow more realistic.

The talk you get from scissors is always to the point. It can be summed up in the taunt: "There's no room here!" Between the steely blades of scissors, nothing can find room—apart from water, that is. Water's capable of inconceivable squirmings and can wriggle through the gap between the blades without taking the slightest drubbing.

Everything else, however, has to back off, guilty of being either too fat or too slow. And if a thing doesn't choose to back off, it's forced to. That's what scissors do. Like a keel in seawater, they thrust things aside and clear a path for themselves. They work like a pair of hefty shoulders, easing others aside. Bit by bit, they overthrow the opposition. They struggle body to body with one adversary, knock him over, and go on to the next. As noiselessly as surgeons, they open a way through, not by demolishing but by leveling off, removing one foundation after another, subtracting supports. Scissors are specialists in deepening a crisis.

They are creatures of evening. In the vertical, noonday light cast on a smooth surface, in a confrontation with the central expanse of an object, they're as useless as eunuchs. But let them slink to the edges of the object, to its twilit limits. Then by a series of sly maneuvers, by nipping the heads off the object's sentinels, they'll manage to slide their way silently inward, undermining every defense.

Undermining is a passion with them. They're cursed with a vindictive nature. And it's not hard to see why. Each blade of a pair of scissors loathes the other. They've been coerced into doing their dirty work together. Dirty, because we see no frontal attack, no heroic act of stabbing. Only an oblique act of slicing, undercover and chilling. In short, scissors behave like servile courtiers. Just as a forceful king summons his nobles to court and dominates them by making sure they rub each other the wrong way and whisper behind each other's backs, so these erstwhile daggers, once fervent-hearted and free-spirited until a sovereign crew forced them together, forfeit all their previous ardor in postures now decorous and docile. They grow courtly. They reek of courtliness, living under the sign of self-containment, suffocation, and whispered gossip.

While the underblade vilifies the object-victim, tracing out a thin line of death, the overblade comes down with a choking, chopping action. As the old trick has it, you toss a stone into the darkness, and when your imprudent enemy sticks his head out to see what's going on —whop! You chop it off with your sword.

That's how scissors get ahead in this world, by surprising the opposition, outsmarting it. They attack the lumbar regions, the less sensitive parts. They begin with the youngest watchman, or the sleepiest, or the most isolated. Once they dispose of him, nothing can stop them. Yield them one single weak point, and they can find the rest of themselves. They are masters of deduction. They link one premise neatly to another and never for a second lose the thread. *They skip nothing.* They move with mathematical assurance.

They live their lives wide awake, almost on tiptoe, their bitter eyes fixed on tomorrow. They resent the actual, the present tenses of verbs, the surrounding landscape. They are intoxicated with things subsequent. The word "tomorrow" sums up their whole methodology. "Forward! Faster! Push ahead!" squeaks the steel of their blades. "Into the future! Tomorrow, here we come!"

And yet, by means of two fingers and a glance, they allow themselves to be manipulated, nicely, neatly, like elderly spinsters, as if they weren't in direct contact with you but were items of a venerable delicacy at the end of a dizzying perspective of anterooms. Maybe that's why they won't tolerate clumsy or inexpert handling the way other tools will. They condone neither error nor fraud. In they go and out they come. And that's that. They stay tense.

It's not uncommon to see children close one eye and study the action of scissors, first opening the blades, then shutting them. They want to discover which blade is the more culpable, to unravel the mystery of scissors, to find their center of gravity, the point of hesitation. Maybe they intuit a secret softness in them, something like a heart that throbs away under all that hardness, a seed, however tiny, of self-surrender and extravagance. And, as usual, the kids are onto something. Frequently, while scissors are immersed in their work, while they're duly providing satisfaction, the blades get along with each other famously. They keep a date with heart, with art, with a genuine finesse. They contract nickel-plated matrimony, each partner forgetful of its lost bohemia. While they are opening up a careful path through seas of cloth, of cardboard, of paper, suddenly they discover that they're no longer playing tricks or sowing seeds of calumny and terror, but are purely and simply *congratulating one another.*

Translated from the Spanish by Geoff Hargreaves

BRUCE SMITH

Catullan IV

Too much or not enough.
The blade-thin letter
from you, Hippolyta,
cuts nothing
not even the wrists.

Stop, I've had enough,
I imagine the letter
says. Or *I was wrong,*
Hippolyta
Or it says *Nothing*
you say makes these wrists

come back to you. Enough
is never enough. The letter
I don't read, Hippolyta,
I send back. Nothing
but a stamp. Slit your own
wrists.

Catullan VII

Don't think I wouldn't have you back
in a heartbeat, Hippolyta, your face
shiny with his cum, creased from the sack.
It would be the privilege of my disgrace
to feel, by proxy, his cock
on my lips as I kiss you,
although now my heartbeat
is set to the work of eternity.

Catullan VIII

I'm done subtracting three
hours from the time of day
to find out how the light
strikes you in the West, Hippolyta.
Early or late. You're asleep
next to him; I'm up.
I'm thrashing in my sleep,
night sweat, no dream,
you're offering three
orifices to him.
Leave me out of it.
Subtract one.
Stick a fork in my ass,
I'm done.

JOSÉ LUANDINO VIEIRA

The girl with golden braids looked at him, smiled, and held out her hand.

"Agreed?"

"Agreed," he said.

They both laughed and went on walking, stepping on the violet flowers that were falling from the trees.

"Violet-colored snow . . ." he said.

"But you've never seen snow . . ."

"Of course not, but I think it falls like that . . ."

"It's white, very white . . ."

"Like you!"

And a sad smile bloomed timidly on his lips.

"Ricardo! There's also gray snow, dark gray."

"Remember our agreement. No more—"

"Yes, no more talking about your color. But you mentioned it first."

When they arrived at the end of the sidewalk, they turned around and returned along the same route. The girl had blond braids with red ribbons.

"Marina, do you remember our childhood?" And he turned suddenly toward her.

He looked her in the eye. The girl lowered her gaze to the tip of her black shoes and said:

"When you used to build carts with skate wheels and push me around the neighborhood? Yes, I remember . . ."

The question that had pursued him for months finally emerged:

"And do you think everything is like it was then? Like when we used to play blind man's buff or hide-and-seek? When I was your friend Ricardo, a clean and well-mannered black boy, as your mother put it? Do you think—"

His own words were agitating him. His eyes shone and his brain was emptying because everything he had built up was pouring out in a torrent of words.

"—that I can go on being your friend?"

"Ricardo!"

"That my presence in your house—in your yard, seldom inside it!—won't spoil your family's plans for your relationships . . ."

He was being cruel. Marina's blue eyes said nothing to him, but he was being cruel; the sound of his own voice made him see that. Abruptly, he stopped talking.

"Sorry," he said finally.

He turned his gaze to his own world. On the other side of the paved street there was no sidewalk. Nor trees with violet-colored flowers. The earth was red. Agaves. Wattle-and-daub houses under the shadow of strangler fig trees. The winding, unpaved streets. A light cloud of dust borne by the wind covered everything. His house was at the rear. It was visible from where he stood. Yellow. Two doors, three windows. A fence made from barrel staves and hoops.

"Ricardo," said the girl with golden braids, "why did you say all that? Have I ever said I wasn't your friend? Have I ever deserted you? Not what my girlfriends say, nor the teachers' veiled advice, nor even my family, which has turned against me—"

"All right. Forgive me. But you know, this is inside us. Sometimes it has to come out."

And he recalled the time when there were no questions, answers, explanations. Before there was the asphalt frontier.

"Good times," he found himself saying. "My mother was your washerwoman. I was the washerwoman's son. I was little Nina's clown. Little Nina with the blond curls. Wasn't that what they called you?" he shouted.

Marina fled for home. He stood there, his eyes brimming with tears, his hands fiercely shut and the violet flowers falling on his black, kinky hair. Then, with resolute steps, he crossed the street, angrily treading the red sand and disappearing into the disorder of his world. Illusion remained behind.

Marina watched him walk away. Friends since they were small. He was the washerwoman's son who amused little Nina. Later, school. Both of them in the same school, the same class. Their great friendship was born.

She took refuge in her room, slamming the door. Around her, a luminous, smiling scene, a happy atmosphere, the soft warmth of the pink walls. And there on her study desk, "Marina and Ricardo, friends forever." The pieces of the photograph lifted in the breeze and scattered on the floor. She threw herself on the bed and lay on her back, staring at the ceiling. It was always the same light fixture. Walt Disney characters. The figures swam in her tear-filled eyes. And everything became covered with fog. She and Ricardo playing together. She was running happily, her dress up to her knees, and her blond curls glistened. Ricardo's eyes were large. And suddenly she began to think about the world on the other side of the asphalt. And once again she saw the wattle-and-daub houses where numerous families lived. In a bedroom like hers, Ricardo's four brothers and sisters slept—why? Why couldn't she go on being his friend, as she had been in childhood? Why was it different now?

"Marina, I have to talk to you."

Her mother came in and stroked her daughter's blond hair.

"Marina, you're not a child anymore, and you have to understand that your friendship with that . . . with your friend Ricardo can't continue. That's very nice for children. Two children. But now . . . a Negro is a Negro. . . . All my friends are talking about how I've neglected your upbringing. That I let you . . . Well, you know it's not because of me!"

"All right, I'll do whatever you want. But now leave me alone."

Her heart was empty. Ricardo was nothing but a distant memory. A memory linked to some pieces of a photograph that were blowing along the floor.

"Stop walking to school with him, coming home from school with him, studying with him . . ."

"All right, Mother."

She turned her head to the window. In the distance she could make out the dark stain of the tin houses and the fig trees. This brought her back to Ricardo. She turned suddenly to her mother, her eyes flashing, her lips arrogantly pursed.

"It's all right, it's all right, you hear?" she shouted.

Then, burying her head in the bedspread, she cried.

On that moonlit night, Ricardo, under the fig tree, remembered. The clove trees and blind man's buff. The carts with skate wheels. And he felt the overwhelming urge to talk with her. He had grown too accustomed to her. All those years of camaraderie, of studying together.

He found himself crossing the frontier. His rubber shoes squeaked on the asphalt. The moon gave a raw color to everything. A light in the window. He leaped over the fence. Dead leaves rusted under his feet. Toni snored in his doghouse. He went slowly toward the veranda, went to the window, and cautiously tapped on the pane.

"Who is it?" Marina's voice came from inside, intimate and frightened.

"Ricardo!"

"Ricardo? What do you want?"

"To talk to you. I want you to explain what's going on."

"I can't. I'm studying. Go away. Tomorrow at the school bus stop. I'll go early. . . ."

"No. It has to be today. I need to know everything right now."

From inside came Marina's mute reply. The light went out. She could be heard crying in the darkness. Ricardo turned around slowly. He ran his hands nervously through his hair. And suddenly the beam of a flashlight from the Portuguese policeman struck him in the face.

"Stop right there! What are you doing?"

Ricardo felt fear, the fear of the black man for the police. With one leap he landed in the yard. The dead leaves gave way and he slipped. Toni began to bark.

"Halt, Negro! Stop. Stop, Negro!"

Ricardo rose and ran to the wall. The policeman ran after him. Ricardo jumped.

"Stop, stop, you Negro!"

Ricardo did not stop. He leaped over the fence. He landed on the sidewalk with a force muffled by his rubber shoes. But his feet slipped when he made the leap into the street. He fell and his head struck the edge of the sidewalk.

Lights came on in all the windows. Toni barked. In the night the blond wail of the girl in braids could be heard.

The moon shone with the color of blue steel, a cruel, clear light. Standing over him, the policeman bared the fallen body with his flashlight: Ricardo, lying on this side of the frontier, under the violet flowers of the trees along the sidewalk.

In the distance, cashew trees arching over the wattle-and-daub houses extended their twisted shadows in his direction.

—Angola, July 7, 1955

Translated from the Angolan Portuguese by Clifford E. Landers

MICHAEL O'BRIEN

Snow

The snow's di-
agonals
drift across
the imagined
space of the
city's co-
ordinates

& what stirs
as if to
meet them is
the desire
for oblit-
eration:
that it all

come down, not
just the snow
but the space
& the laws
that predi-
cate it, that
it be ef-
faced, along

with the con-
sciousness of
its devis-
ing: blackout,
sleep, the wear-
ing away

of every
thought of who
we are or
meant to be,
the very
zero of
our setting

forth, lost in
that hushed, crys-
tal softness,
whispered noth-
ing, drifted
smudge of a
wet eyelash.

MONA HATOUM

SHIFTING GROUND

Doormat, 1996.
Straight pins, canvas, and glue.

[ABOVE] *Installation: + and -*, 1994.
Sand, wood, stainless steel, and motor.

[BELOW] *Installation: + and -* (detail), 1994.

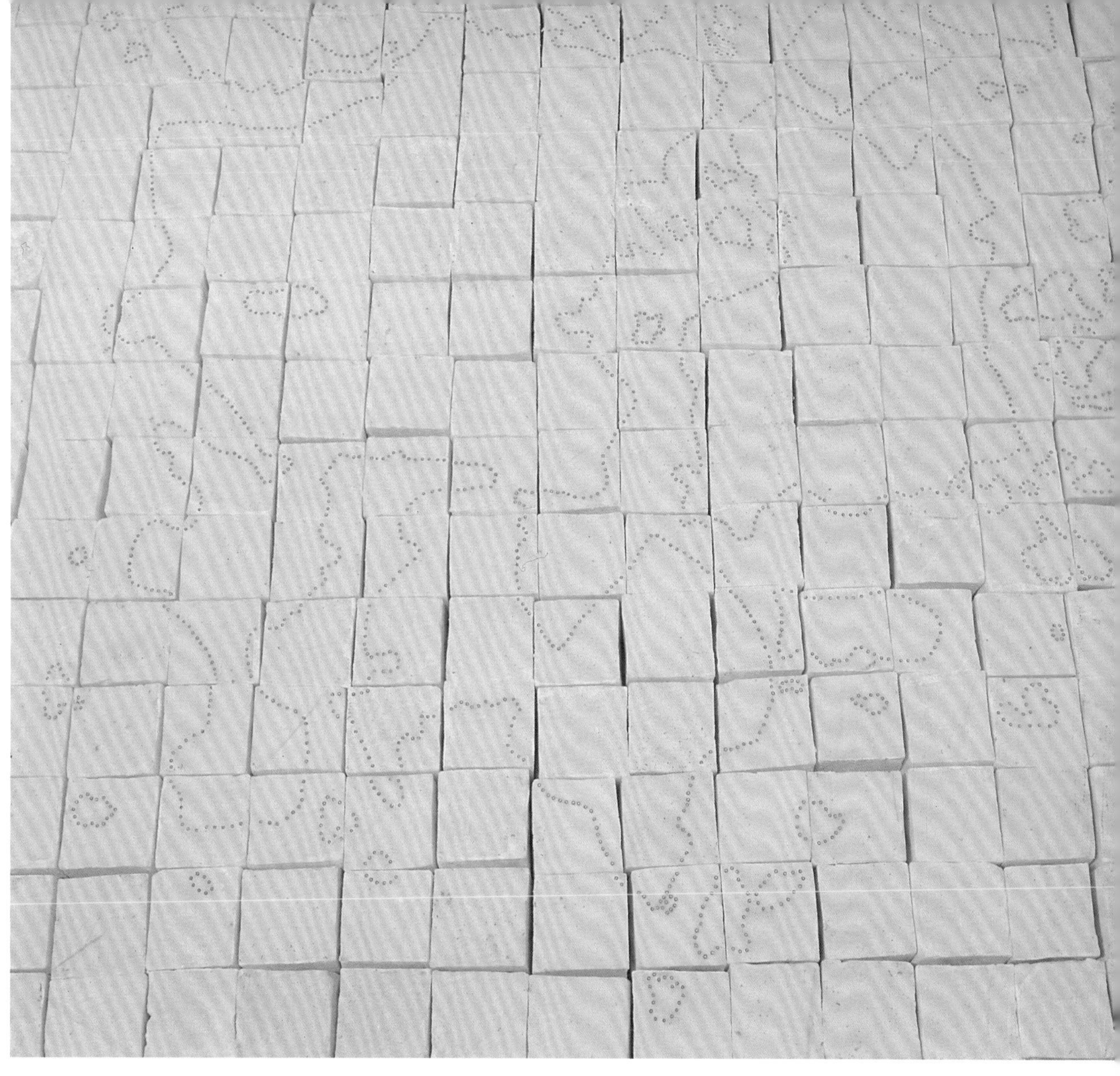

Present Tense (detail), 1996.
Soap and red glass beads.

Marrow, 1996.
Rubber.

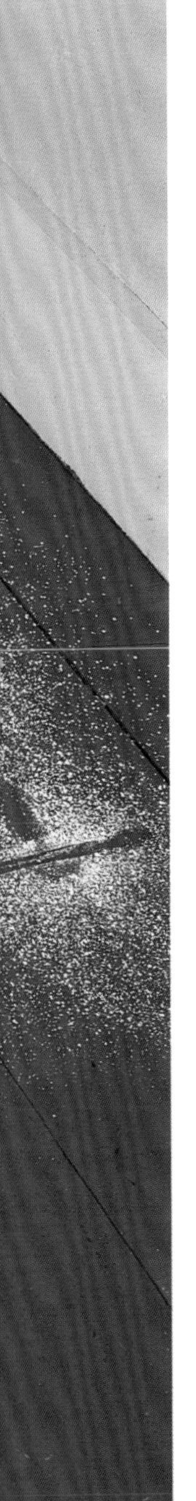

[LEFT]
First Step (detail), 1996.
Wood, metal, paint, and powdered sugar.

[ABOVE]
Large Shaker Colander, 1996.
Rubbing on wax paper.

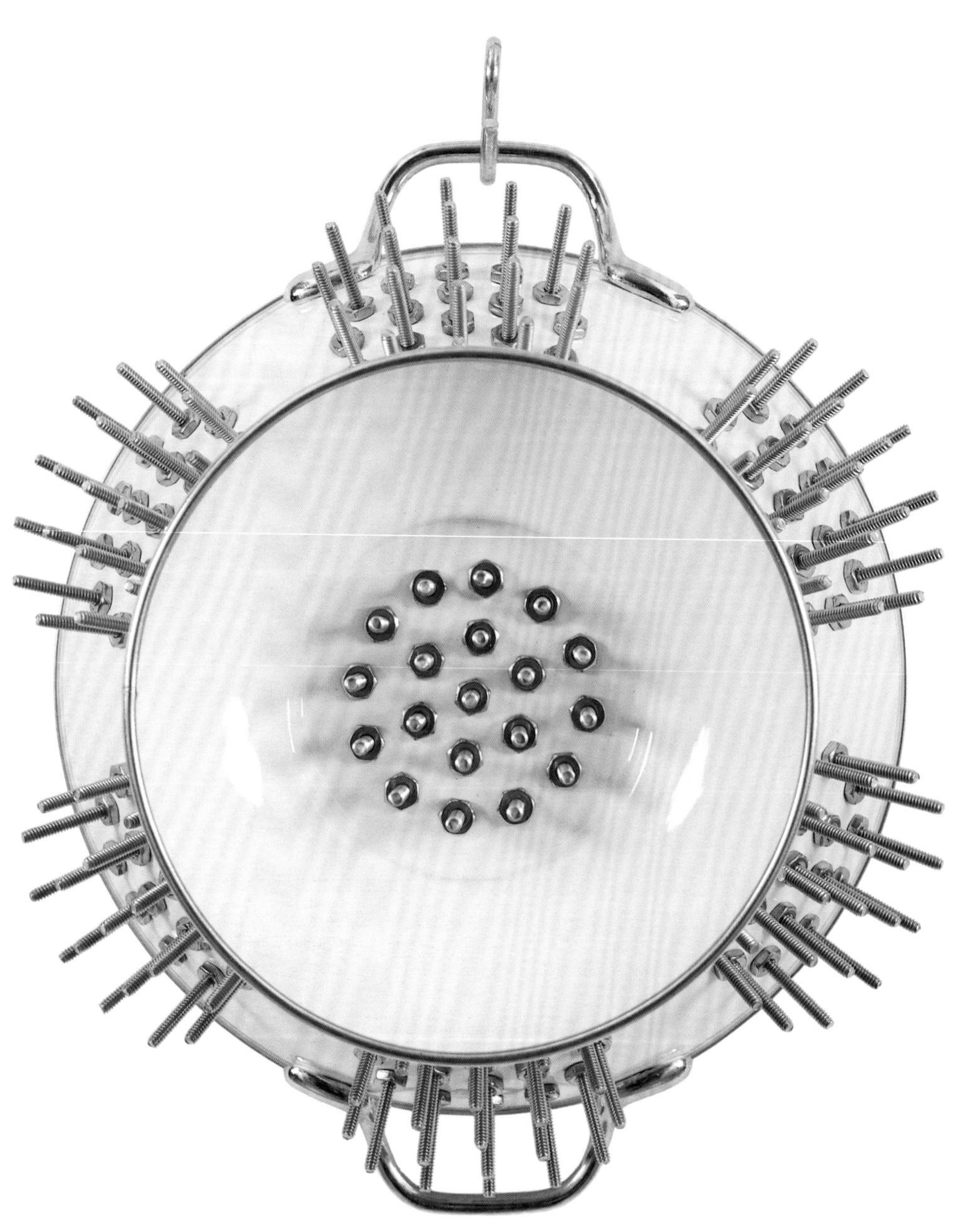

No Way II, 1996.
Enamel and steel.

MONA HATOUM

The condition of exile is one of wariness, characterized by a close reading of the texture and seams of meaning laced through language and objects, the vernacular and the quotidian. The exile can never go home, nor can he or she ever fully come to a psychological rest in the new country; yet an understanding of the transmissions and tremors of received meaning, cultural mores, and social referents can inure him or her against being pegged as different.

Born in 1952, into a family of Palestinian exiles living in Beirut, the artist Mona Hatoum became doubly exiled when, in 1975, during her first visit to Britain, civil war erupted in Beirut and she was prevented from returning home. In her work, Hatoum uses diverse media—performance, installations, sculpture, and video—to sift for the allusions and connotations created by the friction of fractious cultures coming together to form new, tertiary constructs.

In Hatoum's *Doormat* (1996), thousands of small stainless-steel pins push through each hole in the weave of its cloth backing in an arrangement that spells out that most obsequious of suburban greetings: WELCOME. Another piece, in a series of carpet works, has a compass embedded into an Islamic prayer mat, also made of pins, which allows the devout to orient themselves toward Mecca. *Marrow* (1996) is an institutional-type cot, evocative both of childhood confinement and dreams. Cast in rubber, the structure seems to have collapsed under its own heavy load of signification. A floor sculpture installed in a gallery in East Jerusalem, *Present Tense* (1996), is made with blocks of the locally produced, olive-oil Nablus soap. Red beads pressed into the rectangle of soap cubes delineate the small parcels of land which, according to the Oslo peace accords, were supposed to be handed back to the Palestinian authorities. If there is nothing that so molds a nation as its geography, then Palestine's divided physical geography is to a large extent the key to its embattled history. Also in 1996, Hatoum produced a series of rubbings on wax paper at the Shaker community's residence at Sabbathday Lake, Maine, another community of exile. Taken from handmade domestic utensils, such as colanders, the rubbings' uniform but irregular patterns are captured through the simple act of frottage. Hatoum also stopped up drainage holes in a colander and ladle with nuts and bolts in *No Way* and *No Way II* (1996). What was to be prevented from draining away?

Installation: + and - (1994) has two motor-driven blades, sharing the same axis, one with a serrated edge, and the other smooth, revolving through a shallow circular sand pit. The production of variance—the highs and lows of the rippled edge—is, in turn, followed by the act of smoothing out. Such difference and heterogeneity haunt each other in all of Hatoum's work.

Jackie McAllister

Hurt Me Not

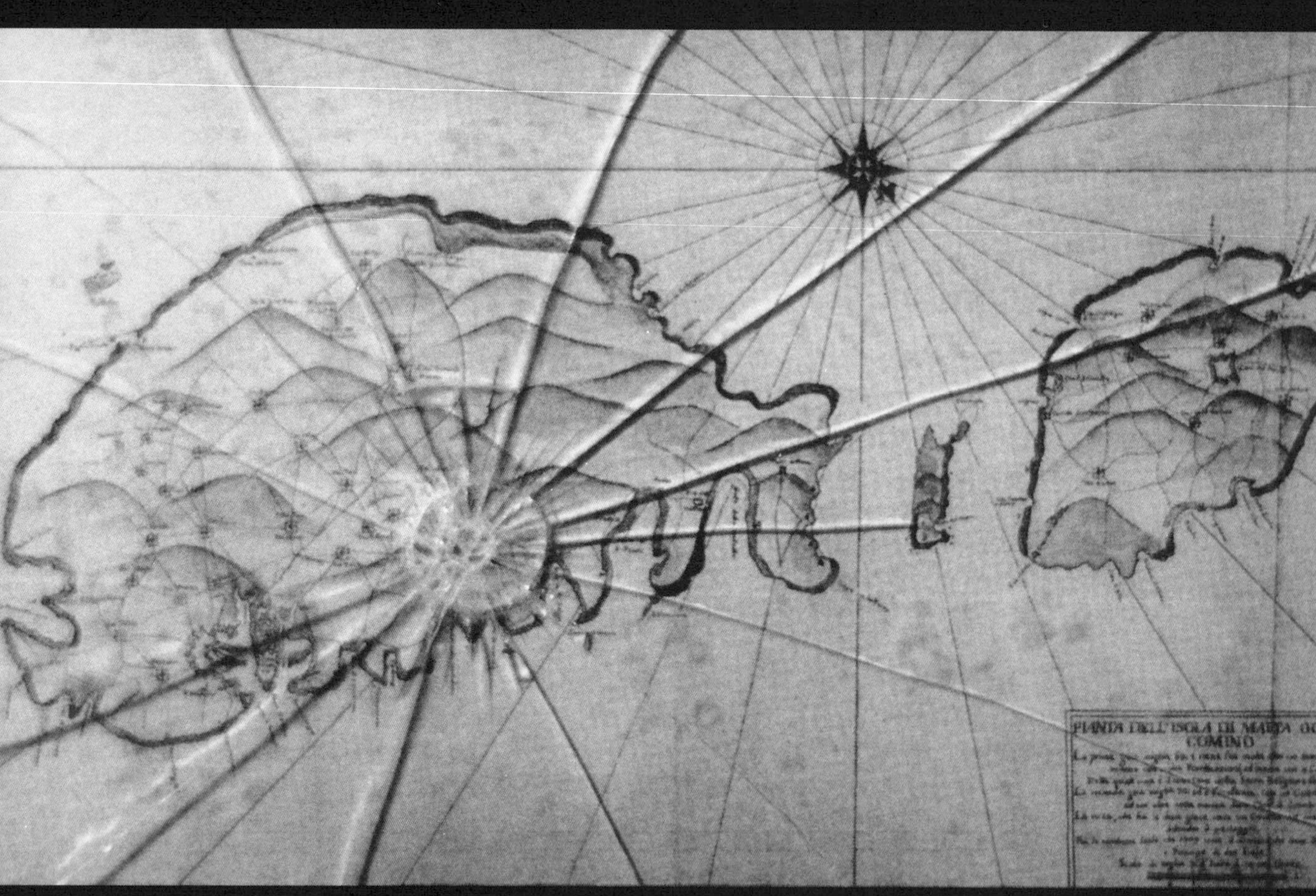

BILGE KARASU

This is the tale of a man who longed to be naked in a world where all people —we should probably say "most people"—live and toil to clothe themselves, if not to weigh down their backs with folds of cloth, then to keep warm in the bitter cold of winter.

*

He came here naked, thinking that the people on this warm island would not find his nakedness odd or subject him to insufferable questions. Yes, the island had its share of winters and the occasional harsh winds from the open sea. When absolutely necessary, he could wear a sweater, after all. He wanted nothing else, although, quite strangely and despite his efforts, his wealth gradually increased.

He neither traded nor stole; nor did he try to flatter his neighbors on the hill to save on meals or heating.

> The hill's residents were the grandchildren of those who had, after the great earthquake centuries ago, moved their dwellings up, away from the shore, fearing that the island would sink; the descendants of the oldest settlers, they fostered a tradition of giving, generously opening their homes, tables, and coffers to others.

He lived by the water, in the part of the neighborhood that was the closest to the schools. He worked for all the schools, teaching various subjects. After all, teaching in as many areas as he could and giving away his knowledge was also part of becoming naked.

> Through nakedness, one achieves bare skin, pride, self-respect. Although it is difficult, he who has committed to the task of becoming naked knows when to take the last inevitable step and die. Yet he wants to take this final step among those who understand the value of such an event. It is a sad, sad tale when one mistakenly believes it is time and attempts the last act in unworthy company.

In addition to teaching, he was also asked to help with official correspondence because of his eloquence and penmanship.

> There was plenty of correspondence. Everything from drinking water to flour was imported to the island. The islanders exported fish. The people on the hill worked together with their neighbors on the shore. Bread was still baked in ovens by the sea and sent up the hill. The people on the hill believed that their forefathers had displayed acute wisdom by relocating after the earthquake. The island's order was nearly perfect. People diligently nursed their fear of earthquakes and made it their duty to pass that fear on to later generations. In the earthquake, the shores had crumbled and sunk. Most of the islanders had perished, their homes were destroyed and swept away. The survivors had moved their dwellings up the hill, and the inland stores spared by the earthquake had managed to continue their business. In later years, newcomers to the island were permitted to settle only by the sea; much later, the few oldest families were allowed to relocate to the hills.

In his native land, people did not know earthquakes or, if they did, they had long forgotten them. They worked the dependable soil to generate the best harvest, to reap the most robust seed from each seed sown. The rivers ran and the rains fell as abundantly as expected. Where necessary, giant transparent domes were built—over cities, over entire regions—to insure a mild, everlasting ecosystem for humans, animals, and vegetation.

As the vegetation grew, so did the insects. The people fought against them but could not exterminate them altogether. Although the insects became fewer in number, they grew larger in size.

> He dropped the water glass. He dropped the glass he took from the table. This was a significant event for the man who wanted to strip himself naked. It was unlike him to break or tear something deliberately. In the past, he had reprimanded himself and grieved for hours over a broken glass or an accidentally torn shirt. Not because of the loss, not even if it was significant, but because of his own absentmindedness. That he could be so careless. Yet, today, he picked up the glass from the breakfast table, held it for a moment four feet above the stone tiles, then loosened his grip; the shattering of glass sounded as familiar to him as the sea's steady rustling, as pleasant as the waves breaking against rocks. That he had cherished the glass, that it was a precious memento he had chosen after seeing it take shape in the hands of a master craftsman in a faraway land famous for its glassworks—none of that even crossed his mind.

Other animals also grew bigger. Although there were fewer of them, they kept consuming in larger quantities. The harder the people worked to reap the robust seed, the more they resented the theft of their food by overgrown rats and insects. Then began the migrations. Having heard fantastic stories for years about the wealth and grandeur of the valleys and the cities, people from faraway mountain villages started to move down. Not that they cared to claim a share of the wealth. It was not their style to covet what they knew did not exist. When asked, they said, we came to see your human-size ants, your elephant rats. Although they soon realized that they had been mistaken, few moved back to the mountains. Instead, they joined the fight to save the wheat fields from rats that were, after all, as big as dogs and ants as big as mole crickets. They gradually got used to life in the lower regions, although they never quite overcame the shock of having left their villages because of fairy tales about giant beasts.

Year after year, people came up with new methods of protecting the seeds and the vegetation, at ever-increasing cost. Each attempt succeeded only briefly and the rats and insects always managed to survive and to resume the onslaught with an even greater appetite for destruction. People could not understand that the comfort they sought for themselves also suited other creatures and, as changing their way of living never occurred to them, they kept searching for new solutions to the problem. Their constant courage was eclipsed by the abject futility of their solutions. In the meantime, an inventive new generation came along and proposed new ways of living. Some of these ideas proved successful but eventually led to even greater problems. As success lured people from villages to towns, and from towns to cities, snakes, rats, and ants roamed freely around the abandoned homes and fields in the country; and, when there was nothing left to deplete, these creatures, too, migrated to the cities—to find greater bounty or death, perhaps.

At the time, he was about to graduate from one of the best schools in the largest domed region. One night at two A.M., he was returning home. He walked along the rows of brightly lit stores. Tall garbage cans, filled to the brim, lined the sidewalk. A large mercurial dog with a radiant coat stood on its hind legs, searching through one of the cans with its paws and tossing scraps of food at another dog—smaller but more beautiful—that was prancing around it. He stopped and watched the dogs for some time. Suddenly, the small dog hopped off the sidewalk and was caught by a fast moving car. The large dog chased the car for a hundred and fifty feet, until the small one could free itself. The car vanished from sight. The small dog's shriek vanished into the darkness of the sidewalk on the other side of the street. He couldn't see the large dog anymore either. That night in his dreams, cars flew by, dragging human beings and dogs, tossing them off at a distance. Mutilated, humans and dogs became indistinguishable, and the indifferent cars stuck to their terrifying, important race. The next day, he began to pack, and, three days later, he was on the road.

On the day he began teaching at one of the island schools, the small dog's howl was still in his ears.

> He stood up without even thinking of picking up the shards, walked toward the door, glass crackling under his feet, and left for school. He was preoccupied. It took him some time to notice his students' agitation.

He never moved out of the first house he had settled in, the one on the topmost row of houses by the sea, near the schools. The other teachers were natives of the island. Some lived by the sea, others on the hill. Because the schools were located between the hill and the coastal neighborhoods, they were out of danger. He was told so. He could live in one of the schools since he did not own a house. . . . But he turned down the offer. He had heard that the residents of the hill felt much pride at their seniority. Those on the hill did not particularly enjoy becoming the minority because of the migrations to the island. But the distinction seemed minor. He had not witnessed any hillside-seaside rivalry. Both the hillsiders and seasiders alike insisted sternly that the newcomers observe the island's rules. But that was all.

For him, the earthquake bore no reality. He noticed that many newcomers easily assimilated the sense of imminent danger that the island nursed so diligently, perhaps because they brought with them their own fear of past earthquakes. He was puzzled by this but tried not to show it.

Here is how matters stood on the island: If another earthquake were to occur and the shore were to crumble and perish, some of those living by the sea would perhaps be spared, but the boatyards, the docks, the bakeries would be destroyed; yes, the people on the hills would save their homes and lives, but they would face hunger and abject poverty. As for those who lived by the sea, if they were to perish, they would prefer their bakeries and ships to perish along with them, and they refused to hear any—albeit occasional—proposal to move the businesses up the hills.

Along with the population of the island, businesses also multiplied and no one complained about unemployment or over-employment. The teacher's work also didn't seem to increase or decrease. Both his earning and his buying power seemed to stay the same. Yet, perhaps because he succeeded in remaining true to his principle of casting everything off, his few modest needs must have grown even fewer, as his wealth was actually increasing. At first he was intrigued; gradually he became anxious, seized by fear.

His wealth was increasing faster and faster, it seemed. He did not understand it. He thought of ways to deplete his wealth, but all promised worse complications. If he bought more and more, he would either increase his possessions and betray his longing to be naked or he would attract others' attention to himself. What was worse: to be perceived as a madman or as someone who distrusted the stable order of the island and therefore saved his money or attempted to exchange it for durable goods? He was an outsider but not like those who came from nearby islands. Back where he came from, people knew poverty, they knew of those who struck it rich and lost it all to start over with pennies. . . . Yet, here, such twists of fate were terrifying. He had been spared the stern greeting with which the island initially welcomed newcomers. Now to be perceived as an outsider and in the harshest manner imaginable would destroy the life that had taken him so long to build. Had he really built a good life, or was he merely imagining that he had? This question, too, started to preoccupy him.

> The end of May was near. Vacation would start soon. This morning, he opened the curtains that he kept closed to keep out the mosquitoes. A strange smell filled the room and his lungs. Like the smell of a garden, like the smell of railroad tracks, like the smell of an auto-repair shop. Smells that would not match or blend. Yet all fused together into one smell. He thought of gardens, railroad tracks, he thought of auto-repair shops; a rush of images left over from different stages of his childhood swarmed into his head, before his eyes. Then the images overlapped, drew together his distant childhood, the sea surrounding his present country, its smell, sounds, its people, and became a single image embracing all in its overarching design. It was as though all the fragments of his life had come together once again. This wholeness lasted for perhaps two minutes as he ardently inhaled the smell that came through the window. When, overtaken by the joy of this wholeness, he left the window to go to the kitchen sink, he could not believe that he had to let go of this emotion, that this letting go was the most important step in becoming naked. Long after he had dropped the water glass, he understood . . . On his way to school . . . He suddenly realized the meaning of breaking the glass. But it was too late. The feeling of having brought his fragments together, the joy of having become whole, had already taken root in him. It could not be uprooted. He had failed to let go at the most crucial point. And the glass, he had broken it as if to pay retribution but there was nothing he could do

> anymore. Even his students' agitation did not catch his attention for some time. His stupor intensified, so did his numbness.

On the island, madness was no laughing matter. It was viewed as the gravest transgression, the worst illness. They cast madmen into the sea from the top of the rocky cliff on the other side of the island. In a land that knew almost no crime and only the lightest punishment, the attitude toward madness was the only thing he could not agree with. The islanders, too, admitted that the punishment was excessive, but refused to change it, arguing that upholding traditions was somehow indispensable to peace on the island.

He had dismissed every solution he could imagine. He had to get used to living with the heart-wrenching problem. He had to concede to the icy indolence dictated by the laws. Knowing only too well that this would be an escape and no solution, he decided to do to his money what the islanders did to madmen.

That evening he climbed the hill and went to the rocky cliff. The money, wrapped tightly in a handkerchief, felt as if it were piercing through his skin under his shirt. When he reached the top, he hesitated. Nobody would see him tossing his money into the sea, but where the waves carried the money would be another matter. If someone were to find the money, others would certainly hear about it, and the prospect of finding himself surrounded by gossip and having to pretend innocent curiosity to avoid raising suspicion terrified him. He decided to bury the money instead, amazed that he had not thought of it earlier. Taking out his pocketknife, he dug out a large stone, widened the hole underneath, and buried his money; he pushed the soil back into the hole and replaced the stone. Descending in the dark, he felt a deep sense of satisfaction. After eating his dinner, he sat in a café, worked a little, then went to bed. He slept deeply. In the morning, he opened the curtains that he kept closed to avoid mosquitoes and . . .

> At first, when he noticed the students' agitation, he tried to ignore their curious behavior and continue with the lesson, since he knew they worked hard and respected learning. Soon, however, he wanted to know the reason for their anxiety, and, trying not to appear too

concerned, he asked them. All the children started talking at once:

> Early that morning, a student who lived in one of the houses by the sea, the house right between the bakery and the docks, had gone to get octopus and fish—go get an octopus, his mother had told him—the boy was very good at this, his mother had already put the pot on the stove, the water would boil by the time he returned, he went to the bay, the same one he always went to, between Twin Rocks, though you would not know it existed because of the steep cliffs on both sides, but the children, and we discovered it as children, too—if you want, we can take you there, not that there is a lot of fish but climbing the rocks is hard and fun—and the boy arrived there . . .

What he could gather was this:

When the boy arrived there, he was startled, wondering at first if he had come to the wrong place. The bay was filled with soil, the rocks that rose above the water now rose above the soil. The cliffs on both sides had not collapsed or anything; they remained in place. The trees he knew, the brushwood he knew, they were all in place. Nor could the sea have simply receded. The soil was dry and packed hard. When the boy returned home, the water in the pot had been boiling for a long time. His mother was at first angry and scolded him, but when she heard what he had to say, she sent the neighbor's son who was three years older than him. When he returned, the neighbor's boy declared that the bay had vanished and then left in a hurry, rushing to tell his friends at school. The woman was all the more perplexed because her son told her that he had had to walk fifteen or twenty steps past the bay to reach the sea and catch the octopus.

He also drew the following conclusion:

The bay used to be narrow but deep. So it was unlikely that the sea could recede without anyone noticing and just as unlikely that strangers (or one stranger) could fill the bay. Since the boy had also mentioned that the trees and rocks were still in place, an erosion was out of question.

"What do you think, sir?" What could he think? Everything he had been told had reached every other islander's ears within thirty minutes, or at most an hour. Even as the students were entering the classroom, the island's leaders were sailing to inspect the bay from the sea. It would be best to reach a decision after the inspection.

That afternoon, nobody on the hill or by the sea talked about anything else. Those who had sailed out to inspect the bay had encountered the same situation in two other places. The sea was not receding at all. The new soil was hard, with almost no gravel or sand. It was also dry.

The needles on the finest seismometers at the earthquake station had not registered even the slightest tremor. Those who had grown accustomed to living with the fear of their island's destruction and had organized every aspect of their existence according to such an eventuality were rendered speechless in the face of this strange occurrence. Suddenly, a voice broke through the murmuring crowds in the cafés lining the square by the harbor. It was a sharp, child's voice, although it was not loud. The child was standing beside the teacher. Everybody realized then: people had been whispering, probably because they were afraid. Perhaps what the child said was childish. "Our island is growing," he said. They hushed him. Later, when they went to bed, they felt more frightened than ever. Sleep did not come easily.

The teachers did not sleep that night; they searched the books and their memories until daybreak. At dawn, they descended to the shore.

They had to believe their eyes. The sight surpassed their worst fears. The docks still extended to the sea but, on both sides, boats were grounded in the soil. The island seemed to be growing like a living creature, its body expanding in all directions.

In two days, the problem was identified. It was indeed a form of growth. It occurred at night and stopped during the day. The watchmen used high-powered flashlights and torches to investigate the phenomenon and witnessed the way a boat lingering in the water one moment was enveloped by a mass of dry soil the next. That was all they could witness. The number of watchmen had to be increased to make sure they slept soundly during the day and remained alert while on duty. But watches, diagnoses, the search for a solution, all this cost many precious days. On the morning of the third day, the islanders realized that they could not wait any longer. The sea in front of the docks had begun to disappear in places. They had to dig up the soil to salvage twelve fishing boats. The excavation took time. Commerce was interrupted. On the fifth day, the cause of the growth was still unknown. People began to throw malicious glances at those who had thoughtlessly complained at one time or another about the smallness of the island. To be fair, more than a few people must have at some point thought or said that the small island was indeed small. And those bothered by the accusing glances and words countered their accusers with, "you, too, that day, don't you remember, during geography course . . . in the café . . . on the ship," trying to remind them of their own words—words that the accusers must have forgotten or perhaps never uttered.

The Councilmen issued a decree banning the overconsumption of water and bread. They announced to the public that expert scientists had been summoned and would arrive in three days. The islanders became increasingly pessimistic about the possibility of finding a solution.

They had settled on this island even before written history and had managed to create order after centuries of fighting against the neighboring islands. The memory of these events still survived in hazy fables and legends. Once a year, for seven consecutive evenings, they would gather by the largest sandbank and listen to the bards who revived the fables and legends of the past without forgetting a single word. The number of bards had not changed for centuries. There were seven of them, each of whom recited for one night. Since they were forbidden to repeat the same narrative in successive years, each would complete the legend cycle in seven years and begin again in the eighth year. In the middle of the second seven-year cycle, each bard would begin training a new pupil. The training would last about seventeen years. Any bard who was exhausted before daybreak had to relinquish his place to his pupil.

The island's growth sent the bards into turmoil as well. They had always ended their fables at the point where school history books began. But now they wanted to seize the matter before the books did and avenge the mistreatment their words had received at the hands of history. History had to end at this point. The word had to belong to the bards and, when and if history resumed again, they had to fill in the gap with their stories. In a mad effort, they began piecing together a new legend. The next festival would have to last eight days. An eighth bard would join them. They decided to train the lowest ranking pupil, without worrying about confusing his young mind. They would train him regardless.

Now the islanders decided to have a daytime meeting by the same sandbank. A meeting of students, teachers, fishermen, bakers, and water carriers who had all left work for the occasion. The only people absent were the bards, or more precisely, the bards and their pupil. . . . They could predict what would be discussed, or so they presumed. If a decision were reached, they would comply with it anyway. They wanted to prepare the words that would recount the time after history came to an end.

Those who spoke at the gathering first summarized the bards' legends, then the accounts in history books; later, they expressed their feelings and thoughts concerning the island's expansion. Then the teachers reported on their research and observations to date and announced that they had started to search for preventive measures.

Right then, the red-winged bird of fear circled, gliding over the hills of the island.

There was no end to the speakers; the speeches became hurried and increasingly incomprehensible.

The expansion could incite greed among the neighbors; losing the new lands stood out as the worst of their fears; some were convinced that nothing good could come out of the growth since the island had lived for years planning against its dissolution; they could starve, die of thirst; they were not used to change; suddenly they were facing their limits; the dread of poverty seized them; if they failed to solve the problem, their forefathers would not forgive them; had the disciplined work of all these years ended up turning the ancestral land into a desert?

Everyone was speaking at once. The ancestors had established the order. It could not be destroyed, was being destroyed, must not be destroyed.

It would be destroyed.

As the red-winged bird of fear glided in the sky and disappeared, the chestnut-maned horse of revolt stirred up a sand cloud. Almost invisible, it ran the length of the sand and cast itself into the sea.

The shouts, "It will be destroyed," were swallowed by a vast silence that lasted a long time. Who had shouted this? The speakers had to come forth.

They were the sons of the oldest families who lived on the hill. There were eight of them. They began speaking with one voice, each facing a different direction.

"Our esteemed bards toil to add a new legend to their cycle. They struggle so that we won't forget our origins, but they don't join the meeting to save our land. We ask you, can those who behave in this way be truly concerned about the ancestral land?"

The silence continued. The bards had come to be seen as semisacred over the years. The youngsters were charging them with a crime that was barely less than madness. That itself was madness.

"At best, they deserve our contempt," the young men jeered. A wind of anger swept through the crowd. From all chests rose voices of derision that stirred the rocks and the soil.

"If the guards sleep, doesn't it mean that the ancestral order is bound for destruction?" asked the young men.

Another round of jeers followed, echoing through the land. The bards, sitting in their caves at the opposite end of the island, decided that the noise was too loud for them to continue working and took a ten-minute break from composing the fourth section of the fable they were preparing for the eighth evening.

"We have been talking here for three hours. Not a single boat has sailed, nor has the dough been kneaded. No one is attending to the ships approaching the harbor. How can the Council members who summoned us here claim to be concerned about the land?"

Ten Council members from the hill, another ten from the shore, the three teachers' representatives to the Council, all looked at each other; drawing together, they began to say, "We . . ." but, unprepared for the jeers, they quickly collapsed and were trampled on by the islanders.

"Enough!" shouted the youngsters. The crowd fell silent. "The bards and the Council have no power, as you've seen," they continued. "You were angry with us for shouting, 'It will be destroyed,' yet what hasn't been destroyed? Ask yourselves. Bakers, fishermen, water carriers, who among you had the good sense to say, 'Let's not all go to the gathering. Half of us should stay behind and do our jobs'?"

Silence. Even the birds circling above them were frightened and flew away. Some of the workers lowered their heads and scurried back to the marketplace. The eight young men continued to accuse others. As the silence lasted longer and longer, fewer and fewer people remained by the sandbank. The last few slowly grew confident that they would not be accused. The young men then began to soften their talk. They wanted to save the island from stagnation, from ancestral traditions that proved vulnerable and no longer meaningful; they were determined to create a new understanding, a new way of thinking. To this end, they would seize control of everything and cooperate with the only group that deserved no accusation of wrongdoing: the Research Team made up of eight teachers. Yet the teachers should not overestimate the meaning of this cooperation. They would merely provide guidance and conduct the necessary investigations.

That evening, the sixteen men put their heads together to discuss the state of the island and to debate solutions. First and foremost, they decided, the expansion had to be stopped. More precisely, the eight teachers saw no choice but to agree with the eight young men who had made the decision. They were not about to disappoint their former students. Only this was certain: none of their research or investigations had succeeded in illuminating the cause of the expansion. So what could be done? There were still fifty-seven hours before the experts were due to arrive. Not that it was certain that they would be able to do anything. When the young men increased the pressure on the teachers to come up with a solution, one of the teachers, perhaps feeling cornered, blurted out something to the effect that if they did not want the island to grow, it had to be halted, excavated. The young men responded with laughter. What were the teachers thinking?

But the teacher continued to speak—on what impulse even he knew not—defending his proposal excitedly. From time to time, he would glance at his colleagues, gesturing with his eyes and face, asking for support. He was amazed at his own vigor. He described an elaborate excavation project, detail after fine detail, as if he had been thinking and planning for days. He did not worry whether his listeners found anything worthwhile in his words. Was his mind in charge, or was his tongue working on its own? He could not tell. Then, he said, "that's it . . ." and stopped, as if the spring of his mental machine had snapped unexpectedly.

He pulled himself together. Out of fear, he could not look at anybody and fixed his gaze at the floor. The silence that followed gave him courage. They were not laughing any longer. Clearly they were considering his words. Raising his head, he came eye to eye with one of his colleagues. The vague smile breaking through the perplexed look made the familiar face somewhat alien to him.

How could he know that his friend was thinking of a broken glass, a pouch of money buried in the ground?

One of the youngsters interrupted the silence. "Let's adjourn, think carefully, and meet again in two hours to decide."

They adjourned.

> Money, glass, the island.
>
> But the island did not belong in the same string of words.
>
> His head was throbbing. He felt as though he were being forced to think in overused clichés, like "throbbing head." For the first time, he viewed madness, was able to view madness, in the rigid mold of the island's traditions. There was no point now in thinking like a teacher, in an educated, enlightened way. He had to be able to think like the rest who knew nothing, who *at this moment* knew nothing yet. But could he?
>
> Even this was nonsense. Madness. Worse madness than that of the bards who declared that history had stopped. He had to start over. The islanders had faced no difficulty until now. They had been able to live. Perhaps due to the feeling of transience they shared because of their fear of earthquakes. And this expansion was the exact opposite of what they had feared and awaited. The exact opposite of perishing by crumbling: what they had hoped would not happen, and, as it had not happened for centuries, what they had slowly begun to believe (though they did not have the heart to tell anyone) would not happen. Just when they were becoming convinced that their worst fears would not come true (though they acknowledged this conviction only now), they were facing something that had not even crossed their minds. A double disappointment of sorts. After spending centuries devising plans and measures against the devastation, the best they could do now was come up with one crazy idea. A solution that was even worse than the crazy, nonsensical one he had thought up a few days ago in order to get rid of his money

> He was sad that he could feel so detached, as though he were a tourist on the island and could leave whenever he wanted to. Not that he would. He had no place to return to. But that an unforeseen calamity could destroy the island
> But why destruction? Why didn't anyone seem to think of adjusting to the new condition? Perhaps this itself would be the cause of destruction. But to disclose his thoughts, to speak them out loud
> He could when the meeting resumed
> To perish in an unforeseen way like this would mean his own destruction as well. A dissolution. One that might even suit him.

When the group members reconvened, he asked to speak, and proposed his idea. They could wait to see whether the expansion would stop or not. Instead of using inadequate information to come up with a solution, when facing a natural phenomenon of unequaled character

> before his eyes paraded giant monstrous beasts, humans accustomed to hunger, still worse, to a life that had lost its balance

to observe the occurrence closely and find a fitting solution

The uproar overwhelmed his thoughts. When the young men calmed everyone down with extraordinary effort, he could not believe what he heard. It was obvious that he received little respect even as a teacher. Those who opposed him were his own students.

To begin with, everyone favored excavation, he had to accept this. Also, to be so indifferent to the fate of the island, as a stranger

He did not want to hear the rest. If he could abandon everything and sail away with nothing but his shirt on

Then again, the expanding land could be cultivated, the nature of our sea trade could change; besides in two days, the experts

His desperate attempt was cut short by stern voices. "Either you leave at once, or you obey our decision and follow every one of our measures."

He told them he would not leave.

His first job was to contact the experts. They were no longer needed. The islanders had already solved the problem by themselves. Afterward, the teacher was expected to join in the preparations for the excavation project.

He agreed. Why, he did not even want to know.

Before dusk, teams were assigned the task of excavating the island's docks, the three most important bays, and other areas where further land expansion would prove the most dangerous. The five-member teams would each work for three hours, and the shifts would last through the night.

The next morning, when the workers rested, the fishermen easily sailed off and the ships carrying flour docked and unloaded easily. The water carriers were able to transport water up the hill. The island returned to life.

In the Council room, the young men and the teachers had pushed the extra chairs to a corner and were sitting more comfortably than the old Council used to. There was no avoiding the vainglory of the teacher who had first proposed the idea of excavation. Since the solution seemed successful, the group wanted to attend to other matters. In two hours, all matters were settled.

The group met again in the afternoon and received neighborhood delegates who wanted to express their joy. Later, the group decided to increase the number of excavation teams and dig out other areas that had previously expanded.

On the morning of the third day, the Executive Committee, for so they called themselves, sat in the meeting room and waited to receive news of final victory. No one showed up. Toward noon, after finishing work, the members adjourned somewhat disappointedly. Yet what they heard brought them back together within less than an hour. On account of the additional excavation teams, daily work on the island had been interrupted. The sandbank where all the residents had gathered had transformed into a vast plateau because no excavation work had been done there. After weighing options, some islanders ventured: "Let's farm the land. It could be profitable." Who gave them the idea, others asked. The teacher was accused, threatened, told that his punishment would be severe if he encouraged such thinking. At the same time, no one wanted to be too harsh with him since, after much debate, all admitted that the idea of cultivating the land was not so outlandish as to require outside provocation. Nevertheless, it was officially declared on behalf of the Committee that participating in the excavation effort was, for the time being, a more pressing duty than farming. And thus was the initiative suppressed. In the evening, fishermen returning from the sea reported that boats from surrounding islands were sailing disturbingly close to the island. There was nothing startling about this, they were told. As the island widened, it grew closer to the other islands.

The Executive Committee realized that matters were becoming complicated.

It was decided that work would continue around the clock and the teams would be organized to remain on duty day and night; fewer workers would be responsible for the daily business of the island; shifts would be increased from three to six hours; given the general fatigue induced by such intense labor, minor interruptions in daily routines would have to be tolerated.

The Executive Committee had no time to assess whether its thinking was sound.

Now the island was growing during the day as well.

The teachers on the Committee proposed that the schools be closed. In turn, the eight young men asked the hill residents to move into tents that were set up on the shore. This way, services would be provided more easily.

In four days, the pickaxes no longer proved adequate for the task. One of the teachers designed a machine that would excavate in one hour what it took ten people three hours to dig. With the limited resources available, however, only three machines could be constructed, provided that twenty-nine people worked twelve-hour shifts for three days. The work started immediately.

Depositing the excavated soil and rocks in the sea was, of course, out of the question. That much had become clear. Initially, the workers had tried to load the excess soil into boats and ferry it to the open sea, but as the task soon proved unmanageable, they began to transport it to the uninhabited rocky area behind the town. Now, as they looked up from their work, they saw all around them strange new formations: tall mounds of soil overtaking the terrain.

The Executive Committee saw no reason to impose rigid rules in addition to those governing steady labor. But the edict issued on the morning of the twelfth day was quite shocking. It prohibited all forms of sexual activity. For obvious reasons, it stated, the island's population had to remain unchanged until the situation was brought under control. More important, at a time when the residents had to work two six-hour shifts daily, they had to resist the demeaning frailty of sexual desire and preserve their energy for the solemn and pressing task of digging.

The people were perplexed by this edict. The meeting of two people at home, in the same room, had already become nearly impossible. The very young children had been put on alarm-clock duty and were required to wake up the adults for their shifts. Day after laborous day divided between digging and six hours of sleep had brought the islanders near to complete exhaustion.

By the time the machines were ready, they had to be used not to excavate but to push the spreading mounds of excess soil farther away from the shore.

People dug and dug, finding no time even to notice their surroundings. Because of the mounds piling around them, they did not leave the work site at breaks and curled asleep wherever possible. Nothing was visible but the forever rising mounds.

On the morning of the fourteenth day, one of the machines was taken to the shore to demolish the first row of houses that used to overlook the sea.

The ongoing investigations—whoever was conducting them, no one knew, except perhaps the Executive Committee members, as the diggers saw no one but the other diggers—the ongoing investigations confirmed that the worst expansion was occurring by the mansions along the shore (that is, what used to be the shore). Therefore the work had to concentrate on that area.

While the demolition of houses continued, the hill (its outline gradually disappearing between the rising mounds) was overtaken by the terrific roar of the other two machines.

That evening, the workers noticed the sound slowly dimming, as if it were traveling through heavy fog; they stopped digging and clawed their way up the mounds. They were surprised to see the machines still running at full speed. As night descended upon them, they realized that they had lost much of their hearing and were almost deaf. "Because of the noise of the machines," they told themselves and continued digging.

The next morning, they worked in perfect silence. They were now as deaf as nails. To their right, to their left, the mounds continued to pile up: the sole evidence that others were still working. Food tents were set up close to the work sites. When the shifts ended, the workers would go to eat before sleeping or trying to look after their own business, that is, if they were near the stores. For those stationed too far from the stores, there was nothing to do but dig. They could still switch shifts, but among the mounds, finding their way around or locating the food tents had become increasingly difficult. Each passing day, there was less and less to eat and it had less and less taste to it.

Shifts were increased again; rest became little more than a promise on paper. Aside from the written directives that somehow always reached the work sites, communication ceased. People had neither the time nor the energy to hear from one another.

They were asked to work harder and harder, to sleep and rest on the site, and then plunge themselves back into work. No time could be wasted on the roads. Children would deliver the food. These were the last of the written directives which were also broadcast on the radio, although the radio employees were probably the only ones on the island who still had their hearing. Yet, because exactly who could and could not hear was never determined, the radio announcements were repeated a few times daily.

On the third day of deafness, one of the workers died while operating the excavation machine stationed on the steep incline. He fell to the ground, as though struck by lightning. It was a heart attack. The workers had moved the machine to this site after demolishing the shoreline houses. The death did not cause confusion at the work site because an official directive had already spelled out the due process. His friends buried him reasonably well under a nearby mound, assigned another worker to operate the machine, and promptly returned to their tasks. They worked until a little girl arrived with their meal. They sent with her the news that they were one fewer. Toward evening, as the team began its second shift, the teacher arrived as his replacement. The workers were very intrigued: had it been decided that the Executive Committee members, too, had to work, or was the teacher sent for another reason? But they did not ask; they had no time to ask.

The teacher did not tell his teammates that, three days ago, the rocky cliff behind the island had collapsed because of the mass of excavated soil heaped against it; that the part of the hill once leaning against the rocky cliff had caved in, destroying an entire neighborhood along with the schools; that many had died, many trapped under the avalanche of soil. There was no way of knowing the extent of the devastation because the only place from which the entire island could be seen had become unreachable since the landslide. The Executive Committee had run out of measures to enact and decided to assign its members to the teams so that they could both work and assess firsthand the state of the shoreline. It was not even clear whether the Committee would reconvene after the assessment was complete. But the teacher did not mention any of this either. Besides, no one could hear well enough to understand. The Executive Committee was deaf now, like everybody else.

When the little girl who brought their meal did not show up in the evening, they were not worried. Perhaps she would be a little late, or perhaps they felt hunger sooner than usual. Having nothing else to do, they worked until it started to get dark. When the girl did not come, they opened their reserve supply and ate one ration. When it was completely dark, they decided that sleeping would be the sensible thing to do and lay on the ground.

At daybreak, the teacher woke up, his body aching all over, as if he had been badly beaten overnight. He noticed the sharp smell of wet soil. He picked up his pickax. No one was in sight bringing food. Should he venture to find the food tent? He was reluctant to. He took out his second ration and ate it. The mounds of freshly dug soil appeared to have changed shape in the course of the night. As he ate, he stared around drowsily; he could see the change but could not pinpoint exactly what had happened. And how exhausted he was! Since he had woken, his feet had been in water. He did not even wonder why the others did not wake him up. But, after some digging, he noticed that none of his team members were around. The mounds were changing shape but not expanding, he was sure of that. He circled a couple of them and saw the tips of a few pickaxes and two or three pairs of feet. His friends were trapped underneath.

He remembered the silent movies. Again. The showings of silent films of his youth. The faint music had served to remind them that they were not deaf. When the rocky cliff collapsed, nobody had either heard the roaring fall or felt any tremors. They had discovered the devastation afterward. This particular landslide, too, must have occurred silently—without tremors, of course. . . . Anyway, it was not unusual not to have felt tremors; the soil was loose. Why had he escaped death, he wanted to understand. But he hesitated. He would continue digging instead.

The sun had risen; his arms were spent.

For days (or was it for hours, he could not tell) he had found no time to think. Now he could rest and think.

The landslide had missed him; obviously, it was because the soil had slid toward the sea. The other workers must have fallen asleep close to the water. Quite possible, it seemed. He tried to envision how they had looked the last time he saw them. He had fallen asleep farther back, on top of a mound. He had slept through the first rays of sunshine and was awakened only when his feet got wet. Now the water was up to his ankles. It seemed as though the mounds were dissolving. Staring blankly, he noticed that the water was rising.

He was exhausted enough not to wonder whether or not he should be afraid. He tried to climb the heaps of loose soil, away from the sea, away from the approaching water. He was surprised to find that he could move without too much effort. He was walking, but the sea was following him.

Apparently, the expansion had stopped. The excavation project had reached its goal, and perhaps exceeded it. He managed a vague smile.

From where he stood, he could see the entire coastline. All of it. He must have reached the top of the hill. The hill that had disappeared among the rising mounds of soil. Everywhere, he could see mounds collapsing, toppling, dissolving. The water was fast approaching him. Emerging from the soil, a flat stone caught his eye. He went and sat on the stone. He felt dizzy. The water ebbed and flowed, loosening more of the soil around the stone. Suddenly among the wavelets, he noticed paper bills floating. In the corner of his mouth, he felt a sharp twinge. Perhaps these were his bills. The money he had buried a few weeks ago. Perhaps they belonged to someone else. . . .

He felt the twinge again.

His knees were now in the water. Around him, the sea spread endlessly, almost calm. The water rose to his waist. He did not move.

A torso, then just a head. The only thing left behind. It would not last much longer. . . .

Translated from the Turkish by Aron R. Aji

Have the gods cursed me?
At the gate
someone has planted a mango.
Its leaves are poison.
When the first fragrant bud unfolds
my womb begins
to itch madly for love.

My lover
stepped toward the bed.
Somehow the skirt
clung to my hips
but the knot came undone by itself.
What can I say?
Nothing makes sense in his arms—
not who I am
not who is taking me.
Is it me that comes?
Is it him?

You ignored
the turning seasons of love,
shook off advice
and treated your lover with
cold disregard.
You gathered the bright
coals of betrayal
against your own bare breasts,
yet cry wildly in rage
a wounded
beast in the forest.

Vikatanitamba
(circa early 9th century)

Those long first days of
untempered love
my body and
your body were never apart.
You came to be my cherished lord,
I the desolate mistress.
The seasons turned.
Now you're the husband
I'm the wife—
what have the years wrought?
Life must be cruel as a thunderbolt
if this is
how it ends.

Bhavadevi
(date unknown)

Black swollen clouds
drench the far
forests with rain.
Scarlet *kadamba* petals toss on the storm.
In the foothills
peacocks cry out and make love,
and none of it touches me.
It's when the lightning
flings her bright
veils like a rival woman
that a flood of
grief surges through.

Vidya
(circa 6th century)

Translated from the Sanskrit
by Andrew Schelling

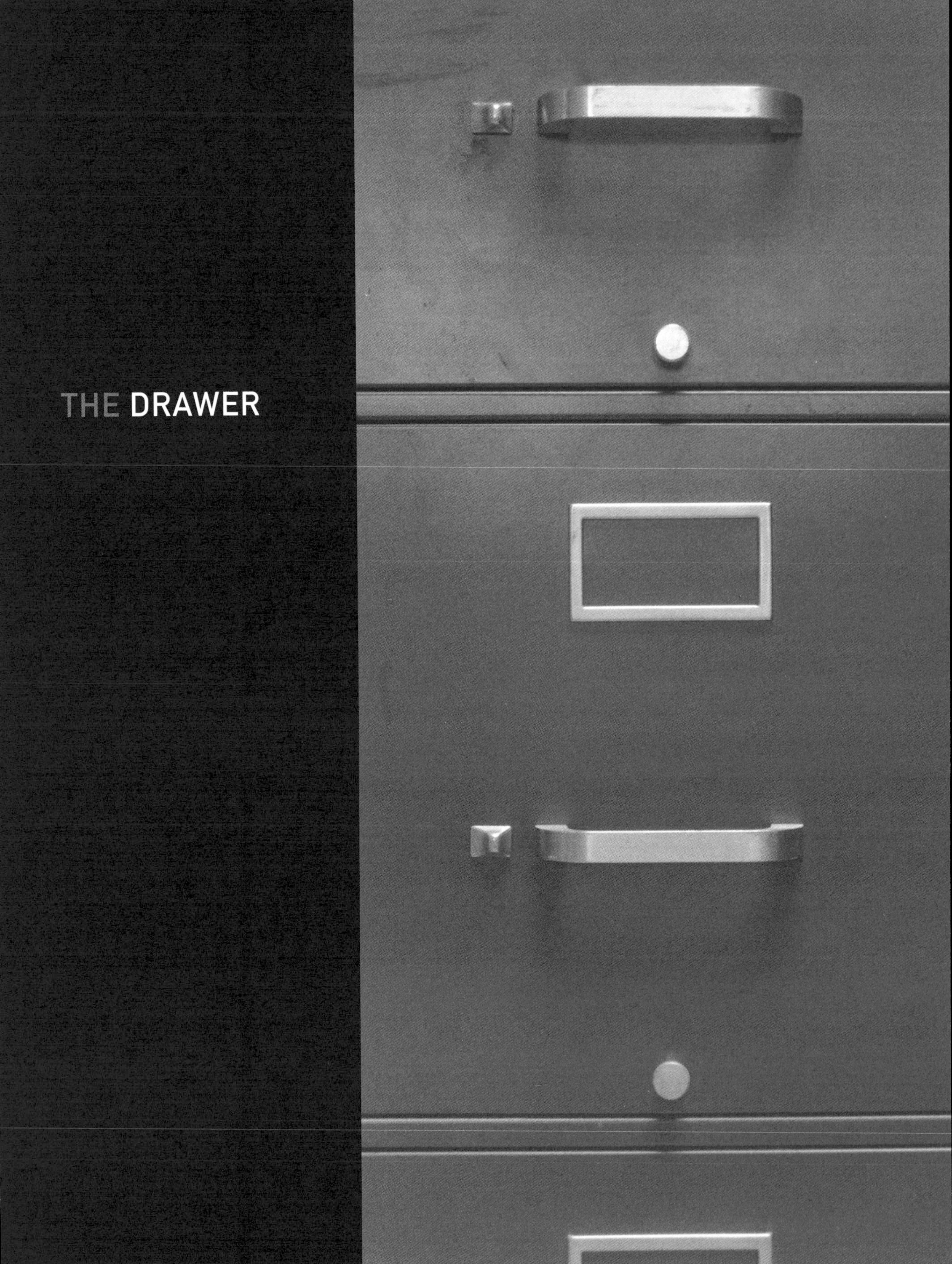

THE DRAWER

ALINA DIACONÚ

I'll tell you: it was about a month ago. I walked into my office as usual.

The day was perfect; one of those days when all the impossible ideas that you ever had pass through your mind: get into the car, for example, and take a road, any road, and drive straight until you arrive somewhere, anywhere, even the most remote, prosaic little village, where a giant void sits in a town plaza with three lonely trees and an ugly white chapel, an absurd and insipid place, but one that can suddenly become sublime; and then something grows inside you, and you feel somewhat like the master of time, a hero of insignificance, and the plaza is no longer a plaza but the garden of Versailles, and the chapel is no longer a chapel but Reims Cathedral, and for some strange reason you don't understand, you dream up an element of happiness for the end, because, after all, what's more important than greasing the wheels of those hidden mechanisms of invention, the ones that bring you closer to that thing, that great thing called freedom.

I'm telling you all this, really, to explain somehow the crazy urge that swept through my mind that day, a little over a month ago, and that's just what it was: the urge to escape.

I have a comfortable office, with a big picture window overlooking the Plaza San Martín. My feet sink into the mustard-green plush carpet, my arms rest on top of the jacaranda desk, and that is exactly how I am supposed to appear, as seen from the other side of the desk: a solemn persona with a powerful demeanor; nevertheless, despite the luxury, the lovely, panoramic view, and everything else, something was disturbing me that morning and I didn't know exactly what it was: the sun that beckoned me to adventure, the monotony of passing through another day on the calendar, another day like so many others, the jacaranda desk, the mustard-green carpet, the image of the Plaza San Martín, the café *ristretto* in the blue ceramic cup, the voice of my secretary, and her unbearable perfume that invaded my nose. I don't know if it was this or the meeting, a long conversation in English that would last three hours minimum, and who knew how many hours maximum, with the usual break to "informally" eat finger sandwiches and turkey canapés at the table in the conference room, or to go to the corner and have a boring, rich, indigestible business lunch with our guests at a four-star restaurant. It all depended on what our guests wanted or what our president wanted—although recently he had become a little indecisive.

Impossible to get into the car, put on a good tape, and drive straight, always straight, following that elusive horizon, fortunately elusive, for that is where the secret of true adventure resides.

Impossible to believe in the magic of paths, in unexpected and definitive encounters, an ethereal creature with a wicker basket filled with daisies and a decadent floppy hat or a girl with long brown hair and a necklace made of conch shells, with teeth of pearl and small sharp breasts. Impossible, the islands and the fans and the palm trees and warm smiles; impossible, too, that small-town plaza with three lonely trees where I was going to recreate the garden of Versailles, the *vitraux* of Reims Cathedral, the kaleidoscope of my forbidden dream. I am a man with no time.

I sat back in my swivel chair, resigned to the everyday routine, and I glanced, distracted, over to the wooden in-box that held my "unfinished business" papers—how could I finish anything at all, with a mind that wanted only to drift away somewhere? Automatically, I took out my keys to open my desk drawer.

Precisely at the moment when I was placing the key in the lock, I discovered to my consternation that my drawer no longer existed. My finger attacked the intercom button furiously and my secretary, with her innate, mechanical efficiency, was in my office before I had even finished transmitting my message.

I made her come over to where I was sitting and ordered her to look. Her grayish eyes grew bigger, and the unbearable perfume emanated from her in waves, destroying the olfactory integrity of my nose. And my fury was so overwhelming, so thunderous, that I felt capable of anything; of opening the window, for example, throwing myself into the Plaza San Martín, like one of the thousands of doves that I saw there every day, and posing on the shoulder of an illustrious statesman or on a horse's mane. I don't think I really cared. At that moment I didn't really care about anything.

"What happened to the drawer?" I cried, and I actually scared myself when I heard my own voice rebounding off the glass windows, off the hollow walls painted with lacquer (that ultra-modern, African-brown lacquer), onto the most hollow walls, which were even more fragile than my own cranial cavity.

Her face took on a rather intense shade of fuchsia that dominated her cheeks, her gray eyes welled up, her head inclined downward toward the mustard-green plush carpet, and her shoulders rose in a desperate "I don't know."

I tried to calm down. I opened my top shirt button and loosened my elegant new Lanvin tie, and I observed her. I felt pity for her, felt pity for myself, and finally stammered:

"I'm sorry, but . . ."

The sentence had no meaning, but for her it was gospel, and immediately she raised her eyes and smiled sweetly; her fingers wiped away the tears that had formed shining rivulets on her rose-colored cheeks, and she whispered:

"I will find out, sir. I will find out."

Needless to say, the drawer did not reappear that day.

During a night of insomnia, from one Valium to another, from the thousands of miles my bare feet traveled from the living room to the music room to the library, as I walked through my house, inch by inch, measuring it unconsciously, I nearly went insane trying to remember exactly which papers had been in that goddamned drawer—papers that might reveal the reasons why this had happened to me. The only papers that came to mind were the gas, electricity, and phone bills I had put in the drawer the previous day, some photographs of my wife and son that I had taken the previous year in Oslo, a few packs of cigarettes, some loose tobacco, two pipes, the folder with the rejected proposal for a future industrial project. What else? My mind went blank.

Obviously, there wasn't anything too important in that drawer, aside from the project in question and my bills; the project was not a real project anymore, and the bills, they would be easy enough to replace.

Nevertheless, for some reason, that drawer had been taken away. The true cause of this larceny was something my memory failed to recall. Espionage, corporate competition, a conspiracy.

All right, a few bars of Debussy and then I will remember. A bit of Debussy and surely I'll understand the motive for the crime, the name of the criminal, everything.

Slowly, I turned on the Debussy recording and closed the door. I leaned back on the sofa, lit a cigarette. And I waited. I waited a while, through the entire *Prélude à 'L'après-midi d'un faune'*, but for once Debussy didn't help me. Nothing became clear, not the crime nor the name or names of the delinquents in question. It was all an endless vortex of hypotheses, of imaginary persecutions, until the second Valium began to take its cloudy effect on me, and everything was lost in the fog of drowsiness from which I emerged two hours later, waking up in the same spot where I had fallen asleep, in the music room, with the lights and the stereo still on.

I'm sorry. Let me get back to the story. I don't want to bore you.

That same morning I arrived at the office early, anxious to hear of any news, but I found myself in the same situation as the previous day. My secretary had spoken with everybody. She had filed a report with Security, in all the other divisions of the company—even the president was required to notify her if he knew anything. Apparently nobody knew a thing about the drawer.

Distraught, I went into my office. I sat down again at my jacaranda desk and looked down again, to the right, at the rectangular hole that used to be my beloved drawer, and a series of shivers traveled up and down my anguished body. On the windowsill, two doves were making love. Everything was the same. The plaza. "What color is San Martín's white horse?" I asked myself, in an effort to revive my sense of humor and penchant for levity. Fruitless. Everything was the same: the Roux painting before my eyes, the walls painted in African brown, the mustard-green plush carpet, the chamois chair, the cheap plastic table, and the enormous fern. Everything was the same. Except me.

A few moments later, my secretary would delicately carry in the cup, the small blue ceramic cup with coffee—freshly ground, made by her own industrious hands with their short fingers and painted nails.

"A wonderful *ristretto*."

The sky was irate, like me. Dark clouds mounted above the plaza, threatening the statesman's peace.

A fireplace . . . a fireplace inside a cabin, that was all I wanted now, all I wanted in the whole world. Me, sitting on the floor, with a glass of cognac, watching the flames, and listening to a thousand drops of rain hammer down onto the roof. The thick raindrops hurtling down in an infernal symphony, the frightening and incredible music of nature.

What leisure. A slow fog was rolling in over my eyelids; no, I didn't even care where I was, if it were a cabin in Bariloche or in Switzerland, if I were alone or with someone. No, better alone . . . no, better to be with a pretty girl, a mute young lady, a mysterious woman wrapped in tulle, eyes half-closed, pale lips, all in white, white and silent, impenetrable, impossible to know, a human being truly impossible to know, that was what I wanted more than anything that day as it rained. And a cabin. And a fireplace. And a cognac.

All of a sudden, a long and terrifying clap of thunder, and the drops began to fall deafeningly between violent gusts of wind. My secretary entered my office (I had long forgotten the coffee), interrupting my idyllic dream of the mute Garbo and the cabin and the fire and the rain.

"Why are you sitting in the dark?" she asked.

She had a point. I stood up from my swivel chair to turn on the light. But another surprise awaited me that morning, a morning that had seemed like every other. The lamp was no longer sitting on my desk. There was no lamp sitting on my desk.

"I can't take it anymore!" I shouted, terrified.

"Where is his lamp?" I could hear my secretary murmuring, while my screams came one after the other, growing louder each time. Then she came over to me:

"Calm down, sir, please . . ."

My lamp, my lovely lamp with the delicate vellum shade, my incomparable handmade lamp, made to order and ordered by me, made from the old silver candlestick holder bought at the flea market in Paris.

"Where is my lamp . . ." I mumbled weakly.

"Where is his lamp . . ." she repeated moronically.

Days passed. After the drawer and the lamp, the two glass ashtrays, the cheap plastic table, the telephone, the chamois chair, the carpet, the intercom, the television, the computer, the Roux painting.

This morning, when I went into my office . . . You won't believe me. Please believe what I say. This morning, when I entered my office, or workplace, or whatever you want to call it, even my desk had disappeared. There was nothing. And what was there wasn't even an office anymore, but rather an empty space. Emptied. My secretary borrowed a chair for me and I sat down, alone in that deserted field.

I looked out the window. Some doves flew around San Martín's shoulders.

I know: What I would like is to get into the car and take a road, any road, and drive straight until I arrive somewhere, anywhere, even the most remote, prosaic little village, and then . . . then . . . what pleasure, to sit on a park bench by the three lonely trees and the chapel in front of them, and be free, nothing more, be free and look up at the sun. But I am a slave, tied to a chair, a man with no time, in the wrong place, at the wrong time.

Translated from the Spanish by Kristina Cordero

CONTRIBUTORS

Aron R. Aji is an associate professor of Comparative Literature at Butler University in Indianapolis. He is the editor of *Milan Kundera and the Art of Fiction* (Garland Press) and has published articles on Salman Rushdie, Milan Kundera, Chinua Achebe, and others.

Teresa Allen is a journalist who has held staff reporting positions at a number of metropolitan newspapers and news organizations, including the *Marin Independent Journal*, *The Seattle Times*, and *The San Jose Mercury News*. She has twice been named Best Writer of the Year by the Gannett Newspaper Company. Since 1994, Allen has been an associate professor of Journalism at Boston University. She has also taught Reporting and Writing at San Francisco State University and at the University of Colorado at Boulder. Since she was assigned to cover California's San Quentin Prison in 1985, she has come to focus on and specialize in crime reporting, prison culture, and death-row issues. Her interview with Andrea Hicks Jackson published in this issue of *Grand Street* will appear, in different form, in her book *Honey, This Ain't No Country Club: Women Doing Hard Time*.

Nuha Al-Radi was born in Baghdad in 1941. She trained as a ceramist at Chelsea Pottery in London, and has had many solo exhibitions in Iraq, Lebanon, Jordan, Kuwait, the United Arab Emirates, the United Kingdom, and the United States. After thirty years as a ceramist, she began painting, etching, and sculpting. Excerpts from the diary she kept while living in Baghdad during the Gulf War appeared in *Granta 42*. *Diary of an Embargo* is the sequel to her *War Diary*.

Marcel Beyer was born in 1965. His first novel, *Das Menschenfleish*, was described by the *Süddeutsche Zeitung* as a masterpiece. He received Germany's Ernst Willner Prize for his second novel, *Flughunde* (Suhrkamp Verlag), from which the passages published in this issue of *Grand Street* were excerpted. *Flughunde* will be published as *The Karnau Tapes* (Helen & Kurt Wolff/Harcourt Brace) in the fall of 1997. Beyer lives in Dresden, Germany.

John Brownjohn's hundred book translations, among them best-sellers such as *The Night of the Generals* and *The Boat*, have won literary awards on both sides of the Atlantic. He is also a screenwriter whose credits include *Tess*, *The Name of the Rose*, and *Bitter Moon*. His latest film, written in collaboration with Roman Polanski, is currently in preproduction. He lives in Dorset, England.

Kristina Cordero is a writer, translator, and editor living in New York City. In 1993, she received a Bachelor's degree in Romance Languages from Harvard University. Since then, she has contributed to *Let's Go: Spain and Portugal*, *Let's Go: Europe*, *Salon Magazine*, and *Condé Nast Traveler*. Her first book, *Frommer's Complete Hostel Vacation Guide to England, Wales, & Scotland*, was published in 1996. She has translated Alberto Fuguet's *Bad Vibes* (St. Martin's Press) and Ray Loriga's *My Brother's Gun* (St. Martin's Press), and is currently at work on her third translation.

Laura Dail's most recent translations include *Four Hands* by Paco I. Taibo II and a manuscript attributed to Eva Peron and published in the collection *In My Own Words: Evita*. She holds a degree in Linguistics from Duke University and a Master's degree in Spanish Literature from Middlebury College. She is a literary agent in New York.

Connie Deanovich is the author of *Watusi Titanic* (Timken Publishers) and editor of *B City*. Her 27-section poem documenting the lunar and imaginative cycles, *The Spotted Moon*, is receiving wide serial publication in journals such as *New American Writing*, *Hambone*, and others.

Lewis deSoto is an artist who works in San Francisco and New York. His work has been exhibited at Metronóm, Barcelona, Bill Maynes Contemporary Art, New York, and Christopher Grimes Gallery, Santa Monica. His work is included in the collections of the Museum of Modern Art, New York, the Museum of Contemporary Art, Los Angeles, and the Des Moines Art Center, Iowa. He is currently completing a public project for the San Francisco Arts Commission at the San Francisco Municipal Courthouse. He received a National Endowment for the Arts Fellowship in 1996.

Alina Diaconú was born in Bucharest, Romania. In 1959, she and her parents emigrated to Buenos Aires, Argentina, where she obtained Argentine citizenship. Her poetry has appeared in translation in *Exquisite Corpse*, and she is the author of seven novels, published in Argentina, several of which have been translated into foreign languages. She is also a columnist for the Argentine magazine, *Cultura*, and a frequent contributor to other major newspapers. She has received several awards and honors, including a Fulbright Fellowship, which brought her to the International Writers Program at the Iowa Writers Workshop in 1985. Diaconú lives in Buenos Aires. *The Drawer* appeared in Spanish in her first collection of short stories, *¿Qué nos pasa, Nicolás?* (Editorial Atlántida).

Eugenio Dittborn has been working on *The Airmail Paintings* series since 1984. *The Airmail Paintings* travel to and from Chile, via airmail, with their exhibition itinerary recorded, along with an explanatory text, on the exterior of the envelope. Seven multi-panel paintings were recently exhibited at the New Museum of Contemporary Art, New York, and an extensive selection will be shown at the Museum of Fine Arts, Santiago, in March 1998. Dittborn lives and works in Santiago, Chile.

Geoff Hargreaves was educated at the Universities of Oxford, North Wales, and Victoria. He has taught in Spain and Mexico. He currently teaches at Frances Kelsey School in Mill Bay, British Columbia, Canada.

Mona Hatoum was born in Beirut to Palestinian parents and has lived in London since 1975. Her work has appeared in the group exhibitions: *Sense and Sensibility* at the Museum of Modern Art, New York; *Cocido y Crudo* at the Centro de Arte Reina Sofia, Madrid; *Identity and Alterity* at the Venice Biennale; and *Rites of Passage* and *The Turner Prize '95* at the Tate Gallery, London. A solo exhibition of her work was held at the Centre Georges Pompidou, Paris, in 1994. The first solo museum presentation of her work in the United States opened at the Museum of Contemporary Art, Chicago, in the summer of 1997, and will travel to the New Museum of Contemporary Art, New York, in December 1997.

Laird Hunt is the author of *Snow Country: Fragments for Radio* (Rodent Press).

Anna Indych is a doctoral candidate at New York University's Institute of Fine Arts, who specializes in the field of Latin American and Latino Art. She is also currently an adjunct instructor at New York University's College of Arts and Sciences.

Andrea Hicks Jackson was born in 1958. She was convicted for the murder of a police officer and sentenced to death in 1984. Since then, she has been an inmate at the Broward Correctional Institute in southern Florida. Her sentence has been reversed and reinstated twice since 1989.

Frank Janney is the president and founder of Ediciones del Norte, a publishing house devoted to Latin American writers. He teaches and performs classical guitar and raises horses in Vermont.

Ronald R. Janssen teaches Modern Literature at Hofstra University. He is currently translating Zhang Cheng Zhi's *A History of the Soul*.

Bilge Karasu was born in Istanbul in 1930. Upon receiving his degree in Philosophy from the College of Literature at Istanbul University, he worked at the National Office of Publications and at the Foreign Correspondence division of Ankara Radio. He held a Rockefeller Grant from 1962 to 1963, and, in 1974, he assumed a faculty position at Hacettepe University in Ankara. Karasu's translation of D. H. Lawrence's *The Man Who Died* won the Turkish Language Association's translation award. Among his works in Turkish are *Death in Troy* (1963), *A Long Day's Evening* (1970), *The Garden of Migrant Cats* (1979), *The Kiosk Called Kismet* (1982), and *The Guide* (1992). In 1991, his novel, *Night* (Louisiana State University Press), won the international Pegasus Award. Karasu died in 1995.

Clifford E. Landers is a professor of Political Science at Jersey City State College. His translations from Brazilian Portuguese include novels by Rubem Fonseca, Jorge Amado, João Ubaldo Ribeiro, Patrícía Melo, Chico Buarque, Jõ Soares, and Marcos Rey, as well as shorter fiction by Lima Barreto, Rachel de Queiroz, and Osman Lins. He is currently translating the nineteenth-century romantic classic, *Iracema*, by José de Alencar.

José Luandino Vieira was born in Portugal in

1936 and grew up in a shantytown in Angola, where he was educated by Jesuit priests. He served eleven years in prison for his participation in the Angolan independence movement. *The Asphalt Frontier*, like all of his writing published to date, was originally composed in prison and rewritten from memory. It appeared in Portuguese in his collection *A Cidade e a Infância* (Edições 70, 1978). Luandino Vieira lives in Angola.

Marcello Mastroianni was born in Fontana Lira, Italy, in 1924. The son of poor peasants, he was sent to a German labor camp during World War II. After the war, he went to Rome, where he worked as an accounting clerk and began acting with a university troupe. In 1947, he made his screen debut in an Italian version of *Les Misérables* and, the following year, joined Luchino Visconti's stage stock company. He went on to star in such films as Visconti's *White Nights*, Fellini's *La Dolce Vita* and *81/2*, Antonioni's *La Notte*, and Germi's *Divorce, Italian Style*. Mastroianni was named Best Foreign Actor by the British Film Academy for *Divorce, Italian Style* and *Yesterday, Today, and Tomorrow*, and he won the Best Actor Prize at Cannes for *The Pizza Triangle* and *Dark Eyes*. He died in Paris in 1996. *Like an Old Elephant* appears in his book *I Remember*, which will be published in Italy by Baldini & Castoldi in the fall of 1997.

Jackie McAllister recently collaborated with artist Diana Balton to design a new national flag for Scotland. Their design was one of ten selected by the *Stirling Flag Project*, organized by Edinburgh's Independent Public Arts, to be enlarged (to one by two meters) and produced as a flag that was flown at different public sites in Stirling, Scotland, in July 1997.

Charles Merewether is curator of Spanish- and Portuguese-language cultures at the Getty Research Institute. He has taught at the Universidad Nacional de Bogota, the University of Sydney, the Universidad Autonoma, Barcelona, and the Universidad Iberoamericana, Mexico City. He is the author of the forthcoming *What Remains: Ana Mendieta*, as well as *Art and Social Commitment: An End to the City of Dreams 1931–1948* (Art Gallery of New South Wales, 1984). He has written extensively on the reinvention of modernism in non-European cultures, especially in Latin America, on violence and the aesthetics of redemption, and more recently on cultural memory and monuments. He is currently writing a book on art and the archive.

Christopher Middleton is an English poet and translator. His most recent book is *Intimate Chronicles* (Sheep Meadow Press). A collection of short prose, *In the Mirror of the Eighth King*, will be published by Green Integer, and Sun & Moon Press is reissuing his collection, *Andalusian Poems* (David R. Godine).

Fabio Morábito was born to Italian parents in Alexandria, Egypt, in 1955. He spent his childhood in Milan and, in 1969, moved with his family to Mexico. He writes all of his works in Spanish, his second language. In 1985, his book of poems, *Lotes baldios*, won the Carlos Pellicer Prize. His latest book, a work of allegorical fiction, *Las panteras no eran negras* (Siruela), won the 1997 White Raven Prize for Children's Fiction in Munich. An English translation of his book

Toolbox, from which the passages published in this issue of *Grand Street* were excerpted, is forthcoming from Crown Publishers in the fall of 1998. Morábito will participate in the German Writer's Program in Berlin from 1998 to 1999.

Peter A. Nagy is an artist who divides his time between New York and New Delhi.

Shirin Neshat was born in Iran. She received a Master of Fine Arts degree from the University of California, Berkeley, in 1983. Her most recent solo exhibitions were held at Annina Nosei Gallery, New York, Lumen Travo Galerie, Amsterdam, and Lucio Amelio Gallery, Naples. She has participated in numerous group exhibitions, including *Le Masque et le Miroir* at the Museum of Contemporary Art, Barcelona, and *foto text/text foto* at the Museum of Modern Art, Bolzano, Italy, and the Frankfurt Kunstverein, Germany. Her work has been featured in the 1996 Sydney Biennale, the 1995 Venice Biennale, and the 1995 Istanbul Biennale. Her work will be part of the 1997 Johannesburg Biennale. A monograph of her work was recently published by Marco Noire Press in Turino, Italy. Neshat lives in New York City and is represented by Annina Nosei Gallery, New York, and Hosfelt Gallery, San Francisco.

Michael O'Brien's most recent book of poems, *The Floor and the Breath*, was published in 1994 by Cairn Editions, New York.

Pepón Osorio was born in Puerto Rico and moved to the South Bronx, New York, in 1975. His recent installations include *The Scene of the Crime (Whose Crime?)*, which was included in the 1993 Whitney Biennial, *En la barbería no se llora (No Crying Allowed in the Barbershop)*, which was commissioned by Real Art Ways, Hartford, Connecticut, *Badge of Honor* (1995), which was commissioned by the Newark Museum, New Jersey, and *El Cab* (1997), a public-art project circulating throughout the South Bronx and Manhattan. Upcoming exhibitions include *Fear & Denial*, an installation at Centro Cultural/Arte Contemporáneo, Mexico City, and the installation of *En la barbería no se llora* in a 1997–98 major exhibition tour in Japan. He is currently working on a fictional installation, *Las Twines*, about twin sisters of different skin colors.

Cristina Peri Rossi was born in Montevideo, Uruguay, in 1941. She is the author of twenty books, including *Dostoevsky's Last Night* (Picador) and *The Rebellion of Children*, a collection of stories that includes *The Milky Way*. She was recently awarded a Guggenheim Foundation grant. She has lived in Spain and worked as a journalist since 1972.

Elena Poniatowska is the author of more than forty works, including her recent novel based on the life of Tina Modotti, *Tinisima*, and the classic *Massacre in Mexico*, as well as the novels, *Dear Diego* and *Hasta No Verte, Jesus Mio*. A novelist, essayist, and journalist, she was the first woman to win Mexico's prestigious National Journalism Award. Born in Paris, she lives in Mexico City.

Martin Prechtel, a musician, painter, and healer, was born in New Mexico and raised there, largely on the Santo Domingo Reservation. In 1976, he traveled to Guatemala to help in earthquake relief work and settled in Santiago Atitlán, where he mastered the language, apprenticed himself to leading shamans and healers, began practicing natural medicine, and participated in Atiteco ritual, initially as a flutist. He eventually rose in the native hierarchy and, in 1979, was appointed Primer Mayor, the official responsible for the vast complex of Holy Week rituals. Soon after, the civil war in Guatemala sent him into hiding until he was able to return to the United States. He lives in Santa Fe, New Mexico. *Scandals in the House of Birds*, the book from which *Stories of the Early Earth* was excerpted, will be published by Marsilio in October 1997.

Robert Rauschenberg was born in Port Arthur, Texas, in 1925. After studying Pharmacology at the University of Texas and serving in the U.S. Navy during World War II, he attended the Kansas City Art Institute and the Académie Julian in Paris. In 1948, he attended Black Mountain College in North Carolina, where he studied with Joseph Albers. He also participated in John Cage's *Theatre Piece #1*, which has since been acknowledged as the first "happening." He moved to New York in 1949, and his first solo show was held at the Betty Parsons Gallery in 1951. He has been involved in theater and dance since the early 1950s, designing sets and costumes for Merce Cunningham, Paul Taylor, Viola Farber, Steve Paxton, Trisha Brown, and others. Most recently he produced *Immerse*, the set for the Merce Cunningham Dance Co.'s *MinEvent*, which debuted at the Joyce Theater, New York, in 1994. In the mid-1960s, Rauschenberg experimented with the use of electronics in his art, and, in 1966, co-founded Experiments in Art and Technology to promote cooperation between artists and engineers. His five-part construction, *Oracle*, owned by the Centre Georges Pompidou, Paris, and *Soundings*, owned by Museum Ludwig, Cologne, are outgrowths of this collaboration. Major solo exhibitions of his work have been held at the Whitechapel Gallery, London, the Museum of Modern Art, New York, the National Collection of Fine Arts, Washington, the Tate Gallery, London, the Whitney Museum of American Art, New York, and the Menil Collection, Houston, among other museums. A major retrospective of his work will open at the Guggenheim Museum, New York, in September 1997. For many years, his work has been shown at the Leo Castelli and Sonnabend Galleries in New York.

Rosângela Rennó was born in Belo Horizonte, Brazil, in 1962. She received a Bachelor of Fine Arts degree from the Escola Guignard, Belo Horizonte, and a Ph.D. from Escola de Comunicações e Artes, Universidade de São Paulo. Solo exhibitions of her work have been held at the Museum of Contemporary Art, Los Angeles, the De Appel Foundation, Amsterdam, the North Dakota Museum of Art, and the Galeria Luis Adelantado, Valencia, Spain, among other exhibition spaces. She lives in Rio de Janeiro and is represented by Lombard/Fried Fine Arts, New York.

Robin Robertson is from the northeast coast of Scotland and now lives in London. His poetry has appeared in a number of American magazines, including *The New Yorker*, *Grand Street*, *The Southern Review*, and *The Yale Review*. A selection of his work will appear in *Penguin Modern Poets 13*. His first book, *A Painted Field*, was published in Britain by Picador and will be published in the

United States by Helen & Kurt Wolff/Harcourt Brace in April 1998. It is shortlisted for the Forward Prize for Best First Collection of 1997.

Juan Rulfo was born in Sayula, Mexico, in 1918. His parents, who had been wealthy, lost most of their possessions in the Mexican Revolution, and died when Rulfo was very young. He was placed in an orphanage for four years, then moved to Mexico City, where he studied law briefly, then worked as an immigration agent before devoting himself to his writing and photography. His first collection of short stories, *El llano en llamas* (translated into English as *The Burning Plain and Other Stories*), was published in 1953, and his novel, *Pedro Páramo*, followed in 1955. His work has been translated into nine languages, and he received the Premio Xavier Villaurrutia (1956), the Premio Nacional de Letras (1970), and the Premio Príncipe de Asturias (1983). Rulfo died in Mexico City in 1986.

Peter Sacks is the author of three collections of poems, most recently *Natal Command* (University of Chicago Press), and of the critical study *The English Elegy*. He is a professor in the English Department at Harvard University.

Edward W. Said teaches literature at Columbia University. His recent books include *Culture and Imperialism* (Alfred A. Knopf), *The Politics of Dispossession* (Pantheon), and *Representations of the Intellectual* (Pantheon).

Vicki Satlow is a translator and an editor at Baldini & Castoldi, Milan. She graduated from Barnard College at Columbia University and currently lives in Italy.

Andrew Schelling teaches poetry, Sanskrit, and wilderness writing at the Naropa Institute in Boulder, Colorado. His recent books include *Old Growth: Poems and Notebooks 1986–1994* and *Songs of the Sons & Daughters of Buddha* (with Anne Waldman). He is completing a volume of translations from the classical Sanskrit, titled *The Cane Groves of Narmada River*, in which the poems published in this issue of *Grand Street* will appear.

Bruce Smith is the author of three books of poetry, most recently *Mercy Seat* (University of Chicago Press).

Vivan Sundaram was born in Shimla, India, in 1943. His work was included most recently in the 1997 Havana Biennale, the 1997 Kwangju Biennale, and the 1997 Johannesburg Biennale. Solo exhibitions of his work have been held at the Winnipeg Art Gallery, the Vancouver Art Gallery, the British Council Art Gallery, Delhi, and the Sakshi Gallery, Bombay, among other galleries. He lives in New Delhi.

Matthew Sweeney was born in Donegal, Ireland, in 1952. He has published seven books of poetry, including *Blue Shoes* and *Cacti* (both Secker & Warburg), and for children, *The Flying Spring Onion* and *Fatso in the Red Suit* (both Faber & Faber). Jonathan Cape will publish his eighth book, *Bridal Suite*, in the fall of 1997. A selection of his work will also appear in *Penguin Modern Poets 12*.

Nathaniel Tarn was born in Paris and educated at Cambridge University, the École des Hautes Études, Paris, Yale University, the University of Chicago, the London School of Economics, and the London School of Oriental & African Studies. He is a poet, translator, editor, critic, and anthropologist. He has published some twenty books of poetry and many volumes of translation, including three best-selling collections by Pablo Neruda. As an anthropologist, he has specialized in the Highland Maya area and Southeast Asia, and has also worked in the Himalayan Region, China, Japan, Cuba, and Alaska. Tarn retired as Professor Emeritus of Modern Poetry, Comparative Literature, and Anthropology at Rutgers University in 1985, and now lives north of Santa Fe, New Mexico. *Scandals in the House of Birds*, the book from which *Stories of the Early Earth* was excerpted, will be published by Marsilio in October 1997.

Milagros de la Torre was born in Lima, Peru. She received her Bachelor of Arts in Photography from the London College of Printing. Solo exhibitions of her work have been held at the Museo de Arte y Diseño Contemporaneo, San Jose, Costa Rica, the Universidad de Salamanca, Spain, the Galeria Ramis Barquet, Monterrey, Mexico, and the Palais de Tokyo, Centre National de la Photographie, Paris, among other venues. She lives and works in Mexico.

Robert McLiam Wilson was born in Belfast, Northern Ireland, in 1964. He is still alive.

Can Xue was born in the Hunan Province of China in 1953. Her father was the editor of the *Hunan Daily News* until 1957, when, as head of the "Anti-party clique," he was transferred to the Hunan Teachers' College to reform through labor. At the age of thirteen Can Xue was forced to leave school and, during the Cultural Revolution, she worked at a machine factory. Later, she taught herself to sew and she and her husband became self-employed tailors. She has been writing since 1988 and her work has been published in China, Japan, France, and Germany. Three of her books have been translated into English: *Dialogues in Paradise*, *Old Floating Clouds* (both Northwestern University Press), and *The Embroidered Shoes* (Henry Holt & Company, fall 1997), which will include her story, *Apple Tree in the Corridor*.

Jian Zhang is assistant chairperson of the Communication and Arts Department at the Brentwood Campus of Suffolk Community College, SUNY.

Grand Street would like to thank **Bradley Jeffries**, **Denise LeBeau**, and **David White** for their assistance with Robert Rauschenberg's *Seen of the Crime*. We would like to thank **Carolina Ponce de Léon** and **Octavio Zaya** for their assistance with the portfolios of art in this issue.

Grand Street would like to thank the following people for their generous support:
Edward Lee Cave
Cathy and Stephen Graham
Barbara Howard
Dominic Man-Kit Lam
The New York State Council on the Arts
Betty and Stanley K. Sheinbaum

Scandals! Publicity Stunts! Libel Suits!

Melrose Place? No!

Victorian England!

The manic fans who greeted Dickens on his first American book tour, the romantic rumors swirling around Thackeray and Charlotte Brontë, Anthony Trollope and Thomas Hardy's scheme to get bigger advances—all precursors of modern publishing.

The author of *What Jane Austen Ate and Charles Dickens Knew* **explores the outrageous publicity stunts, bitter rivalries, rows and general mayhem perpetrated by this group of supposedly prudish—yet remarkably passionate and eccentric—authors and publishers.**

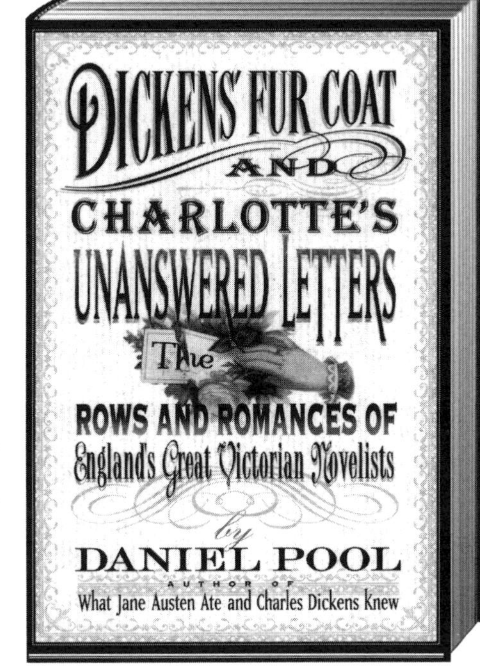

"*Great Books* **meets celebrity gossip: a rare literate entertainment."**—*Kirkus Reviews*

"Informative and engaging... Pool is a social historian of uncommon literary wit."
—*New York Times Book Review*

Order from your wholesaler today!

HarperCollins*Publishers*

ILLUSTRATIONS

Front Cover
Shirin Neshat, *Offered Eye*, 1997. Silver-gelatin print and ink, 10 x 8 in. Artwork courtesy of the artist and Annina Nosei Gallery, New York.

Back Cover
Pepón Osorio, *En la barbería no se llora (No Crying Allowed in the Barbershop)* (detail), 1994. Mixed-media installation. Collection of the Wadsworth Atheneum, Hartford, Connecticut. Photograph courtesy of the artist and Ronald Feldman Fine Arts, New York.

Title Page
Vivan Sundaram, *Box One: Father*, 1995. Teak-board box fitted with woolen lining and notebook of Umrao Singh Sher-Gil, 19 11/16 x 13 3/8 x 17 11/16 in. Photograph courtesy of the artist.

Table of Contents
Juan Rulfo, *Untitled*, circa 1950. Silver-gelatin print. Courtesy of the Rulfo family and the Asociación Juan Rulfo, A.C., Mexico, D.F.

pp. 17–21 Robert Rauschenberg, *Seen of the Crime*. Titles and dates appear with images. **p. 17** Fresco, 111 x 75 in. **p. 18** Fresco, 38 1/2 x 38 1/2 in. Both copyright © Saff Tech Arts/Robert Rauschenberg. Licensed by VAGA, New York. Photographs by George Holzer. **p. 19** Vegetable dye transfer on polylaminate, 61 x 41 in. **p. 20** Vegetable dye transfer on polylaminate, 121 1/8 x 121 in. Both copyright © Robert Rauschenberg. Licensed by VAGA, New York. Photographs by Ed Chappell, Inc. **p. 21** Handwritten text by Robert Rauschenberg. All photographs and text courtesy of the artist.

pp. 24, 26, 29, and 32 All images courtesy of Nathaniel Tarn.

pp. 37–46 *Archives of the Fallen*. Titles and dates appear with images. **pp. 37, 38, 39, and 45** Four works by Eugenio Dittborn. **p. 37** Paint, charcoal, stitching, and photo silk screen on two sections of non-woven fabric, 84 1/2 x 110 1/4 in. **p. 38** Paint, monotype, wool, and photo silk screen on wrapping paper, 68 x 57 in. **p. 39** Photo silk screen on wrapping paper, 68 x 57 in. All photographs courtesy of the artist and Alexander and Bonin, New York. **p. 45** Paint, photo silk screen, and stitching on 6 sections of non-woven fabric, 137 3/4 x 220 1/2 in. Photograph courtesy of the artist and the New Museum of Contemporary Art, New York. **pp. 40, 41 and 46** Six photographs by Rosângela Rennó. From an installation of 40 black-painted, orthochromatic film prints, 10 color prints, aluminum, iron frames, bolts, and white-painted iron letters, each iron frame 23 5/8 x 15 3/4 in. All photographs courtesy of the artist and Galeria Camargo Vilaça, São Paulo. **pp. 42, 43, 44, and 46** Fifteen toned silver-gelatin prints by Milagros de la Torre. **pp. 42, 43, and 46** Five prints, 16 x 16 in. **p. 44** Ten prints and pigment, 3 x 6 in. All photographs courtesy of the artist.

pp. 48–49, 52, 54, and 55 Photographs courtesy of Reuters/Corbis-Bettman. **p. 51** Photograph courtesy of Ruth Chin/Corbis-Bettman. **p. 58** Courtesy of the artist. **p. 61** Photograph courtesy of AP/Wide World Photos.

pp. 68–72 Vivan Sundaram, *The Sher-Gil Archive*. Mixed-media installation. Titles and dates appear with images. **p. 68** Wooden boxes covered with etched glass containing autochromes by Umrao Singh Sher-Gil of the Sher-Gil family in 1924, converted into translites, 26 3/4 x 22 7/16 x 72 7/16 in. **p. 69** Teak-board box fitted with plastic case, mirror, and gabardine cloth, with framed photographs in water, 19 11/16 x 13 3/8 x 17 11/16 in. **pp. 70 and 71** New prints made by the artist from Umrao Singh Sher-Gil's negatives and photographs. **p. 72 (left)** Photograph, 24 x 20 in. **(right)** Silk screen on woollen cloth, 96 x 30 in. All photographs courtesy of the artist.

pp. 89–92 Lewis deSoto, *Kalpa*, 1997. Mixed-media installation. Casts of human bones, paint, flocking, coyote bones, stainless-steel cable, redwood and canary wood, 6 x 8 x 1,080 in. (position variable). **pp. 89 and 92** Installation views. **pp. 90 and 91** Video stills. Courtesy of the artist and Bill Maynes Gallery, New York.

pp. 94 and 96 Photographs by Robin Holland. **pp. 97, 99, and 101** Photographs courtesy of the Metropolitan Opera Archives, New York.

p. 107 Photograph courtesy of Photofest. **p. 109 (top right)** Photograph courtesy of UPI/Corbis-Bettman. **p. 109 (all others)** Photographs courtesy of Photofest. **p. 110 (clockwise from top left)** Photograph courtesy of UPI/Corbis-Bettman. Photograph courtesy of Photofest. Photograph courtesy of Photofest. Photograph courtesy of UPI/Corbis-Bettman. Photograph courtesy of UPI/Corbis-Bettman. Photograph courtesy of Photofest.

pp. 113–116 Pepón Osorio, *Más is More*. Titles and dates appear with images. **p. 113** Mixed media, 78 x 48 x 48 in. Collection of the National Museum of American Art, Washington, D.C. **pp. 114–115** Mixed-media installation at the 1993 Whitney Biennial, the Whitney Museum of American Art, New York. **p. 116** Mixed-media installation, approximately 405 square feet. Bed, 75 x 67 x 78 in. Photograph by Tony Velez. Collection of El Museo del Barrio, New York. All photographs courtesy of the artist and Ronald Feldman Fine Arts, New York.

p. 135 Photograph by Sabu Quinn.

pp. 141–144 Shirin Neshat, *Women of Allah: Secret Identities*. Four silver-gelatin prints and ink. Titles and dates appear with images. **p. 141** 45 x 74 in. Photograph courtesy of the artist and Annina Nosei Gallery, New York. **pp. 142 and 143** 10 x 8 in. **p. 144** 8 x 10 in. Artworks courtesy of the artist and Annina Nosei Gallery, New York.

pp. 169–176 Juan Rulfo, *Nothing of This is a Dream*. Eight silver-gelatin prints. Titles and dates appear on **p. 177**. Courtesy of the Rulfo family and the Asociacíon Juan Rulfo, A.C., Mexico, D.F.

p. 192 Paint and photograph by J. Abbott Miller and Paul Carlos.

pp. 201–208 Mona Hatoum, *Shifting Ground*. Titles, dates, and materials appear with images. **p. 201** 1 x 28 x 16 in. Edition of 6. **p. 202** 12 1/2 x 157 x 157 in. **p. 203** 1 3/4 x 117 1/4 x 95 in. **pp. 204–205** As installed, 12 x 45 x 57 in. **p. 206** Cot, 37 1/4 x 41 3/4 x 23 1/2 in. Installation, 37 1/4 x 85 x 45 1/4 in. **p. 207** 21 1/2 x 27 in. **p. 208** 10 3/4 x 8 3/4 x 5 in. Edition of 6. All photographs courtesy of the artist and Alexander and Bonin, New York.

pp. 259, 260, and 261 Photographs by Peter Berson.

In *Grand Street* 60, the caption on page 239 was erroneously printed as "August 1986." It should have read "April 1996." Peter Fend's contributor's note should also have included the show *Chernobyl Solutions*, installed at Steffany Martz Gallery, New York, which ran from April 25 to May 25, 1996, and marked the tenth anniversary of the accident in Chernobyl.

In *Grand Street* 61, the footnote on page 8 mistakenly identified La Casa de las Américas as the Cuban government publishing house. It is actually a literary organization that arranges conferences and meetings between Cuban and Latin American writers and gives annual prizes to works, which are then published and distributed.

American Short Fiction

JOSEPH E. KRUPPA, Editor,
University of Texas at Austin

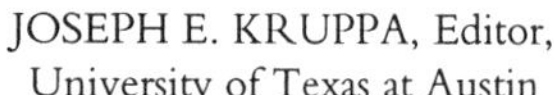

National Magazine Award for Fiction
1993 and 1995 Finalist

Stories you'll love to read.
Stories you'll remember.
Stories that will make you think.
Long stories. Short stories.
Short short stories. And nothing but stories.

American Short Fiction is published in
Spring (March), Summer (June), Fall (September), and
Winter (December)

Subscriptions: Individual $24, Institution $36
Canada/Mexico, add $6; other foreign, add $14(airmail)

Single Copy Rates:
Individual $9.95, Institution $12,
Canada/Mexico, add $2; other foreign, add $4(airmail)
Prepayment only, please.
Refunds available only on unshipped quantities of current subscriptions.

To subscribe, or for more information, write:
University of Texas Press
Journals Division
Box 7819, Austin, Texas 78713-7819
journals@uts.cc.utexas.edu

POETRY SOCIETY OF AMERICA

10 more reasons to join

For complete guidelines, membership & program information, Call the PSA toll free at

(888) USA-POEM

THE WRITER / EMILY DICKINSON AWARD of $100 for a poem inspired by Dickinson though not necessarily in her style. Past judges include Garrett Hongo, Susan Howe & Peter Sacks. *Members only.*

LYRIC POETRY AWARD of $500 for a lyric poem on any subject & in any style. Past judges include Deborah Digges & Dara Wier. *Members only.*

CECIL HEMLEY MEMORIAL AWARD of $300 for a lyric poem on a philosophical theme. Past judges include Michael Collier, Alice Fulton, Wayne Koestenbaum & John Yau. *Members only.*

LUCILLE MEDWICK MEMORIAL AWARD of $500 for an original poem on a humanitarian theme. Past judges include Nina Cassian, Jayne Cortez, Susan Hahn & Yusef Komunyakaa. *Members only.*

ALICE FAY DI CASTAGNOLA AWARD of $1,000 for a manuscript-in-progress of poetry, prose or verse-drama. Past judges include Robert Creeley, Peter Davison & Barbara Guest. *Members only.*

LOUISE LOUIS / EMILY F. BOURNE STUDENT POETRY AWARD of $100 for the best unpublished poem by a high school student from the United States. Past judges include Lucie Brock-Broido, Safiya Henderson-Holmes & Carl Phillips.

GEORGE BOGIN MEMORIAL AWARD of $500 for a selection of four or five poems that reflects the encounter of the ordinary & the extraordinary. Past judges include Rachel Hadas & Alan Shapiro.

ROBERT H. WINNER MEMORIAL AWARD of $2,500 for a brief manuscript of poetry by someone in mid-life who has not yet received substantial recognition. Past judges include Marie Ponsot, Donald Revell, W. D. Snodgrass & Gerald Stern.

NORMA FARBER FIRST BOOK AWARD of $500 for a first book of poetry written by an American and published in 1997. Past judges include Sandra Gilbert, Thylias Moss, Mary Oliver & James Tate.

WILLIAM CARLOS WILLIAMS AWARD of a purchase prize between $500 and $1,000 for a book of poetry published in 1997 by a small press, non-profit or university press. Past judges include Lucille Clifton, Jorie Graham & Donald Hall.

SALT

SUBSCRIPTION FORM

Salt, a leading international poetry journal is published biannually. Subscribe now, and receive a FREE copy of *Salt 9*.

I would like to subscribe to *Salt*. Please send me:

❑ the next two issues for $33.95
+ postage and packaging (please specify)
within Australia ❑ $6
overseas: airmail ❑ $20
surface mail ❑ $8

❑ the next four issues for $67.80
+ postage and packaging (please specify)
within Australia ❑ $12
overseas: airmail ❑ $40
surface mail ❑ $16

❑ backlist issues, *Salt* numbers .... @$16.95 per copy
+ postage and packaging per copy (please specify)
within Australia ❑ $3
overseas: airmail ❑ $10
surface mail ❑ $4

I enclose a cheque / money order (all payments to be made in Australian dollars) or please debit my credit card (delete as applicable)

Mastercard / Bankcard / Visa

Credit Card no. ____ / ____ / ____ / ____

Expiry Date: __ / __

Name: ______________________________

Address: ______________________________

____

Signature: ____________________ Postcode: ________

Please send to: Fremantle Arts Centre Press,
PO Box 320, South Fremantle, 6162, Australia.
Fax: (08) 9430 5242 Email: facp.iinet.net.au

mtc•new•season

Manhattan Theatre Club.

Be guaranteed seats to an exciting new season and you'll never run the risk of being sold-out of the shows everyone will be talking about!

Corpus Christi

by Terrence McNally
directed by Joe Mantello

Terrence McNally, three-time Tony Award-winning author of "Kiss of the Spider Woman," "Love! Valour! Compassion!" and "Master Class," as well as this year's critically acclaimed "Ragtime," returns to MTC with the World Premiere of his latest work.

Alligator Tales

written & performed by Anne Galjour
directed by Sharon Ott

Deep in the Louisiana bayou, a Cajun community experiences love, loss and miracles in hurricane season in this startling, funny and moving new play.

Disappeared

by Phyllis Nagy

A young woman vanishes. Was she murdered, or did she run away? A comic, eccentric crime story with an off-beat look at the mysteries of urban life.

Captains Courageous, The Musical

music by Frederick Freyer
book & lyrics by Patrick Cook
based on the motion picture "Captains Courageous".
Originally produced by Ford's Theatre, Washington D.C. 1992.
directed by Lynne Meadow

Batten down the hatches for the New York Premiere of a new musical based on Kipling's classic tale of a young boy on the high seas.

Three Days of Rain

by Richard Greenberg
directed by Evan Yionoulis

Author of the critically acclaimed MTC productions of "Eastern Standard" and "The American Plan", Richard Greenberg returns with the New York Premiere of his new romance.

And two more production to be announced.
Program, series, dates, and venues are subject to change.

There are two subscription packages available:

I. SuperSeries = All 7 plays (4 plays in Stage I, 3 plays in Stage II)
II. 5 Play Series = 4 plays in Stage I, 1 play in Stage II

You may also visit our website at www.mtc-nyc.org and follow the simple directions for ordering on-line.

Subscribe Now! Call us today:
(212) 399-3030

RAIN TAXI

review of books

reviews • interviews • essays

DJUNA BARNES • RIKKI DUCORNET • STEPHEN DIXON • ARNO SCHMIDT • • MINA LOY • PAUL BOWLES • AMIRI BARAKA • JANE MILLER • ATLAS PRESS SAMUEL R. DELANY • ANTONIN ARTAUD • LESLIE SCALAPINO • IVAN KLIMA • • ROSARIO CASTELLANOS • ROBERT WALSER • DAVID FOSTER WALLACE CAROLE MASO • MIROSLAV HOLUB • JOHN WIENERS • PAUL METCALF • • PETER HANDKE • RUSSELL EDSON • CHARLES FORT • BURNING DECK

One Year Subscription (4 issues) $10, International Rate $20
Send Check Or Money Order: RAIN TAXI, PO Box 3840, Mpls MN 55403

Acclaim for *The Reader's Catalog*

A Book-of-the-Month Club Selection

"*The Reader's Catalog* is the best book without a plot."—*Newsweek*

"The most attractively laid out and compactly informative guide that I know of to books that are currently in print." —*The New York Times*

"A catalog of 40,000 distinguished titles, organized in 208 categories, for readers who hunger for the quality and variety available in today's mass-market bookstores. Hallelujah!"—*Time*

"A browser's paradise."
—*Library Journal*

"The scope of the endeavor is, as the kids are wont to say, awesome."
—*The Baltimore Sun*

"It must be called a triumph."
—*The Los Angeles Times*

"A valuable literary tool that's not only a reader's resource, but also a browser's delight."
—*Parade Magazine*

"The best reading-group and bookstore guide available."
—*Time Out*

"The catalog is discriminating yet expansive, a feat of editing that anyone who has wasted time rooting out data in the weeds of the Internet will appreciate." —*Newsday*

YOUR GUIDE TO THE 40,000 BEST BOOKS IN PRINT

TO ORDER: CALL 1 800 733-BOOK OR VISIT YOUR LOCAL BOOKSTORE TODAY

$34.95 • Distributed by Consortium

poliester

una revista de arte contemporáneo de las américas
a contemporary art magazine of the americas

germán nadin ospina. *archaic critic*, 1993

upcoming issues:
venezuela (winter 95-96)
art & architecture (spring 96), biennials (summer 96)

$40 1 year / 4 issues / usa

$50 1 year / 4 issues / europe & south america

name

address

city state country

zip code telephone

make checks payable to mireles cemaj, s.c. and send to poliester
av. michoacán 139 col. condesa méxico, d.f. 06140 tel. 525 211 4044 fax 525 211 4039

GRAND STREET BACK ISSUES

36

Edward Said on Jean Genet; Terry Southern & Dennis Hopper on Larry Flynt
STORIES: Elizabeth Bishop, William T. Vollmann; PORTFOLIOS: William Eggleston, Saul Steinberg; POEMS: John Ashbery, Bei Dao.

37

William S. Burroughs on guns; John Kenneth Galbraith on JFK's election
STORIES: Pierrette Fleutiaux, Eduardo Galeano; PORTFOLIOS: *Blackboard Equations*, John McIntosh; POEMS: Clark Coolidge, Suzanne Gardinier.

38

Kazuo Ishiguro & Kenzaburo Oe on Japanese literature; Julio Cortázar's HOPSCOTCH: A Lost Chapter
STORIES: Fernando Pessoa, Ben Sonnenberg; PORTFOLIOS: Linda Connor, Robert Rauschenberg; POEMS: Jimmy Santiago Baca, Charles Wright.

39

Nadine Gordimer: SAFE HOUSES; James Miller on Michel Foucault
STORIES: Hervé Guibert, Dubravka Ugrešić; PORTFOLIOS: *Homicide: Bugsy Siegel*, Mark di Suvero; POEMS: Amiri Baraka, Michael Palmer.

40

Gary Giddins on Dizzy Gillespie; Toni Morrison on race and literature
STORIES: Yehudit Katzir, Marcel Proust; PORTFOLIOS: Gretchen Bender, Brice Marden; POEMS: Arkadii Dragomoshchenko, Tom Paulin.

41

Nina Berberova on the Turgenev Library; Mary-Claire King on tracing "the disappeared"
STORIES: Ben Okri, Kurt Schwitters; PORTFOLIOS: Louise Bourgeois, Jean Tinguely; POEMS: Rae Armantrout, Eugenio Montale.

42

David Foster Wallace: THREE PROTRUSIONS; Henry Green: An unfinished novel
STORIES: Félix de Azúa, Eduardo Galeano; PORTFOLIOS: Sherrie Levine, Ariane Mnouchkine & Ingmar Bergman—two productions of Euripides; POEMS: Jorie Graham, Gary Snyder.

43

Jamaica Kincaid on the biography of a dress; Stephen Trombley on designing death machines
STORIES: Victor Erofeyev, Christa Wolf; PORTFOLIOS: Joseph Cornell, Sue Williams; POEMS: Robert Creeley, Kabir.

44

Martin Duberman on Stonewall; Andrew Kopkind: Slacking Toward Bethlehem
STORIES: Georges Perec, Edmund White; PORTFOLIOS: Fred Wilson, William Christenberry; POEMS: Lyn Hejinian, Sharon Olds.

45

John Cage: Correspondence; Roberto Lovato: DOWN AND OUT IN CENTRAL L.A.
STORIES: David Gates, Duong Thu Huong; PORTFOLIOS: Ecke Bonk, Gerhard Richter; POEMS: A. R. Ammons, C. H. Sisson.

46

William T. Vollmann on the Navajo-Hopi Land Dispute; Ice-T, Easy-E: L.A. rappers get open with Brian Cross
STORIES: David Foster Wallace, Italo Calvino; PORTFOLIOS: Nancy Rubins, Dennis Balk; POEMS: Michael Palmer, Martial.

ORDER WHILE THEY LAST.

CALL 1-800-807-6548

Please send name, address, issue number(s), and quantity. American Express, Mastercard, and Visa accepted; please send credit-card number and expiration date. Back issues are $15 each ($18 overseas and Canada), including postage and handling, payable in U.S. dollars.

Address orders to GRAND STREET, Back Issues, 131 Varick Street, Suite 906, New York, NY 10013.

47
Louis Althusser's ZONES OF DARKNESS; *Edward W. Said on intellectual exile*
STORIES: Jean Genet, Junichiro Tanizaki;
PORTFOLIOS: Barbara Bloom, Julio Galán;
POEMS: John Ashbery, Ovid.

OBLIVION
48
William T. Vollmann: UNDER THE GRASS; *Kip S. Thorne on black holes*
STORIES: Heinrich Böll, Charles Palliser;
PORTFOLIOS: Saul Steinberg, Lawrence Weiner; POEMS: Mahmoud Darwish, Antonin Artaud.

HOLLYWOOD
49
Dennis Hopper interviews Quentin Tarantino; Terry Southern on the making of DR. STRANGELOVE
STORIES: Paul Auster, Peter Handke;
PORTFOLIOS: Edward Ruscha, William Eggleston; POEMS: John Ashbery, James Laughlin.

MODELS
50
Alexander Cockburn & Noam Chomsky on models in nature; Graham Greene's dream diary
STORIES: Rosario Castellanos, Cees Nooteboom;
PORTFOLIOS: Katharina Sieverding, Paul McCarthy;
POEMS: Robert Kelly, Nicholas Christopher.

NEW YORK
51
Terry Williams on life in the tunnels under NYC; William S. Burroughs: MY EDUCATION
STORIES: William T. Vollmann, Orhan Pamuk;
PORTFOLIOS: Richard Prince, David Hammons;
POEMS: Hilda Morley, Charles Simic.

GAMES
52
David Mamet: THE ROOM; *Paul Virilio on cybersex and virtual reality*
STORIES: Brooks Hansen, Walter Benjamin;
PORTFOLIOS: Robert Williams, Chris Burden;
POEMS: Miroslav Holub, Fanny Howe.

FETISHES
53
John Waters exposes his film fetishes; Samuel Beckett's ELEUTHÉRIA
STORIES: Georges Bataille, Colum McCann;
PORTFOLIOS: Helmut Newton, Yayoi Kusama;
POEMS: Taslima Nasrin, Simon Armitage.

SPACE
54
Born in Prison: an inmate survives the box; Jasper Johns's GALAXY WORKS
STORIES: Vladimir Nabokov, Irvine Welsh;
PORTFOLIOS: Vito Acconci, James Turrell;
POEMS: W. S. Merwin, John Ashbery.

EGOS
55
Julian Schnabel: THE CONVERSION OF ST. PAOLO MALFI; *Suzan-Lori Parks on Josephine Baker*
STORIES: Kenzaburo Oe, David Foster Wallace;
PORTFOLIOS: Dennis Hopper, Brigid Berlin's *Cock Book*;
POEMS: Amiri Baraka, Susie Mee.

DREAMS
56
Edward Ruscha: HOLLYWOOD BOULEVARD; *Terry Southern and Other Tastes*
STORIES: William T. Vollmann, Lydia Davis;
PORTFOLIOS: Jim Shaw, ADOBE LA;
POEMS: Bernadette Mayer, Saúl Yurkievich.

DIRT
57
John Waters & Mike Kelley: THE DIRTY BOYS; *Rem Koolhaas on 42nd Street*
STORIES: Mohammed Dib, Sandra Cisneros;
PORTFOLIOS: Langdon Clay, Alexis Rockman;
POEMS: Robert Creeley, Thomas Sayers Ellis.

DISGUISES
58
Anjelica Huston on life behind the camera; D. Carleton Gajdusek: THE NEW GUINEA FIELD JOURNALS
STORIES: Victor Pelevin, Arno Schmidt;
PORTFOLIOS: Hannah Höch, Kara Walker;
POEMS: Vittorio Sereni, Marjorie Welish.

TIME
59
Mike Davis on the destruction of L.A.; John Szarkowski: LOOKING AT PICTURES
STORIES: Naguib Mahfouz, Nina Berberova;
PORTFOLIOS: Spain, Charles Ray;
POEMS: James Tate, Adonis.

PARANOIA
60
Fiona Shaw on life in the theater; Salvador Dalí on the paranoid image
STORIES: David Foster Wallace, Nora Okja Keller;
PORTFOLIOS: Tom Sachs, David Cronenberg;
POEMS: Fanny Howe, Lawrence Ferlinghetti.

ALL-AMERICAN
61
William T. Vollmann tracks the Queen of the Whores; Peter Sellars: THE DIRECTOR'S PERSPECTIVE
STORIES: Reinaldo Arenas, Guillermo Cabrera Infante;
PORTFOLIOS: Rubén Ortiz-Torres, Doris Salcedo;
POEMS: Octavio Paz, Aimé Césaire.

Some of the bookstores where you can find

GRAND STREET

Magpie Magazine Gallery, Vancouver, CANADA

Newsstand, Bellingham, WA
Bailey Coy Books, Seattle, WA
Hideki Ohmori, Seattle, WA

Looking Glass Bookstore, Portland, OR
Powell's Books, Portland, OR
Reading Frenzy, Portland, OR

. . . On Sundays, Tokyo, JAPAN

ASUC Bookstore, Berkeley, CA
Black Oak Books, Berkeley, CA
Cody's Books, Berkeley, CA
Bookstore Fiona, Carson, CA
Huntley Bookstore, Claremont, CA
Book Soup, Hollywood, CA
University Bookstore, Irvine, CA
Museum of Contemporary Art, La Jolla, CA
UCSD Bookstore, La Jolla, CA
A.R.T. Press, Los Angeles, CA
Museum of Contemporary Art, Los Angeles, CA
Occidental College Bookstore, Los Angeles, CA
Sun & Moon Press Bookstore, Los Angeles, CA
UCLA/Armand Hammer Museum, Los Angeles, CA
Stanford Bookstore, Newark, CA
Diesel, A Bookstore, Oakland, CA
Blue Door Bookstore, San Diego, CA
Museum of Contemporary Art, San Diego, CA
The Booksmith, San Francisco, CA
City Lights, San Francisco, CA
Green Apple Books, San Francisco, CA
Modern Times Bookstore, San Francisco, CA
MuseumBooks–SF MOMA, San Francisco, CA
San Francisco Camerawork, San Francisco, CA
Logos, Santa Cruz, CA
Arcana, Santa Monica, CA
Midnight Special Bookstore, Santa Monica, CA
Reader's Books, Sonoma, CA
Small World Books, Venice, CA
Ventura Bookstore, Ventura, CA

Honolulu Book Shop, Honolulu, HI

Page One, SINGAPORE

Asun Bookstore, Reno, NV

Sam Weller's Zion Bookstore, Salt Lake City, UT

Bookman's, Tucson, AZ

Baxter's Books, Minneapolis, MN
Minnesota Book Center, Minneapolis, MN
University of Minnesota Bookstore, Minneapolis, MN
Walker Art Center Bookshop, Minneapolis, MN
Hungry Mind Bookstore, St. Paul, MN
Odegard Books, St. Paul, MN

Chinook Bookshop, Colorado Springs, CO
The Bookies, Denver, CO
Newsstand Cafe, Denver, CO
Tattered Cover Bookstore, Denver, CO
Stone Lion Bookstore, Fort Collins, CO

Nebraska Bookstore, Lincoln, N

Kansas Union Bookstore, Lawrence, KS
Terra Nova Bookstore, Lawrence, KS

Bookworks, Albuquerque, NM
Page One Bookstore, Albuquerque, NM
Salt of the Earth, Albuquerque, NM
Cafe Allegro, Los Alamos, NM
Collected Works, Santa Fe, NM

Book People, Austin, TX
Bookstop, Austin, TX
University Co-op Society, Austin, TX
McKinney Avenue Contemporary Gift Shop, Dallas, TX
Bookstop, Houston, TX
Brazos Bookstore, Houston, TX
Contemporary Arts Museum Shop, Houston, TX
Diversebooks, Houston, TX
Menil Collection Bookstore, Houston, TX
Museum of Fine Arts, Houston, TX
Texas Gallery, Houston, TX
Bookstop, Plano, TX

Bookland of Brunswick, Brunswick, ME
University of Maine Bookstore, Orono, ME
Books Etc., Portland, ME
Raffles Cafe Bookstore, Portland, ME

Pages, Toronto, CANADA

Dartmouth Bookstore, Hanover, NH
Toadstool Bookshop, Peterborough, NH

Northshire Books, Manchester, VT

Wootton's Books, Amherst, MA
Boston University Bookstore, Boston, MA
Harvard Book Store, Cambridge, MA
M.I.T. Press Bookstore, Cambridge, MA
Cisco Harland Books, Marlborough, MA
Broadside Bookshop, Northampton, MA
Provincetown Bookshop, Provincetown, MA
Water Street Books, Williamstown, MA

Main Street News, Ann Arbor, MI
Shaman Drum Bookshop, Ann Arbor, MI
Cranbrook Art Museum Books, Bloomfield Hills, MI
Book Beat, Oak Park, MI

Afterwords, Milwaukee, WI

Accident or Design, Providence, RI
Brown University Bookstore, Providence, RI
College Hill Store, Providence, RI

Farley's Bookshop, New Hope, PA
Faber Books, Philadelphia, PA
Waterstone's Booksellers, Philadelphia, PA
Andy Warhol Museum, Pittsburgh, PA
Encore Books, Mechanicsburg, PA
Encore Books, State College, PA

Yale Cooperative, New Haven, CT
UConn Co-op, Storrs, CT

Rosetta News, Carbondale, IL
Pages for All Ages, Champaign, IL
Mayuba Bookstore, Chicago, IL
Museum of Contemporary Art, Chicago, IL
Seminary Co-op Bookstore, Chicago, IL

Encore Books, Princeton, NJ
Micawber Books, Princeton, NJ

UC Bookstore, Cincinnati, OH
Bank News, Cleveland, OH
Ohio State University Bookstore, Columbus, OH
Student Book Exchange, Columbus, OH
Books & Co., Dayton, OH
Kenyon College Bookstore, Gambier, OH
Oberlin Consumers Cooperative, Oberlin, OH

Indiana University Bookstore, Bloomington, IN

owa Book & Supply, Iowa City, IA
rairie Lights, Iowa City, IA
niversity Bookstore, Iowa City, IA

Box of Rocks, Bowling Green, KY
Carmichael's, Louisville, KY

Louie's Bookstore Cafe, Baltimore, MD

Xanadu Bookstore, Memphis, TN

Bridge Street Books, Washington, DC
Chapters, Washington, DC
Franz Bader Bookstore, Washington, DC
Olsson's, Washington, DC
Politics & Prose, Washington, DC

Daedalus Used Bookshop, Charlottesville, VA
Studio Art Shop, Charlottesville, VA
Williams Corner, Charlottesville, VA

ibrary Ltd., Clayton, MO
Vhistler's Books, Kansas City, MO
eft Bank Books, St. Louis, MO

Community Bookstore, Brooklyn, NY
Talking Leaves, Buffalo, NY
Colgate University Bookstore, Hamilton, NY
Book Revue, Huntington, NY
The Bookery, Ithaca, NY
A Different Light, New York, NY
Art Market, New York, NY
B. Dalton, New York, NY
Coliseum Books, New York, NY
Collegiate Booksellers, New York, NY
Doubleday Bookshops, New York, NY
Exit Art/First World Store, New York, NY
Gold Kiosk, New York, NY
Gotham Book Mart, New York, NY
Museum of Modern Art Bookstore, New York, NY
New York University Book Center, New York, NY
Posman Books, New York, NY
Rizzoli Bookstores, New York, NY
St. Mark's Bookshop, New York, NY
Shakespeare & Co., New York, NY
Spring Street Books, New York, NY
Wendell's Books, New York, NY
Whitney Museum of Modern Art, New York, NY
Syracuse University Bookstore, Syracuse, NY

Paper Skyscraper, Charlotte, NC
Regulator Bookshop, Durham, NC

Chapter Two Bookstore, Charleston, SC
Intermezzo, Columbia, SC
Open Book, Greenville, SC

Square Books, Oxford, MS

Oxford Bookstore, Atlanta, GA

Books & Books, Coral Gables, FL
Goerings Book Center, Gainesville, FL
Bookstop, Miami, FL
Rex Art, Miami, FL
Inkwood Books, Tampa, FL

Lenny's News, New Orleans, LA

And at selected Barnes & Noble and Bookstar bookstores nationwide.

2wice

VISUAL \ CULTURE \ DOCUMENT

Richard Barnes,
Theatre, Legion of Honor, 1994

A NEW MAGAZINE THAT BRINGS
STUNNING PHOTOGRAPHY,
WRITING, AND DESIGN
TO ITS COVERAGE OF VISUAL CULTURE.

NEXT ISSUE: interiors

AVAILABLE AT FINE BOOKSTORES.
TO SUBSCRIBE : TEL 212 228 0540 | FAX 212 228 0654